W9-BYS-563

THE FINAL DECEPTION

THE FINAL DECEPTION

HEATHER GRAHAM

THORNDIKE PRESS
A part of Gale, a Cengage Company

Copyright © 2020 by Heather Graham Pozzessere.
New York Confidential.
Thorndike Press, a part of Gale, a Cengage Company.

ALL RIGHTS RESERVED
This is a work of fiction. Names, characters, places and incidents are either the product of the author's imagination or are used fictitiously. Any resemblance to actual persons, living or dead, businesses, companies, events or locales is entirely coincidental.
Thorndike Press® Large Print Core.
The text of this Large Print edition is unabridged.
Other aspects of the book may vary from the original edition.
Set in 16 pt. Plantin.

LIBRARY OF CONGRESS CIP DATA ON FILE.
CATALOGUING IN PUBLICATION FOR THIS BOOK
IS AVAILABLE FROM THE LIBRARY OF CONGRESS

ISBN-13: 978-1-4328-7679-1 (hardcover alk. paper)

Published in 2020 by arrangement with Harlequin Books S.A.

Printed in Mexico
Print Number: 01   Print Year: 2020

For Josie Blanco, one of the most
giving and generous women I know.
Thanks for being there for
so many people so often!

PROLOGUE

Craig Frasier breathed it in before he could stop himself; the bloodcurdling scent of burning flesh.

Human flesh.

Flames still skittered over the body — an accelerant had been used. As he stood there in the small dark alley, he heard others rushing in: Mike Dalton, his partner, and patrol officers. He heard the sirens; the fire department was coming.

But there was no saving this victim.

Craig was already tamping the fire out; an extinguisher would make the work of the medical examiner more difficult.

But he knew what the medical examiner would find.

The victim had been strangled, then the tongue had been cut out. And then the eyes had been gouged out. Death had occurred, mercifully, before the fire had been set.

The corpses haunted his dreams. Burned

shells, some flesh and soft tissue remaining, charred and clinging to the bones, mummy-like. The mouth in the blackened skull was agape, and those empty, soulless eye sockets seemed to be staring up, as if they could still see, as if they stared at him in reproach . . .

Why hadn't they caught the killer sooner?

He heard a rustling sound. Looking across the alley, Craig saw a shadow moving. Leaving the corpse to others, he took off like a bullet. He pursued the moving shadow at a run . . . running and running for blocks. The city was a blur around him.

He reached apartments on Madison, with a coffee shop and a dress store on the first floor, just as the gate at the street entry to the residential units above was closing. He caught the gate, and he reached the elevator in time to see what floor it stopped on. He followed.

And again, as he arrived, a door was just closing; he didn't let it close.

And there he was: the Fireman, still smelling faintly of gasoline, ready to sit down to a lovely dinner with his family. About to say a prayer before the meal . . . just a husband and a father, and a man who looked at Craig and calmly said, "So, my work is over. But I have obeyed the commandments given me, and I will go with you."

Why did you take so long? The corpse again! In Craig's dreams, the corpse was back, animated, flying at him like a ghostly banshee, issuing a silent scream.

Craig opened his eyes.

He didn't awake screaming or startled — he didn't jerk up. It was almost as if he always knew it was a dream, reliving the day the Fireman had gone down.

He'd had the dream several times before. But, now, it seemed as though it had been a long time. Weeks. He'd thought he'd ceased experiencing it altogether. He'd been doing all the right things: quietly seeing a Bureau shrink a few times, following their advice. He hadn't told Kieran Finnegan, his fiancée, about his recurring nightmare, and while she was a criminal psychologist working with two of the city's finest criminal psychiatrists, he'd made a point of not telling her or her bosses.

He'd thought he'd settled it on his own. It was a little strange and sometimes intimidating being in love with someone who studied the human psyche, and he hadn't wanted Kieran worried about him or trying to analyze him.

Why the hell had the dream come back?

He felt Kieran shift against him. He pulled

her into his arms and she rolled, crystal eyes opening wide when she realized that he was awake.

And aroused. Kieran's tangle of auburn hair was a wild mass around her face, emphasizing her eyes and the quick smile that came to her lips.

"Ah!" she murmured, feeling his arousal against her.

"Your fault," he accused.

"Well, thankfully. What time is it?" she asked with a soft whisper.

He laughed. "Quickie time, or time for a quickie," he said.

Her smile deepened, and there was something so sensual about it that it never failed to increase whatever he had begun to feel.

In her arms, in the liquid burn of kisses here and there strategically placed, in the swift — and intense — blaze of arching and writhing and thrusting, all else faded.

After, Craig headed for the shower. He was an FBI agent in the Criminal Division of New York City's branch of the FBI. He could be satisfied in having brought down several killers. But there would be more; a sad fact of the world and humanity. He was blessed to have his job, his vocation, and it was time to go to work.

10

He shoved the dream into the back of his mind.

Whatever his day held, he'd already seen the worst that this world could offer.

Little did he know.

Chapter One

Two months later

" 'Thou shall not suffer a witch to live'!" Raoul Nicholson said. His voice was low, but passionate. He stared at Kieran Finnegan with eyes that pleaded for understanding.

Kieran sat in a chair across from Nicholson, her hands folded on the simple metal desk between them.

Nicholson was handcuffed, and chained to pegs in the concrete floor at the foot of his side of the table. Nicholson was forty-eight years old, a thin man, but lean-muscled, wearing a full beard and mustache and long, unkempt brown hair.

The man's attorney, Cliff Watkins, stood behind Nicholson, hands folded behind his back, having declined to sit. He'd assured Kieran he would be there just to protect his client, though protecting him seemed a futile effort at times.

13

Kieran liked Watkins. He was clean-shaven and bald, somewhere in his early to mid-forties, wiry in build and calm in demeanor. Despite his client, he wasn't a grandstander; his firm had taken on the case pro bono, but he was doing his best to see that the man was treated fairly.

Trying for an innocent plea of any kind didn't seem to be his game.

Nicholson could never be deemed innocent.

Watkins didn't seem to be concerned with safety issues. He'd shrugged when they'd chained Nicholson down. He'd known a protest would be foolhardy, and for the record alone.

Kieran wasn't sure the security measures were necessary. She didn't believe Nicholson was a threat to her because he didn't believe that *she* was a witch.

Or was it all a ruse for an insanity plea?

She started to speak, but, before she could, he was imploring her again. "Don't you understand? The world is a disaster, because no one adheres to the commandments. Those I executed, they weren't men and women. You must believe me. I killed witches. I helped rid the world of monsters. You must obey the commandments. 'Thou shall not suffer a witch to live'!"

14

"What about, 'Thou shall not murder'?" Kieran asked quietly.

"It refers to *people!*" Nicholson told her, distressed and shaking his head. "You don't understand what I'm trying to tell you. They were *witches.* Satan's minions."

Nicholson had brutally murdered five people: two sex workers, a senior at NYU, a fashion designer, and an accountant. Before they had been murdered, the investigations into their deaths had proved he had delivered each one of them a simple message: *I know what you are; you are going to die.*

The bodies had been found across the city — one downtown, one in the West Village, one in Hell's Kitchen, and two Midtown.

They had been burned, leaving very little to be discovered by the medical examiner. But even with the use of an accelerant, there had been enough left behind for the ME to report that, in each case, the eyes and tongue had been removed. That information, however, had been kept from the public.

The press had given him the moniker the Fireman. Once in captivity, Nicholson had never denied his guilt. He had been on a mission — and in the eyes of his Maker, he had done what needed to be done. He was happy to be a martyr; his reward would

15

come to him, and he would be judged by "He Who Mattered," or his "higher power." What happened in earthly courts didn't matter to him. They had wondered, naturally, if anyone else had been involved — his family, friends, members of his church. But Nicholson had told them time and again that no one else had been involved. They didn't understand. The mission — and it had been a mission — was his, and no one else was part of it, nor did they know about it. Word had come to him alone, and he had acted on his own.

Nicholson owned a furniture repair shop in the village and had a rent-controlled apartment. He had a wife, Amy, and two children, Thomas and John; the elder had graduated from NYU, and John was now studying at Princeton.

His wife was devastated . . . She couldn't stop crying 24/7. They had been a religious family, but she'd had no idea of her husband's homicidal desire to cure the world of witchcraft. Or *so she claimed.*

His pastor, Reverend Axel Cunningham, had been similarly stunned, or *so he claimed,* as well. As had Nicholson's employees at the furniture shop. And according to everyone at Annie's Sunrise, the café where he stopped every morning for a doughnut and a latte, he was always kind and courteous and polite. Annie Sullivan, who owned the place, claimed that he was one of the nicest customers who came in, courteous to everyone around him, making people smile as they started out their day.

To everyone he regularly interacted with, he was just a wonderful person. If he hadn't admitted his guilt, they would have all said he wasn't capable of such violence. Even his attorney had said he'd never met such a sincere man.

"I'm sorry to press, Mr. Nicholson, but I'm trying to understand why you thought those young men and women were witches, and why that allowed you to kill. I'm not making fun of you or doubting you, I'm trying to see it from your perspective."

And determine if you're lying, she thought.

He leaned forward, as if he felt he had found a friend, one who really might not just understand him, but also agree that witches needed to die.

"You must listen to me." He paused to sniff suddenly. "They're not even silly people who practice sanctioned 'Wicca' religions. Witches don't dance beneath the moon in the forest, naked, bowing to their horned god there. Real witches are devious. They wear beautiful shells, and that's how

17

they manipulate men — and women — and cause them to do hurtful things. I heard the voice that told me who they were — and what must be done."

"A voice? God's voice?"

"Perhaps it was God's voice. Perhaps He sent Gabriel or another angel. We all see God differently, but, yes, if you like, it was God's voice. But the point is, I knew what must be done, and as hard as it was, I did it. I was told to be merciful — one does not retrieve a soul by cruelty. I offered them a chance to repent, and I strangled them, as quickly as I could. Then I cut out their eyes and tongues so they would no longer see the devil as they made their way to purgatory, no longer be able to answer his call. And if I am to die for the good I've attempted to bestow upon the world, so be it. I have done as I was commanded."

Watkins spoke up. "You're not going to die, Raoul."

"If there are federal charges, I could be sentenced to death," Nicholson said.

"No, Mr. Nicholson, what we're trying to determine here is just what charges they wish to pursue," Kieran told him quietly. She looked over at the man's attorney. Watkins met her gaze with steady brown eyes.

"The laws of man must be used as man chooses," Nicholson said. "I will answer in the flesh, as such laws command. I only killed witches. I killed nothing but evil."

"You killed people with families and friends and long lives ahead of them," Kieran said.

"The voice was very clear on who must be killed and when. You can't imagine what havoc they might have done to the world. There are more out there, of course. They are the devil's disciples — and you must be afraid, Miss Finnegan, you must be very afraid."

"Mr. Nicholson, I beg you, watch your words!" Watkins warned.

Kieran was startled. She hadn't expected to be on Nicholson's list — in fact, she hadn't even expected to be here.

In a case this serious, her employers, Drs. Fuller and Miro, usually did the interviews, and several of them, for the police or the FBI. They were psychiatrists. Kieran was on their staff as a psychologist, and most often worked when therapy was ordered by the court or the effect of that therapy was to be determined.

But because of the circumstances of this case, they had both already spoken with the accused. And they wanted Kieran's opinion of his mental state, as well. "I'm in danger?" she asked, keeping her voice even and low. Was he a threat to her?

She thought maybe, if he were ever free again. "Witches — slaves of Satan! I fear for you greatly. You don't know the danger they present. You can't imagine what they might do to you! You are in no danger from me — you're a good person. Anyone can see that. But you also must believe that evil is out there. I barely began to rid the world of a tiny portion of the evil."

"Mr. Nicholson, I really want to see all this, see what you're seeing. But your victims — I just can't see what harm they caused anyone."

Nicholson sighed softly. "You don't see, but you will. The young woman I last freed . . . if they haven't discovered it yet, she was spreading a deadly disease. Satan commanded her to spread it as far as she could. The man . . . second, third . . . I don't remember. He killed his father. Satan told him to do so. They were all obeying *their* higher power, Satan. I was charged to stop them!"

Kieran sat back. She didn't know if it was true or not. Could the medical examiner test a burned body for infectious diseases? If that had been the case, she didn't know about it.

"How did you know these things?" she asked.

"The voice told me, of course." He leaned forward again. "You must watch out for evil people — the true murderers, true spawns of Satan. You see, I am afraid. Afraid for you. Not from the voice I hear. The voice likes you. It commanded me to be honest with you — but danger lurks from Satan. His minions foster evil."

Well, at least he thought she was good. And he was talking to her; more even than when he had been interviewed by her bosses.

Back against the wall, Cliff Watkins sighed as if with great patience.

"Mr. Nicholson, how did the voice, telling you to kill, come to you?"

"Different ways. Sometimes in a crowd. I'd hear the whisper, but no one near was talking to me. Once, through my cell phone. Once, I saw the name in the paper, and I knew. And when I dreamed that night, the voice came to me in the dream, showing me what I must do."

He seemed so positive; so certain.

She jotted down some notes. There were fine lines to be drawn between someone who was incompetent to stand trial, and

21

someone who was legally insane.

She was glad all she had to do was report on her findings, give her opinion on his mental state. "Thank you for talking to me, Mr. Nicholson," she told him, and stood, nodding to the guard who stood by the cell door. He opened it for her; another guard waited to escort her out.

Cliff Watkins followed. "He's sick, can't you see? We can take a deal on this and get him into a facility from which he can't escape, where he'll be given the help he needs. Please, I hope you see the truth of the man."

She smiled; she wasn't sure what she saw yet. There was a lot of precedent for this kind of delusion.

David Berkowitz, the Son of Sam killer, had heard voices ordering him to kill.

And, in the 1970s, in Southern California, Herbert Mullin had killed because a voice told him that an earthquake was imminent if he didn't offer blood sacrifices to the earth. Anthony Sowell, the Cleveland Strangler, had killed because a ghost had ordered him to do so. And there were so many more killers who had somehow justified their actions. Nicholson wanted her to see the truth.

What was the truth?

One way or the other, Nicholson would

be locked up for a very long time.

She exited the prison. Dr. Fuller was waiting for her, ready to head from Rikers Island back to the mainland. They would have plenty of time to discuss their thoughts and findings as he drove over the Francis R. Buono Memorial Bridge to Queens, and from there, down to Lower Manhattan. It was a long trip in heavy traffic. At least it was spring, and there would be an occasional pretty sight on the way. People who lived in concrete jungles, as Kieran did, tended to care for every burst of green tree or bright flower.

"I don't think he's lying. I think he believes every word he says," Kieran told Dr. Fuller. "It's hard to judge, but . . ." She pulled out her phone and the notes she had written after studying all she could about the man's life. "He was an avid churchgoer, and his church, Unitarian, is truly fundamentalist. He never danced, celebrated a birthday, or did anything that was slightly fun — from what I can tell — much less indulge in drugs or alcohol or any other vices."

Kieran relayed all the details of her interview with the accused. They continued to talk, and the drive went more quickly than Kieran had imagined it might.

"I just wish I could be sure," Kieran said.

Fuller cast a sideways glance and smiled. "Don't we all? Why do you think Dr. Miro and I had you talk to him as well?" Fuller was an older man with classic Hollywood movie-star good looks, though he was one of the most humble people Kieran had ever met.

They had made it all the way down to Lower Manhattan, Kieran realized. Dr. Fuller was going to pull over for her to get out soon, and they couldn't tarry long on Broadway.

"Write it all up for me, and we'll give it to the prosecutors. They'll have to make the decision on just how to proceed," he told her. He stopped the car.

"Did you want to park somewhere, grab something to eat?" she asked him. Her family owned Finnegan's on Broadway, the pub where they had stopped.

It was barely 4:00 p.m., early for dinner, but it was Friday evening, and the pub would soon be entering cocktail hour, a wildly busy time.

"Thanks, but I have a romantic dinner tonight with the wife!" he told her, smiling. And then he frowned. "Oh, you should see the look you're giving me!" he told her. "Kieran, shake it off. It's the weekend. We

24

deal with horrible things all the time. You'll have to quit thinking about it. Nicholson is off the streets — that's what is most important. Get in there. And enjoy your family, your beau, and your life!"

She saluted him. "Yes, sir!" He grinned as she slid out of the car. She did have to shake off her time with Nicholson, and she knew it.

Her "beau," as Dr. Fuller had called him, was stepping out onto the sidewalk, obviously looking for her, just as she started for the door of Finnegan's.

"Hey!" she said cheerfully. Maybe too cheerfully.

Craig took a stride toward her and pulled her firmly into his arms. It was good; the warmth of him, the strength of him, wrapping all around her.

"Craig, I . . ." Her voice trailed off.

"I know," he said softly. "Don't forget," he added, his voice husky, "I was on the task force that brought him down."

For a moment they stood there, taking strength and comfort from each other, and then they went in.

Kieran's oldest brother, Declan Finnegan, had brought in a great Irish band, the Boys of Shannon. They were playing and the pub was in full swing. From behind the bar,

Declan waved her way. There was a little concern in her brother's eyes. She smiled and waved in turn.

Then she saw that her other brothers, Danny and Kevin, were running around helping. They were apparently short on staff this night.

"Looks like I'd better pitch in for a few minutes," she told Craig.

"Sure."

She served Guinness and Smithwick's and all the pub's specialties: shepherd's pies, corned beef and cabbage, pot pies, and more. And the music touched her — guitars, drums, violin, and keyboard. The night went on. She chatted and laughed. Danny and Kevin wound up sitting with Craig while she ran a bit ragged. Then she announced they were leaving. It wasn't even eight, but her brothers could take over; she'd done her bit.

"You're going to miss the band coming back on," her brother Danny — one time bad boy, petty-thief-turned-historian and New York City tour guide — called to her, grinning.

"Maybe we'll come back. I need a breather after work. And more work!" she said, reminding him she'd been the one waiting tables.

"Hey, I have a tour first thing in the morning!" Danny cried.

She shrugged, taking Craig's arm and leading him out.

Grimacing, Danny stood, assuring one of their regulars he'd be happy to get him another soda with lime.

"Do come back later!" her twin, Kevin, called. "Be social!"

"Sure!"

The pub would still be open for hours — until 2:00 a.m. on a Friday night — but she wanted time with Craig. Though her fiancé had a Bureau car, they walked from the pub. It was merely six blocks to their newest home. They'd moved a lot in the last few years — his place, her place, a place together — but now they were in a new condo and she loved it. Loved that it was theirs and they had chosen it together.

Upstairs, she showered quickly, loving as well that while the previous owner had kept the architectural integrity of the place, he'd installed a new master bathroom with a seriously fine shower nozzle. It seemed to wash the feeling of the day away. Maybe she made it do so in her mind. She stepped out of the bathroom in a thick terry robe, walked over to the windows, and peeked out into the night. The apartment stretched from side to side of the building, so from the living area with its high ceilings they could look out at the skyline, just as they could from their bedroom, which was in an open loft space up a flight of stairs.

Stars were visible, and they were beautiful in the night sky. She heard Craig come in, and she smiled. It was Friday night; it was early. They had hours together here in the new home they loved like a pair of children excited over a new tree house.

She nearly said something about Nicholson but she didn't.

Until he touched her, she hadn't realized Craig was right behind her.

She didn't speak. He lifted her hair, kissing the nape of her neck. She turned to him and the kiss came to her lips, and his hands were on her, teasing on the tie of the terry robe.

Soon it was gone, and his clothing was strewn everywhere. His lips were liquid and afire on her flesh, they became a tangle of limbs on the bed, and they made love.

They lay comfortably together. And for a very long time, they still didn't speak. But then the day began to gnaw at the back of her mind. She was hesitant; she knew Craig had been on the case and he'd seen the results of the killer's work.

"What?" he asked her. "Come on —
something is weighing on your mind."

"Talking to Raoul Nicholson today," she
said.

She felt him stiffen. "I don't understand
why Fuller and Miro asked you to interview
someone like Nicholson."

"They both spoke with him. Then they
asked me to, as well."

"He has to be a madman."

"Or speaking the truth — just as he sees
it. Or he's creating an unbelievably good
con."

He rose on an elbow and looked down at
her. "And?"

She shivered slightly; he held her closer.
"I don't know — there's something about
him. I've heard no one had any idea he was
a killer, no one believed the Fireman might
have been him — not his wife, coworkers . . . casual friends at the coffee shop he
stopped by each morning. And yet . . ."

"And yet?"

"There's something about him. He
doesn't seem delusional on the surface. But
the way he speaks is . . . too passionate. The
voice made him do it. The voice of God, in
his mind. And those he killed were diseased
— or about to kill the innocent. Well, you
know his story. I guess the world knows his

story. He's been written up in every major media outlet in the country, if not the world. The Fireman — apprehended." She grimaced at him. "At least you made the Bureau look great."

"Yeah — because he immediately admitted his guilt, and they finally managed to match a fingerprint at a crime scene," Craig said. "Otherwise . . . I'm not sure how my opening the door to his home would stand up."

"You said the door was open."

"It was," Craig said with a shrug. "Anyway, what will you say at trial?"

"That he needs to be locked up — and never let out."

"But is he competent to sit at trial?"

"Yes, I believe he's cognizant to what's going on around him. He's just living in an alternate world, or as I said, it's possible he's creating the best crazed persona possible to get into a hospital rather than a maximum-security prison, where he would be held without a chance for parole."

"It will be a while before we get to it," Craig said. He remained on his elbow, observing her carefully. He added quietly, "Life — and crime — will go on. But, aside from all that, we've got to . . ."

"To what?" she asked. They were personally involved with several cases. She knew people led normal lives by stepping back when they weren't working, but she and Craig had met because of a string of diamond heists in the city when they'd both wound up a little too personally involved. They didn't ask each other to forget friends, family — or even the problems of those who frequented Finnegan's on Broadway.

This one though . . .

"Step back," he told her.

Yeah, she needed to step back.

She couldn't help but wonder, though, if his thought hadn't been for them both. She'd seen pictures of the victims. He'd seen the real deal.

"We have a wedding we keep putting off planning. People to see, places to go," he reminded her. He was right. "We've been together years. Your brothers are starting to look at me as if they question my intentions."

Kieran grinned and ran a teasing finger down his chest. "I'm sure many a night when we leave the pub, they're well aware of our intentions."

He smiled at that, drawing her closer. "So, the wedding."

"Want to run away to Vegas?"

"I'm not into being hated the rest of my life."

"Well, your intentions will have been honorable at the very least!"

"Seriously, it is absolutely foolish to even consider having the reception anywhere but the pub," Craig said, rolling on an elbow to smile at Kieran. "You would break your brothers' hearts — not to mention those of your regulars, who must, of course, be invited." He grinned. "We should head back over tonight, let them know we still haven't figured out a date, but there's no question about the reception. Make them happy. And Danny can give us his latest historical discovery, and we can see what Kevin is up to — it is a Friday night, and it's still early. We should be free and clear."

"Sounds good. Maybe. Maybe not — let me mull on that."

Kieran stretched and rose and walked to the window, just slightly opening the drapes. Their loft was on Reed Street, once part of an industrial complex, a massive tailoring shop, converted to apartments, and now apartment/condos. There were large plate-glass windows that looked over the street. Downstairs, the living area offered high ceilings and more intricate little architectural details. The apartment was perfect. She liked their neighbors. New York was amazing, and while she had traveled to many places, she still found her native city to be one of the most diverse, historical, and fascinating places she had ever seen. The view out the window was always intriguing. They had something of a neighborhood; she saw the same people in the little deli down the street all the time.

Life is good. Forget Nicholson.

She was determined to do so. The night itself commanded she do so — it was beautiful. She turned to look back at Craig, and a real smile came to her lips.

Even after several years and many a strange adventure along the way, she still adored Craig. Her smile became a grin as she observed him with a trace of amusement as he lay stretched out on the bed.

"What?" he demanded, brows becoming an arch.

"You look like a pullout poster."

"What?" he demanded indignantly, starting to rise.

"Not an insult, you look . . . great," she said, and her smile became a laugh. "You just look like a pullout, a pinup, you know? All you need is a come-hither look on your face."

He was long and wire-muscled and bronze

against the sheets — and still naked. Of course, part of his physique was demanded by his job. She knew enough of his friends and coworkers to know that FBI agents did tend to come in athletic and fit — very fit. Naturally, they had to go through the Academy and keep up for their work.

"You want a come-hither look?" he teased. He wiggled his eyebrows. She wasn't sure the look was really all that come-hither, but, then again, the way he was stretched out . . .

Come-hither enough.

She paused to adjust the drapes, and as she did so, she noticed that in seconds, the weather had changed. Dark clouds covered what had been a striking starlit sky. She shivered suddenly; it felt ridiculously like an omen or a foreboding.

It was just rain.

She made sure the drapes were back in place and turned toward the bed. She flew at it, flinging herself on his naked body.

He gasped, groaned, caught her, held her above himself, and laughed.

"My come-hither was okay then?"

"No, it sucked!"

"Ah, I see. But you're coming to me anyway, right?"

"As you pointed out, it's Friday night, and neither of us have work, and I already helped out at the pub, so we can head over when we feel like it — or not — *and so* we have a chance here for sex, which since we live together we should be having far more often, while we're both physically here and awake. The come-hither look we'll have to work on."

"I'm crushed."

"You are not. You're overconfident, if anything. You're certain your look is completely seductive and compelling."

"I don't know about that. Crushed. I am crushed. You're lying on top of me, crushing me."

She grinned and didn't budge for a minute, then she pushed up against his chest and straddled him. "The big, bad agent-guy can't handle it, huh?"

"Oh, he can handle it, all right." Calmly he folded his arms behind his head. "Part of any investigation is to see just how far and where the other party is willing to go."

"Far!" she warned. She eased herself around in a slow and sinuous motion, and then eased slowly back down on his arousal, drawing a groan and tremor from him.

She began to move.

He caught her arms, pulling her down to him, not losing a beat. "Big, bad agent, eh?" And, with a fluid motion, he rolled the two of them together, drawing her beneath him, and then their eyes locked, and their bodies moved.

They lost themselves in each other for a while.

Replete at last, they lay together, damp and shimmering, holding each other still.

Craig's phone rang.

Kieran groaned softly.

Craig hesitated; on the fourth ring, he rolled over, found his phone on the bedside table, and answered it.

He listened; she watched the tension come into his face.

"What is it?" Kieran asked.

"Um, not sure yet. Just a crime scene that I must get to. Kieran, I'm sorry —"

"In for a penny, in for a pound," she told him, and reminded him, "Sometimes it's me. You put up with my crazy family and an entire Irish pub. And still . . ."

"And we wake up together," he said.

"And go to bed at night together. Sometimes." She laughed softly. "It's okay. Go — go! Get to your crime scene."

He gave her a grim smile and rolled to the edge of the bed to rise, and then padded into the bathroom. "I'll see you at the pub. I'm just not sure how late."

"It's open late. Especially on a Friday

36

night. Oh, and I'm tight with the owners. It will be fine."

She lay back down, thinking she could just go to sleep, relax for the night, if she wanted.

But she didn't want to be alone right now, though she would never say so to Craig.

She wasn't usually so unnerved. She'd spoken to murderers before, along with rapists, child abusers, and then occasionally those who really might find a way to go straight.

She'd get up and first go over her notes, because it was necessary. Then she'd head to the pub. She might not be needed to wait on any of the tables, but Declan was always there when she needed him. While she and Danny and Kevin had "day" jobs, they all headed to the pub when they were off, or when they wanted to be with the family, or when they were simply at loose ends.

Craig emerged after what must have been a two-minute shower; he was buttoning his tailored shirt as he emerged. His Glock and holster were already at the small of his back.

He barely finished buttoning his shirt before he reached for his jacket.

He strode to the bed and hesitated, unusually tense. He was accustomed to his work; he dealt with it well.

"I'll keep in touch," he promised. "And

I'll see you as soon as I can get there."

Then he was gone. She lay back down, contemplating the darkened sky. To her, it seemed there was something else about it.

A whisper of warning.

She shook off the thought, rose, showered, and dressed. Later, she would realize just how dark and foreboding the night and the coming days would prove to be.

CHAPTER TWO

The corpse had been burned, Craig Frasier observed, something tightening in his gut.

But the Fireman, Raoul Nicholson, was locked away at Rikers — Kieran had just interviewed him.

"What the hell?" Mike Dalton muttered. Like Craig, his partner must have been feeling a sense of déjà vu. The crime scene was way too much like those they thought they had seen the last of. The apartment was crowded with personnel, including the medical examiner, FBI agents, cops, and the paramedics who'd answered what had gone out as an emergency call.

One of the uniformed cops who had been first on the scene — a very young man whose face was turning an almost cartoon-character shade of green — started to give it up and made a choking sound.

"Get him a bag, now! Kid, get control. You can't vomit on the crime scene," Craig

39

said, grabbing a bag from a quick-thinking paramedic and handing it to the young cop.

Most of the people in the room remained silent. Everyone here was likely thinking the same thing: *they had caught this killer already; this shouldn't be happening.*

They had to forget the past; forget what they thought they knew. Here was a new crime scene.

And a new victim.

Craig gave himself a firm mental shake. They all had to move. Starting with the cop about to contaminate everything around him.

"Kid, we've all been there," Craig said to the young cop, his tone quiet. The man was obviously new to the job; he didn't even look as if he'd been shaving long. He'd probably be ribbed by his fellow cops later. But maybe not too badly. Every first responder had had a moment when they'd witnessed something that was beyond their level of acceptance, and had a gut reaction to the inhumanity of it.

"Hey, someone help him out," Mike suggested.

"And, please, everyone else, clear the room — we've just about compromised the place all to hell here," Craig said. "Unless you're NYPD forensics or photography, get out. Officer Ridley," he said, speaking to the man who appeared to be in charge, "could you start a canvass? See if any of the residents saw or heard anything."

Craig had called it right; Ridley was apparently ranking officer in the room. He nodded gravely to Craig and turned to the uniforms. "You heard him, let's get started. We've access to every floor."

"So is the Fireman capable of astral projection?" one of the cops muttered. "There's one way in, one elevator. It's impossible. Unless he had a key to this apartment."

"It doesn't mean someone didn't hear something. We need witnesses, and this thing called evidence. Come on. Let's act like cops, huh?" Ridley snapped.

People began to filter out.

For a moment there was quiet in the room. Everyone there felt a little shell-shocked — and a little nauseated, as well.

"Let's get on the phone up to Rikers," Craig said. "Confirm that Nicholson is still in custody, or if he made it out somehow. We may have a copycat on our hands."

"I'll make the call," Mike said, stepping back to the little entry hallway right off the elevator. The hall led to a longer hallway, a dining room, and the parlor, where the body lay.

Craig hunkered down by the body, across from the medical examiner. "What can you tell us, Dr. Layton?" Craig asked, looking over at the man.

Soon after he'd gotten the call from his boss, FBI Assistant Director Richard Egan, that evening about the alert from the police precinct, he'd asked to make sure that Layton was put on the case.

Layton had handled the victims of the Fireman.

Frederick Layton shook his head. "Damn. This is all preliminary, Special Agent Frasier, but it sure as hell has all the aspects I saw with . . . yeah. The Fireman."

Craig didn't need the medical examiner or anyone in forensics to tell them the flames in the apartment had been deliberately ignited *on* the body.

Fire hadn't even ruined much of the handsome Upper East Side apartment.

"Time of death can be narrowed down without me," Layton said. Craig knew they had a good approximate time of death because they knew when the man had last been seen alive. The guard on duty at the door to the elegant apartment complex had known that their victim, Charles Mayhew, had arrived home just about three hours ago. About forty-five minutes later, Mayhew hadn't answered a call for a delivery. The guard, Joey Catalano, had become nervous and headed up.

Catalano said he'd smelled fire as soon as he'd got in the elevator; he'd hurried into Mayhew's apartment, which occupied the entire seventh floor. The parlor was visible from the entryway, and Catalano had seen flames and grabbed the fire extinguisher that was right next to the elevator door. He'd called 911 as soon as he'd put out the fire consuming Mayhew's body.

"There's more left than there has been at other times," Layton said matter-of-factly.

The bodies they had found across the city had burned quickly and fiercely, leaving very little to be discovered by the medical examiner.

But if this killer was a true copycat, they would discover the fire had not been set to cause the agony of burning to death. Dr. Layton had told them that on the original cases, the victims had been strangled before death, and then gasoline was used as an incendiary accelerant.

The horrible smell of burned flesh was strong. Craig had a handkerchief with him and was holding it across his nose and

43

mouth until one of Layton's assistants provided him with a mask.

The corpse was black and gray and mottled, giving it an ancient appearance, despite the speed with which the security guard had arrived to spray it with a fire extinguisher. The flame retardant added to the grotesque look of eerie bubbles that had formed over the remains.

And still, one thing was obvious: the eyes had been gouged out. Craig thought that when Layton worked on the body, he would certainly discover that the tongue had been cut out, as well.

He'd seen it all in his sleep, in his dream, his memory — a moving picture within his mind's eye, haunting and terrible, and now, once again, real.

"If Nicholson's still locked up, he had to have been in close contact with someone," Layton said. "This is just . . . too close. I'd almost venture to say identical."

The details of the mutilations had not been shared with the media. Any copycat at work would have had to somehow have learned the specifics. There could have been leaks, of course, but to the best of Craig's knowledge no insider information had ever made the news, in print, online, or on the television. Dr. Layton looked up from the

corpse and straight at Craig. His eyes —
large behind his gold-framed glasses —
betrayed the fact even he was a little unnerved by the discovery, again, of a corpse
in this condition. But he began his professional spiel.

"Anything I tell you is going to be an as-
sumption. The fire inspector is on his way.
Hopefully he can tell you how long the fire
burned. The body has lots of fatty tissue, so
with an accelerant, one can burn quickly.
But I do believe the security guard found
Mayhew almost immediately. He dialed 911
straightaway, patrol came . . . and they sent
for you and me. I'm going to say he was
killed right before he was set on fire. We
know for sure it was in that three-hour
window. I'm going out on a limb a little,
but based on experience, I'll suggest he
might have been killed before he was set on
fire, which would put his death about an
hour ago. I'll tell you close as I can . . ."

Layton paused, and then continued. "This
is unnerving. It really looks like the same
killer — method of body burning exact,
and . . . no tongue. No eyes." He was quiet
a minute. "If Raoul Nicholson is still up at
Rikers, he may have had an accomplice.
Because this is one hell of a copycat."

"The tongue is gone?" Craig asked. "You

checked?"

Layton nodded grimly.

It was bad news having a serial killer at work in the city — any serial killer. The Fireman killings had been exceptionally bad. And now it seemed that they were starting all over again. Craig looked at the notes sent to him by the tech team at headquarters.

Victim: Charles Mayhew, real estate magnate. Fifty-two, divorced, no children, CEO of his own company, Mind Mechanics. Popular with politicians — belonged to numerous social clubs. Residence at the Marchman Building for ten years. Each floor is one apartment — each elevator key brings a resident to his or her apartment. Security personnel do have master keys in case of emergency. In Mayhew's apartment there are three bedrooms, three baths, kitchen, parlor, dining room, and office. Mr. Mayhew had never been arrested; he was a graduate of Yale, was included in lists of important New Yorkers, and his financial status put him into the realm of multimillionaires. He was known for his philanthropic works.

Craig looked around the apartment; nice place for a guy alone in NYC. It was exceptionally fine, and befitting a man of his status.

Known for his philanthropic works.

Dr. Layton cleared his throat and said, "I'm just the ME, and some detectives and agents like to do the theorizing and detecting themselves, but . . . ."

Craig looked at him, nodding, and said, "I'm happy to hear anything you have to say, Doctor. Your opinion is an educated one, and you are more familiar with the evidence than anyone else."

Layton swallowed. "Maybe it is different. Might be a copycat with an agenda." Layton went on quietly, "This was a very, very wealthy man. He wasn't an easy target. Prostitutes on the street are accessible. And even a student, out wandering, shopping. The other victims were a designer and an accountant. They were average people, caught alone — something of a feat in New York City, but still caught alone. If Nicholson wasn't at Rikers, I'd say this was his work, certainly. But this murder was also bolder. You know more about the minds of men, and I don't really have a theory, but more a question. Is that a natural progression for a serial killer? There will be a complete autopsy, of course, but on initial observation it appears the cause of death

47

was asphyxiation. A cursory exam shows the windpipe is crushed. He was killed in the same way the other victims were killed, down to a T. So, if Nicholson's somehow out, is he escalating? Or did he have a partner, and they're growing bolder?"

"Mike is on the phone right now, checking," Craig said.

"If it wasn't him . . ." Layton muttered.

"It was someone who knew him," Craig agreed. "And, yes, this is a step forward — by Nicholson, or someone who studied him. All the victims were different, but they were killed outside, in dark alleys, quiet streets. The killer this time took a far greater chance accessing Charles Mayhew's apartment." There had never appeared to be any external rhyme or reason to the chosen victims previously — only that for some reason, Nicholson had believed they were witches. Was there something else behind the killings they didn't see? A correlation . . . a thread?

"Nicholson's fourth victim, the fashion designer, he was also a drag queen. Had a hell of a following, from what I read," Craig said, thinking out loud. "When the first two came in, both sex workers, it did seem like someone was down on prostitutes . . . playing a different kind of Jack the Ripper. But the murdered student was superior at academics, and shy and studious. No sexual content there, even after all the digging we did. And the accountant was a family man without a whisper of scandal to his life. And now, this man was known for his good works. What I'm wondering is, why the hell would someone think he was a witch, about to do evil to someone?"

"Why indeed," Layton agreed. Despite the clamp and tension in his gut, Craig was still hunkered down by the body across from the ME. The mask he'd been provided helped, but it didn't obliterate the smell. The corpse didn't appear to be real, except the awful smell of burned flesh was a sharp reminder he'd been very real indeed. Historically, witches had been burned in areas of Europe, hanged in others. In the United States, they'd been hanged, not burned. The most infamous slayings had been in Salem, Massachusetts, purportedly by good Puritans convinced the devil was causing their problems. And yet, in retrospect, theories suggested that those accused of being witches also happened to be those holding land the accusers coveted.

So was there something that these victims had in their possession that their killer — Nicholson — had actually wanted? Was there a tie in there he wasn't seeing?

49

It was easy to covet wealth, but who stood to gain from Mayhew's death?

And how had the killer gotten in — and out — of an apartment with one entrance, needing a special key for the elevator to even stop at the floor?

Craig stood as Mike walked toward them, a grim look on his face.

"What is it?" Craig asked.

"We've got a problem," Mike said.

"You know, I never doubted you'd have your reception here," Declan, the eldest of the four Finnegan siblings, told Kieran, grinning. "I mean, you'd have to worry about Mom and Dad rolling around in their graves if you didn't. And, on a lighter side, the price tag is going to be right. Also, seriously, your family, friends . . . everyone comes here."

"Still, it was a decision we had to make," Kieran said. Declan was behind the bar; it was Friday night, so Jimmy Murphy, one of the pub's regular bartenders, was on, but Declan was helping out.

Kieran was at the one stool that sat by the hinged piece of curved bar that allowed for an exit or entry. The siblings referred to it as the "loner" chair, but it was a great place to converse with a bartender and not be annoying to or heard by anyone on the other stools in front of the bar with its two dozen taps.

"The decision you have to make is picking a date — and a church. Or other venue," Declan said firmly. He smiled. Her eldest brother made a great bartender — he was a listener — and often replied with safe advice to be taken or ignored. Of course, he'd taken on "protector" mode where she was concerned, but he liked Craig and respected him.

"It's hard to set a good date," Kieran said. "Something is always happening."

"You're making excuses. You're not afraid of getting married, are you?"

"No, of course not!"

"Just checking."

She sighed. "It's what we do . . . there is always another case."

"Yes, that's the point. There will always be something. So, you choose your date, and whatever comes up, there are many other competent agents who can handle Craig's cases. And Fuller and Miro are not the only psychiatrists on call. You can never find time? You two have to make time."

"Right. Yes, sir!" Kieran said, smiling.

"Hey, you need to be happy."

"I am happy. I love our new place. And,

51

seriously, most of the time I feel good. A lot of my work has to do with reuniting families, making sure people are receiving the treatment or the therapy they need . . . It's not all about crazy murderers!"

Declan nodded. "You can find someone to do the wedding right here — go from wedding to immediate reception. Or there are a lot of fantastic venues in the city. Have the ceremony at a park or up at the Cloisters. But then again, you'd have a long trip with a lot of people from way up the city to downtown."

"A park would be pretty," Kieran mused, noting that Declan was suddenly staring at her hard — and frowning.

She loved her brothers equally, but Declan had quickly taken on the mantle of responsibility when they'd lost their mother years before, and then their father. He was tall and well built, with fine blue-gray eyes and dark auburn hair — a very handsome man. She was incredibly proud of him. Finnegan's had maintained its reputation under his leadership and had been written up by many travel magazines and websites as a go-to venue.

Right now, he looked a great deal like her father — filled with authority and concern.

"What did you just say?" he demanded.

She was startled. "Uh — a park would be pretty for a wedding?"

"No, about crazy murderers. What are you up to now?"

She sighed. "They're still arguing over the charges Raoul Nicholson is going to face. Dr. Fuller has interviewed him, and Dr. Miro has interviewed him. Probably a few police psychiatrists, too. They asked me to speak with him today."

"So, that's why you're here, hmm?" he asked quietly.

"Hey, I'm here all the time!" Kieran protested.

Declan nodded, studying her. "Yeah, but . . . you could have had a nice, relaxing night alone in your great new apartment. That creep got under your skin. There's something about the way he doesn't look crazy that is even more disturbing, like his evil is hidden, devious . . . anyway . . ."

"Yeah, you feel like you need a shower."

"I would think just walking into the facility at Rikers would make you feel like you need a shower."

"Hey, eighty-five percent of the people there are awaiting arraignment or trial — they've yet to be proven guilty. For that matter, Nicholson is still waiting for his trial date."

53

"So much for speedy justice."

"His is an unusual case. He's confessed to the murders, but his mental state and his ability to aid in his own trial are under question. And we try, but statistically, about one hundred thousand people enter Rikers on a yearly basis — that's a lot of people."

"Well, we are on an island of millions," Declan said. "Let's get off the criminals. So what does Craig say?"

"About what?" Kieran asked with a frown.

"The wedding!"

"Oh, he says we should do whatever I want — except, he knows the reception has to be here."

"Of course," Declan said.

"Declan!" a customer called, and Declan excused himself.

Kieran hadn't heard from Craig recently and was about to call him when she felt someone coming close behind her; instinctively, she whirled around on her stool.

"Woah!"

It was Kevin, her twin brother. He was tall like Declan, with slightly lighter hair. She looked up into eyes a blue-green shade like her own.

"Your show over?" she asked, trying to offer him a big smile. He was currently in a new musical that had been running about a month called *A Bite of the Apple,* a play on the history of New York City.

He glanced at his watch. "Yeah, it's late!"

"How was the night?"

"Sold out — a Friday night in New York. And a great audience. You know, I wouldn't be against a role in a big-time drama or sitcom that paid megabills for years and years, but I do love live audiences. So, how was your day?" he asked, sliding around her to lean against the bar.

"Uh . . . well . . ."

"She interviewed Raoul Nicholson today," she heard Declan say. He'd delivered an ale to a man just around the corner from them and returned to eye them both.

"Wow. How'd that go — first time you've met him, right?"

"Yes, it was the first time I saw him. Miro and Fuller wanted me to talk to him. They didn't tell me anything about their reports. They wanted my unbiased take on him."

"And your take was . . . ?" Kevin asked.

She looked at Declan and shrugged. "Disturbed — in a very different way. He doesn't appear to have any other signs of mental illness, but he believes the people he killed were witches. He feels they would have done some terrible evil to others — if he hadn't stopped them. He understands

55

the laws of the state, and that in the eyes of the state, he's guilty. And he isn't remorseful. He did what he had to do as long as he could do it. Or not."

"Or not?" Kevin asked.

She shrugged. "I'm not even sure if he was making it all up — except he hasn't asked for an insanity plea. His attorney wants to go for it."

"And the prosecution?"

"Is still playing around with the exact charges they'll bring into court. He has been charged with murder — but how they'll amend the charges before trial depends on what the prosecution believes they'll be able to prove."

"There's irrefutable evidence against him, and he confessed," Declan said.

"Yes, but his sentencing and the trial will hinge on whether he is or isn't sane. They'd have him executed, I believe, if they could. He has said outright that he would kill again. The thing is, they don't want him getting out, and if a slew of medical experts declare him unfit to stand trial . . ."

"And that hinges on whether he's telling the truth?" Kevin asked.

"Hey, Declan!" someone called. "Turn up the television. I don't believe this! He's out — that bastard Fireman guy. He's out!"

CHAPTER THREE

Craig stared at Mike, incredulous. Then he pulled his phone from his pocket. There wasn't a valid reason he should be worried about Kieran — *except she had interviewed a killer that afternoon, just before he had somehow escaped.* But Nicholson killed those he thought to be witches, and it was doubtful he could think of Kieran as a witch.

Then again, what criteria had the man used to determine who was or wasn't a witch?

Only the voice in his head.

How the hell had the man gotten out? Craig needed to know; they needed to be back on the hunt.

But not until he had spoken with Kieran.

She answered his call on the first ring.

"Where are you?" he asked her.

"The pub — I came right back in after you left, and I'm fine," she told him.

"You know he's out."

"It's all over the news. But keep at whatever you're doing. I'm the last person you need to worry about — Nicholson does not think I'm a witch."

"Yes, but he knows you."

"Craig, he knows hundreds of people, I'm sure. Trust me — he doesn't believe I'm a witch. He told me as much. Craig," she added softly, "we can't do this all the time."

"We don't do it all the time," he said defensively. "Just when there's a credible threat to your safety. You're forgetting other cases."

"Craig, I'm good. And I'm at the pub and —"

He heard her protest as her phone was taken from her.

"She's not leaving here alone," Kevin interrupted. "And it's not just her. You should listen to the people in here. The media got wind of it quickly, and no one is going home alone. There's a group from Wall Street that meets here all the time, and they're divvying up who is going with who to make sure everyone gets home okay. I'll go with Kieran, and I'll stay at your place until you get back."

Craig heard Kieran chastise her brother. "You have a matinee tomorrow!"

"Right, well —"

"We have the guest room all set up," Craig reminded him.

"So I'll sleep at your place," Kevin continued.

Mike was watching Craig. He slowly lifted an eyebrow.

"Thanks, Kevin," Craig said, and hung up.

"So, seems the media has wind of what we didn't know," he said to Mike.

His partner nodded grimly. "I don't know how word got out so fast," he said. "But here's the story — Nicholson is out. He didn't kill anyone during his escape. Apparently he had an interview this afternoon and then complained of violent pain in his stomach. He got himself to the infirmary and drugged a pack of people. But how he got out from there, no one knows. Dressed up as a guard — that's what they're suspecting at the moment. But . . . yeah, he's gone. He's out."

"When did all this happen?" Craig demanded.

"Approximately four hours ago."

"Barely enough time to get from Rikers Island to here, find a way up and kill and set a fire to the body and then somehow escape."

"Barely enough . . . but possible?"

"Possible, but . . . just barely."

"You think someone is setting up a killer — as a killer?"

"If you wanted to kill someone and get away with it, what better way than to set it up on a confessed murderer?" Craig asked.

"But the timing . . ." Mike said, shaking his head.

"Yeah, tough to think that timing works," Craig agreed. "And then again, strangling, the same, tongue cut out, the same, eyes gouged, the same, set afire with gasoline . . . the same. And a man who could make his way out of Rikers . . . well, it's not that far-fetched to think he might have made his way up here." He shrugged. "I want to speak with the doorman."

"We might want to start in the morning," Mike said. "Craig, it's nearly midnight."

"And no better time to strike, right? Midnight. The 'witching' hour," Craig said dryly.

"Okay then," Mike said wearily. "Let's interview the security guard. Officers have been pounding on doors and waking the neighbors . . . and the news is out that Raoul Nicholson has escaped. By morning, the world is going to know about another murder."

"And then we have to go out to Rikers," Craig said.

"Sure, yeah, we'll sleep when we're dead. And partnering with you, my friend, I always figure that might come sooner rather than later."

Kieran and Kevin sat in the apartment on Reed Street. She had wanted to walk — it was an easy enough distance to cover on foot. But she had been overruled; no easy strolls that night. Taking the path of least resistance, Kieran had allowed one of the regulars, Mitch Beattie — who had moved to Brooklyn, but still chose to come to Finnegan's on Friday nights, switching his drink from Guinness to the Guinness non-alcoholic beer, Kaliber — to drive them to the apartment complex. Once there, Kieran had put water on to boil for a pot of tea, and hoped Craig would walk in any minute.

She'd known Kevin was working on writing his own play, and so she tried to draw him out on it. Her questions seemed to be working. Kevin was a fine actor, she thought, and the perfect leading-man type. But he really loved the theater, and would often take a project when he thought the writing was excellent — even if he didn't think it would prove to be a blockbuster.

"It's historical, and I'm going from the beginning of New York — Dutch settlement, all that." He grimaced. " 'No Irish Need Apply,' " he said, quoting signs that had been displayed in the mid-1800s throughout the city. "It's about the country really, and the incredible melting pot that is New York, and how different ethnic groups found their place. By the way, there was no killing of witches here. Salem — as we know — wasn't the first or only place in the colonies women were persecuted, but seriously, most cases were in the Massachusetts Bay Colony — Connecticut and Massachusetts. Makes you wonder how Raoul Nicholson got started on his killing spree. I know he's a fundamentalist, but I do have friends who are fundamentalists, and they're horrified by what happened. It doesn't seem to have anything to do with any recognized religion. He's on his own private mission."

"I think we should talk about the theater," Kieran said.

"I think we should talk about Raoul Nicholson. He's on the streets again."

"Maybe far from New York."

"Madman or liar?" he asked her.

"Either way, your concern for me is just about as crazy — not that I don't love you for it. The man doesn't think I'm a witch.

Honest. And you need a key and a code to get into this building. And our windows and our one and only door are connected to a state-of-the-art security system. I'm safe," she added softly. "So, New York City history — from the Dutch settlement to today. That's a lot to handle!"

She realized he wasn't really listening. He was looking past her to the television; she left him watching the news while she brewed the tea.

The sound was low; Kevin found the remote control and raised the volume.

"We know Nicholson is out," Kieran protested, thinking that watching the same news over and over again wasn't going to get them anywhere. "Kevin —"

"I know where Craig is," he said. "He did it already — Nicholson has killed again!" Kevin said.

Kieran spun around to see the wide-screen TV.

A reporter was standing alongside Central Park on the Upper East Side. She was grave as she spoke. The street was filled with vehicles, cop cars, dark sedans, FBI standard issue, she thought, and vehicles that were labeled as belonging to crime scene forensics units.

There was also an ambulance.

"The police have informed us that multi-millionaire Charles Mayhew was murdered tonight in his guarded apartment here on the Upper East Side. Mr. Mayhew is well-known to New Yorkers for his many philanthropic works. The police are giving us all 'no comment' remarks when we question them regarding the situation. The media, however, was alerted by an anonymous source — someone, we believe, within the building. We know the police can't give out much information on an ongoing investigation, but we can't help but speculate on this murder on the very eve the heinous 'Fireman' has escaped his prison on Rikers Island."

"Lord!" Kevin breathed. "He is out there . . . out here. He's killed again. Already. He escaped what, four hours ago, something like that?"

"Kevin, it would be nice to think Nicholson is the only man in New York who proved to be a killer. Nice, but that's hardly true. Anything could have happened. Mayhew was richer than Croesus. He might have made all kinds of enemies to get that way," Kieran said. "We don't know what —"

"Craig knows," Kevin interrupted. "Call him."

"I'm not calling him — he's working.

And," she told him, "you're going to go to sleep, and so am I. You have a matinee, and you're going to be brilliant and shine."

"Kieran . . ."

"And you're welcome for the tea — the least I can do, with you insisting on staying with me," she said.

"I didn't —"

"Good night, Kevin. I love you. Guest room is all set up."

She walked to him, gave him a kiss on the cheek, and turned to head up the stairs to the loft.

She didn't know if he went into the guest room or not. She really hoped he did. The weekends were hard work; his show offered matinees on both Saturday and Sunday, and then again on Wednesdays, as well.

She loved her twin very much. But she didn't want him harping on about the case. She knew she wouldn't be able to sleep; she hoped Kevin could.

Though she wouldn't admit it, she was as suspicious as he was that Nicholson might be at it again.

But . . . how? How had he gotten from Rikers Island and up to a posh apartment on the East Side in such a short amount of time?

She pulled out her computer, keying in

65

words, trying to find anything regarding modern-day witchcraft, biblical witchcraft, or anything else that might have started Raoul Nicholson on the belief that people walking the streets of New York might be witches.

She was stunned to read an article reporting human rights agencies within the United Nations were working desperately to counter a rising number of persecutions across the globe in the twenty-first century; as recently as 2013, in Papua New Guinea, a twenty-year-old mother had been burned alive — suspected of sorcery. There were dozens more reports from various African countries, and the researchers believe the modern persecutions reached well into the developed Western world.

She leaned back on her pillow.

Not here, she thought. *Not in New York City!*

Was Nicholson just one of many?

She began looking back into the history of executions in the United States, the first on record being that of Alse or Alice Young of Windsor, Connecticut. The woman was hanged in May of 1647. In 1648, Mary Johnson confessed to practicing witchcraft — or "familiarity with the devil." The confession came after a series of beatings, and God alone knew what else. Because

Mary was pregnant, she was allowed to live until her child was born. She wasn't executed until 1650. In all, between the years 1647 and 1697, records showed that thirty-five people were accused of witchcraft. Eleven were executed.

"Unbelievable," Kieran muttered to herself, searching for another article. The author of her next reference suggested that harsh New England winters, the fear of attacks from the native population, and the ravages often left by disease had the settlers looking for a scapegoat.

Not to mention that back in Europe, mass executions were occurring.

An estimated forty thousand to sixty thousand people had been executed in Europe between the 1400s and early 1700s. *But that barbaric practice had stopped.*

She wanted to keep searching, studying the past to try to determine how a man could believe, in today's world, strangers were in league with the devil. But her efforts were to no avail.

She fell asleep with the computer still on her lap.

Joey Catalano seemed to be a decent enough guy. He was about twenty-five, clean-cut, with serious brown eyes, a six-foot frame, and a solid middleweight's body. He was polite, but he also carried a gun. Licensed, he'd assured Craig and Mike right away — possibly because the police had already asked that question.

They met with him in the guard's tiny office in the lobby, next to the elevator. He'd brought in his boss, a middle-aged man, thin and austere, with steel-gray eyes and hair and that matched his demeanor. He was introduced as Simon Wrigley.

He was the Wrigley, apparently, of Wrigley Security Systems, the company contracted by the building, and was ready to help with any answers Joey Catalano couldn't give.

Another man in the security service had been called in to work the door.

Simon Wrigley was probably there, too, because Joey Catalano — despite the fact that he made a great "security" presence with his build and his height — seemed to be unnerved by what had happened. His fingers shook.

Of course, a grisly murder had happened on his watch.

By the fierce way Wrigley looked at him, Joey was probably unnerved by his boss, as well.

"Here's what I don't understand," Catalano told them. "No one came in who didn't live in the building — not until the deliveryman appeared with a package for Mr. Mayhew. That's when I buzzed him. When he didn't answer, I decided just to go up and check on him. And then I got in the elevator, and smelled the smoke and . . ." He lifted his hands.

"You never left your post?" Craig asked him.

"Not even to pee?" Mike added a little indelicately.

But Catalano shook his head. "My shift is 8:00 p.m. to 4:00 a.m. I make it a point to go before I'm on the clock, and watch the liquids before I start, as well. At midnight, I do take a five-minute break. I lock the main doors before I do so, and you see where we are now — and that our toilet is right there. I'm not away for more than a few minutes. I wouldn't be. When residents have visitors, they must check in. Remember, now I can send someone up with the master key, but each resident has keys that only open on their floors."

"So, tell us who came and went once you came on shift," Craig said. "We'll roll the tape at speed, and you can tell us about everyone as we see them."

For a moment Catalano looked confused.

"Joey, they'll fast-forward the footage,"

Simon Wrigley explained. "Somehow, some-one got into this building. Either that, or . . ."

"Or someone who lives in the building killed him," Craig said.

Joey nodded and spun his chair around to the computer, then cued the footage to show at high speed. Each time the door opened, he hit the pause button.

"That's Mr. and Mrs. Mobley, Toni and Teri," he said. He looked back at Craig. "They've been here for six years — nice people. They'd been to the new Italian place on Fifth Ave." He paused. "You know that the police already went through the footage, copied it, and sent it on, right?"

"I'm sure it's at your headquarters by now," Simon Wrigley assured them. "It's like this guy — this killer — was a magi-cian, or Spider-Man. I sure can't begin to figure how he got in here!"

"We'll study it again later," Mike said. "For now, please keep going."

"Okay . . ."

The next stop was for a single young woman. "Sienna Johnson," Catalano said. "Floor number six — she lives alone. Trust-fund baby, but super nice."

"Thank you, go on," Craig said.

The next person they saw was a man in a

hoodie exiting the building. He had a little dog on a leash.

"Mr. Blom, fourth floor — and Ruff. Good little dog. You know how the little ones can be such yappers? Not Ruff — great manners. And a good companion for Mr. Blom. He's a great guy."

"Nice. You know all the tenants," Craig said.

"It's an old building, refurbished," Wrigley explained. "Just eight stories, and now every one of them is an individual apartment. We do know everyone who lives here — as you can imagine. The few tenants pay for us — the security team — and for maintenance. You can figure just what that costs them per month."

"Roll again," Craig said.

Catalano did so. A messenger in a popular courier company's uniform arrived and left.

Mr. Blom — floor four — returned with Ruff.

Then, the UPS man with his package. They saw Catalano try to buzz Mayhew. They watched the video of Catalano dutifully locking the door before heading to the elevator. He hit Stop when his image disappeared as the door closed. They knew what had happened next.

"I know you're going to want to talk to

the tenants again," Catalano said, "but do you think it could wait until morning? If they can sleep, they're asleep. They're all retired or Monday to Friday nine-to-fivers, except for Sienna Johnson, and she's just . . . rich. And Charles Mayhew, except . . . well."

"Yes, that's fine. We'll be back early," Craig said.

"It's out now about Raoul Nicholson," Wrigley said. "You all had him behind bars. And now this. There you are — a perfect argument *for* the death penalty. For a man like Nicholson, who admitted his guilt, who killed so many people, innocent people — he needs to be executed."

"Ah, but new evidence has proven a lot of men on death row or in for life to be innocent," Mike reminded him. "Better for two guilty persons go free than one innocent man be condemned — or something like that."

"Benjamin Franklin took that statement — almost word for word — from Voltaire, I believe," Craig said. He looked at Simon Wrigley. "We don't make the laws, sir. That's the US Congress and the governing body of the State of New York. If this was Raoul Nicholson, we will catch him again."

"And how many will die before?" Wrigley asked. "Poor Joey here is going to live with

Mr. Mayhew's death the rest of his days. You're going to torment the tenants, unnerve them all over again, and Nicholson is your killer. You let that bastard get out, and he got in here somehow."

"Possibly, and possibly not," Craig said flatly. They needed to leave before he lost his temper.

Workers at Rikers did their best with a massive population of detainees — from those who had committed minor infractions to cold-blooded rapists, murderers, child abusers, and more. He wasn't happy about Nicholson's escape, but it wasn't anyone's fault unless someone had knowingly helped him.

"We'll interview the residents bright and early, Mr. Wrigley, if you'll be so good as to make sure they're aware we'll need to see them. We'll be back by 8:00 a.m. Right now, we need to know more about the master keys."

"Key," Wrigley corrected him. "There is only one here. It's passed from guard to guard."

"And there are no other copies?" Mike asked, a frown on his face and doubt in his words.

"One more — but not here, kept in a safe at our office's headquarters on Forty-

Second Street off Broadway," Wrigley said. "My family has been in business since the First World War. We're highly respected. We've learned through the years how to become more and more secure. There's never been any kind of a break-in at this building."

"Until now," Mike said. That caused Wrigley to stiffen.

"You're suggesting it was an inside job? People are vetted before they move in here. My guards are bonded. Our residents are innocent of this. I'd bet my life on it. You people let Nicholson escape — let this death be on you. Somehow, Charles Mayhew himself must have brought this man in. My guards know how important it is that a master key is never — never — out of their hands, except when it is passed on to his shift relief!"

They'd made him angry; there was no point arguing with an angry man.

Craig looked at Joey Catalano. The young man still seemed to carry a light tinge of green about him.

"You're sure you had your key all night."

"Oh, yes, sir, I'm positive."

"Thank you both. There will be an officer just outside all evening. He'll be watching over everyone here," Craig said.

Joey Catalano nodded. Simon Wrigley just glared at them.

As they crossed the lobby, Craig muttered, "Didn't mean to piss him off."

"Oh, he seems like he's just pissy in general," Mike said. "Like it or not, a brutal murder happened while his guard was on duty. He's trying to throw blame at someone else. So he's looking at Rikers."

"Yeah," Craig agreed. He hesitated with his hand on the door. "Just a minute. I want to see the crime scene head. I think it's a guy named Corwin Booth tonight."

"It is. Why?"

"They need to look for a note. Nicholson sent each of his victims a note before he killed them, almost as if he was giving them a chance to change their ways, or at the least confess their sins and die with . . . their souls clean, perhaps, in his mind."

Mike nodded. "I'll get the guard to get us up there."

The new guy was on the door, much older than Joey Catalano, and gray all around. His beard was the color of steel and his buzzed hair matched. His face even seemed to have a cast of the color.

He nodded grimly, though, accompanying them to the elevator, sliding in the flat metal key that would bring them up to the right apartment, and then leaving them on their way in the tiny elevator.

Up in the apartment, Layton and the body were gone. A crew of four techs still worked the scene. Craig quickly found Corwin Booth — a slender man in his early thirties — moving quickly around the room, wearing rimless glasses and a face mask against the lingering smell of burned flesh.

"See if you can find a note, Booth, please," Craig told him.

"A warning note?" Booth asked, clearly familiar with Nicholson's MO.

Craig nodded.

"We'll dig through everything here. My team is good. If it's here, we'll find it."

"Check the trash, everything," Mike added.

Booth smiled with no amusement. "That's a given, Special Agent," he said.

Mike winced. "Sorry. It's just —"

"Yeah, I worked a few of the Nicholson scenes. He sent a note every time. But if we don't find one, it might not mean anything. How could he have gotten such a note out from Rikers?"

"How could he have gotten himself out from Rikers?" Mike replied.

"Touché, Special Agent Dalton, touché," Booth told him. "But . . . so far, we haven't come up with anything. We'll be here through the night though. I'll call if we do find a note. But I have a feeling we won't. I have a feeling this wasn't him."

"You don't think Nicholson did this? What's different?" Craig asked.

Booth shook his head. "Just . . . The other victims weren't found inside. They were found in alleys. So . . . the body is very similar. As for anything else, I'm still looking."

"But what do you think?" Craig asked him.

"Hey, I'm not paid to think. I collect evidence, and evidence speaks for me."

"You interpret it, too," Craig reminded him.

"Yeah, well . . ."

"Yeah, well . . . what?" Craig prodded.

"You can't interpret a hunch, and it isn't evidence. Something feels wrong. Maybe it's just logic. Maybe even if this guy got out of Rikers — and prisoners have escaped from max security prisons — I don't like the timing. This had to have been scoped out and planned. So . . . I don't know. It isn't evidence, and if you prove that Nicholson did it, well . . . I'll accept it."

He looked away uncomfortably.

"Thanks," Craig told him. "Really —

thanks."

He and Mike headed back to the elevator. They didn't need a key to go down; the large *G* was the only button that would respond to any touch.

There had to be more. It wasn't a magician or Spider-Man who had gotten in and strangled, sliced, gouged, and set Mayhew on fire.

It had been a killer, a man or a woman, cold-blooded and calculating . . .

One who had studied the building, the residents, and found whatever it was that Craig and Mike were missing.

In the middle of the night, Kieran rolled over and stretched out an arm, still half asleep, but certain that she would touch a warm body.

There was no one.

That woke her up, and she bolted to a sitting position. The room had a dim glow from the streetlights outside below her windows — she had fallen asleep with the blinds still open.

She fumbled for the TV remote control and quickly searched for a twenty-four-hour news station. It was a national news channel; still, she saw the escape of Raoul Nicholson was still taking center stage, along with the murder of New York entrepreneur and philanthropist Charles Mayhew. As of now, few details were available, other than the man had been murdered in his Upper East Side apartment.

A tidal wave in the Pacific was the next item. So far, it wasn't threatening land.

She turned to the bedside table and found her phone. It was 4:00 a.m.

Worried, she keyed quickly to her messages and breathed a sigh of relief.

Craig had sent a text. He was fine; he wouldn't be home until midday sometime. He asked her to stay with Kevin, suggesting she lend a hand to the waitresses at Finnegan's come morning, or maybe catch Kevin's show again. She read the rest aloud to herself. " 'Don't want you worrying about me, and I don't want to be worrying about you. We'll get Nicholson, but you were one of the last people to see him before he pulled the stunt that got him to the infirmary.' "

She set the phone down, wishing she hadn't awakened.

It was the middle of the night, and now all she would do was sit there and be worried.

Craig hadn't given her any details on the case he was working — she knew it was the murder of Charles Mayhew. Such a thing would keep an agent like Craig out all night.

She started to set the phone down and then realized she also had a message from Craig's immediate superior, Richard Egan.

Kieran, we'll get you down to the offices here tomorrow sometime. You might be able to give us something. Miro and Fuller will come in as well. All hands on deck with Nicholson on the loose.

She stared at the message a long time. She'd been involved with cases before that had brought her in close contact with Egan. He was Craig's boss but a friend, as well.

She wondered, though, if it had occurred to Craig yet that — whether he liked it or not — she was involved in this case, and that Egan might call her in.

She had been the last person to interview Nicholson. Which made her wonder about the time she had spent with the man. He had so freely confessed; he had tried so hard to make her understand his reasons for murder were not just good, they were valiant. But all the while, he had to have been planning his escape. It must have been difficult to manage — not only did he have to get by medical personnel, but guards. And when he got by both, he still had to get out of the facility and off the island.

He had to have been in the infirmary before, watched every move made by the doctors and nurses and the guards there.

She thought about the layout of the place and determined he must have somehow stolen a uniform and ID belonging to someone not well-known — a new psychiatrist, doctor, or perhaps, even a guard. If he'd managed such a feat, then he might have walked right out.

Except his face had been plastered over the news time and time again over the last months.

She rose, finding one of her terry robes, and walked downstairs.

To her surprise, she found Kevin was awake as well, still seated on the sofa, hunched over his phone. She took a seat next to him.

"Hey!" he said, surprised to see her. "You're up."

"I don't have a matinee performance tomorrow," she chastised.

"I'm fine," he assured her.

"Working on something?" she asked.

"Yeah," he said, and then he looked at her. "No."

"What are you doing?"

"Looking up killers who claimed they

heard voices . . . or a higher power or whatever. Did you know there's an annual World Voices Hearing Congress that takes place? Several hundred people take part in it. They eschew the idea that the voices they hear are a symptom of mental illness and instead learn how to get along with them."

"I know many people hear voices, and they may mean many things," Kieran said. "But most people don't allow a voice to tell them to kill."

"It's a common enough defense," Kevin told her. He shrugged. "Makes me glad I'm an actor. I hear voices all the time — but they're lines in reply to mine when I'm learning a script on my own. But for instance the Son of Sam — a dog told him to kill. The BTK killer said a demon got into him at an early age and forced him to kill. I've been reading about dozens of cases — a mom who threw her son off a bridge, a woman who heard the walls telling her she had to kill her neighbor . . . so much more."

"Most of the time, they are suffering from psychosis or schizophrenia," Kieran said.

"Or maybe they're making it up to get away with murder."

She nodded and repeated softly, "Or they're making it up to get away with murder."

Kevin nodded and yawned. "Well, my call isn't until 11:00 tomorrow. I guess I'll try to get some sleep. Are you coming with me in the morning or am I taking you to the pub?"

Kieran groaned. "You don't have to take me anywhere."

"Yes, I do. I don't want to get on Craig's bad side," he said lightly.

Kieran shook her head. "Richard Egan wants to see me — Craig's boss. How does that sound for safe?"

"You never stay safe," Kevin said softly but seriously. "Luckily, if you have a voice, it's some kind of a guardian angel."

"And I'm really not stupid," she said.

He looked at her and shrugged. "There have been moments when you could have fooled me."

She picked up a cushion from the sofa and hit him over the head with it.

He laughed. "Okay, I'm going to bed. Honestly. You should sleep, too."

"I'm going up. Night, bro, love you."

He headed to the guest room; she went back up the stairs.

There was no way she was going back to sleep. She was far too restless. She decided to rent a comedy they'd missed at the movies that she'd really wanted to see.

It barely held her attention. But it did do something for her — it let her fall asleep.

When she woke, this time there was a warm body beside her. She curled close instinctively as she opened her eyes.

Craig was next to her. But he wasn't sleeping. He was staring up at the ceiling.

He realized she was awake and pulled her close. She started to speak but saw his grim expression.

And so, she kept silent and lay next to him.

When he was ready, he would talk.

She was dreading what he was going to have to say.

CHAPTER FOUR

Craig had gotten only two hours of sleep and was surprised he felt better for it. He'd thought maybe he'd just stay up, start the 8:00 a.m. interviews, and then join the task force meeting at headquarters scheduled for 11:00.

He looked at Kieran and smiled. She knew him so well. He rose on an elbow. She hadn't asked the obvious questions; she was waiting. That was one of the things he loved about her; she knew when to give him space.

And so he answered without the questions being voiced.

"Yes, the murder method was the same. Did Nicholson have time to escape and get there? Possibly. But if so, he'd planned on killing Mayhew before. There are all kinds of complications with the building — guards, keys programmed for only one floor — anyway, there's footage . . . lobby footage, front door footage, that kind of thing.

Same burned and mutilated body . . . but it doesn't feel right. Don't know if I believe anything Nicholson says anymore." He studied her face. "Kieran, you're good at what you do, and I know it. Did you believe him?"

She thought about it for a minute; she had truly questioned herself. "Yes."

"But the whole time he was talking to you, he was planning his escape."

She nodded. "Yes, and it's possible he played me, but he still didn't deny what he did. He was ready to face whatever, certain in his own mind he was righteous — he had done what a great higher power had told him to do."

He studied her, remembering the hours he and Mike had spent out at Rikers. Then he told her how it had apparently gone down.

"Soon after you left him, he doubled over, screaming about pain in his abdomen. Apparently he studied someone having acute appendicitis somewhere along the line, because he feigned it perfectly. They brought him to the infirmary. He was chained to the bed, but when he was going in for certain tests, metal had to be removed. They have plastic cuffs and ankle cuffs, but in between, he somehow managed to drug the guard and the nurse working with him while he was in a waiting vestibule. After that he donned a guard's uniform, cap, and badge. And took his gun. But he didn't hurt anyone — he just walked out."

Craig paused, letting out a long breath. "Thing is, in an escape, someone usually gets hurt or killed. Nicholson had it all figured out. He got hold of the drugs somehow before he went to the infirmary, hid them, and used them. He knew right where to be and when. There was barely any time in which he could pull off knocking someone out cold with drugs, and then leave a naked guard in his place under the sheets while he was walking out calmly. Someone said he was whistling. Naturally, they're all over themselves out at the island — not trying to lay blame on one another or the system, just trying to figure out how the hell they failed. They were watching Nicholson. It's almost as if he had help, though everyone involved with him has been grilled, and they all remain at a loss."

"Interesting," Kieran murmured.

"In which way — or all ways?"

"I'm thinking about the fact he didn't kill or cause any real harm to anyone," she said. "It's almost as if he took as much care not to hurt others as he did to get out."

"Okay."

"Well, it does suggest he had help. And . . ."

"And what?"

"I'm wondering if the voice he hears is real."

"You mean he has demons in his head?" Craig asked skeptically.

"No more than we all have our demons," she said. "No, I mean . . . makes me wonder if he has been put up to all this by someone else. He didn't kill the guard or the nurse because he believed they weren't evil. But he got out because . . ."

"Because he was being told someone else needed to be killed. Charles Mayhew? If he was helped somehow by someone on the island, who had visited the island . . . that same person might have been the one to make the plans to get him into Mayhew's apartment to kill him."

"Possibly. Otherwise someone else killed Mayhew but wanted to make sure Nicholson was out to take the blame."

Craig nodded and glanced at his watch. He had to get back to Mayhew's apartment complex to speak to the other residents.

"So . . . ?" Kieran said, watching him rise.

"Stay here. I'll come back for you. We'll go down to headquarters together. I'll let

Egan know what is going on."

Kieran nodded.

Craig hurriedly showered. As he dressed, he was glad Kieran had gone downstairs and was no longer lying in bed, reminding him of where he should be.

He ran down the steps.

"Kevin still sleeping?"

"Yep. I'll let him sleep."

"I'll be back within two or three hours."

"I'll be here," she promised.

As he left, Craig made a point of checking that the alarm was set. Kieran watched him. He turned to see she was smiling.

"What? An alarm system is a good thing."

"Oh, I agree. Honestly, guess what I was thinking? That it's great to be living with an FBI guy."

"Marrying him," he reminded her.

"Yeah, yeah, we'll get to that," she said.

"Hey!"

"Just kidding — we'll get to it soon, I promise!"

He headed out, wondering if it was good for her to be living with an FBI guy. Or if it just always put her too close to the action.

It would have been nice to go back to sleep; Kieran knew she wasn't going to do so.

As soon as they went to the FBI offices,

she would be in the hot seat: she had visited a killer just before his escape, and she hadn't gotten so much as a whiff of his plans.

Then again, anyone who had worked for any amount of time with criminals knew they often came in wily, slippery, and capable of feats that boggled the mind.

She still felt anxious about it. She hadn't seen the most recent crime scene, but she hadn't seen any of the other crime scenes either, not firsthand. The pictures had been enough.

Once dressed, she pulled out her computer. She had files filled with notes on the sessions Fuller and Miro had spent with Raoul Nicholson as well as interviews conducted with his family members, co-workers, and even acquaintances at his favorite coffee shop.

Interviews with his sons had shown what might be expected — it seemed they both loved him, but years of living in his repressive household had also made them long to live their own lives.

More normal lives. Both asked first if their words were in confidence — neither wanted their father or mother knowing what they had to say.

Amy, Nicholson's wife, on the other hand believed fervently in her husband. She hadn't known about his "missions," but she believed if he said he was commanded to kill by a higher power, he was telling the truth. And no matter what the outcome of his confession, trial, or plea deal, she would remain by his side.

Kieran sat back, thinking about Nicholson's words when she had interviewed him, and then went back through the notes made by her colleagues.

He had never mentioned what specific evil he perceived in those he was after. Were they going to kill someone else? He'd briefly said something about those who were diseased — and perhaps about to kill others through careless sex. Such could be the case with sex workers.

But . . . a student, a fashion designer, and an accountant?

And now a very rich philanthropist?

She wasn't sure what it would help or change, but when she was at headquarters today, she meant to find out if there was any possible veracity to Nicholson's claims.

Mike Dalton was waiting on the corner when Craig pulled up for him.

"How are you doing?" Craig asked his partner as Mike got in the car.

"Great. That two hours of sleep I wasn't

expecting . . . magnificent!" Mike said cheerfully before looking at Craig and adding, "Not!"

Craig shrugged. "We have to get him, Mike."

"We will. But we can't stay up all night every night."

"I don't intend to. It all just broke yesterday."

Mike let that slide. "We'll have to divide and conquer our interviews if we're still going to make it to the task force meeting." He pulled up an email on his phone that had details of the building's residents.

"All right."

"You want anyone in particular? I'll take the couple — Toni and Teri Mobley. They're the eighth floor, one above Mayhew's apartment, the highest. Mayhew's place is on the seventh. Sienna Johnson, the single rich girl, is on floor six. I don't mind talking to her. According to this, Yolanda and Derek Ramirez are not in residence — they're on vacation in Mexico. So that's the fifth floor absent. You can start with the fourth floor — Mr. Olav Blom. And Ruff." Mike shook his head. "Little terrier — Ruff. Small dogs never like me."

"Ah, but does that speak well of your personality?" Craig asked.

"Hey, the big dudes like me fine."

"I'll deal with Ruff and his owner and also take floors two and three — ground level is the lobby. Who are the others?"

"Julian and Bernadette Chalice have floor number three. He's in comics and movie production. She's . . . She's just married to a rich guy, I guess. She helps out with struggling theaters."

"Sounds good. And what about floor number two?"

"Two women who made a mint in web fashion — Lindsey Trent and Abigail Wyndham," Mike said. "They partnered with a clothing manufacturer, apparently saved them, and make a bundle on 'clothes for every woman.' They make bathing suits for ladies who want long bike short things for a bottom with choices of tops, and suits that have long sleeves — in case they don't like their arms. They're kind of like modified sheer dive skins. I checked out their website. Pretty cool."

Craig laughed. "I'm so glad to see you're enjoying fashion!"

"Hey, I have a friend I can't get to come to the beach because she has a scar on her left thigh. I'm going to get her onto their site — well, as long as they prove not to be horrible and heinous murderers," Mike amended.

When they reached the posh apartment/condo building on the Upper East Side, it was apparent that Simon Wrigley had stayed up all night, too, or perhaps taken a nap on the small cot in the guard's office.

He'd also seen to it that Joey Catalano had stayed.

Catalano looked the worse for wear. He was cradling a large cup of coffee in a paper cup and blinking a lot. He offered them a weak smile that quickly faded. He was obviously wondering if it was all right to smile when a murder had taken place on his watch.

"Joey will escort you men up," Wrigley informed them.

"Thank you. The residents are expecting us?"

"They are," Wrigley said grimly. "That's Nathan on the door this morning — his regular shift. Joey is at your disposal. I'll give you two our call boxes. They're like little walkie-talkies, light and easy to use, but you can reach Joey, or each other, on any of the floors."

"That's great. Thank you," Craig told him. He and Mike took the small call boxes — about the size of cell phones though their function was more like walkie-talkies. Joey pointed out the keys on the gizmos, and Mike and Craig both thanked him.

"We'll be heading to different floors," Craig said. "Joey, you can drop me and then Mike. I'll work my way up from two, and Mike's working down from the top. We won't be long. I know the residents have already spoken with police officers."

"Yes, they have," Wrigley said pointedly.

"Sorry. We have the lead on this case. FBI and NYPD are task-forcing it together with other agencies involved as well, but Special Agent Dalton and I are where it all stops, so please bear with us," Craig said.

"Sure," Wrigley told them. His expression was tight; he wasn't going to argue with them, but was still annoyed. He felt his clients were being victimized — when one tenant had already become the ultimate victim.

"Hey, don't mind Mr. Wrigley," Joey said when they were alone in the elevator. "I think he's trying to be cooperative. He got a divorce not long ago — third time. He's a hard man, but a fair man. And I know this whole thing is really bothering him."

"I don't blame him," Craig said. "But we do have to find answers."

"Yeah, answers. Good for everyone."

The two entrepreneurs on the second

floor were waiting for Craig, standing at the entry, anxiously holding hands.

He wondered how long they had been there waiting.

He smiled; he always started off pleasantly. The FBI was not out to make enemies with the public, but rather encourage the public to come forward when they had information or needed help.

"Hi. I'm Special Agent Frasier. Ms. Wyndham and Ms. Trent?"

They were an attractive pair, both appearing to be in their midthirties, slender, and almost the same height. One was pale-skinned, blond and blue-eyed, and one had sepia skin, dark brown eyes and soft curling hair that was nearly jet black.

"I'm Abigail Wyndham, and this is Lindsey," the blonde said. They both still stared at him.

"Come in, come in . . . please!" the dark-haired woman, Lindsey, urged.

"Thank you."

He was led to the living room, architecturally the same as Charles Mayhew's. The design was different. Mayhew's place had been filled with heavy leather sofas and chairs. The women had a lighter touch. Drapes in an elegant royal blue threaded with gold covered the windows, and the sofa was a sectional with matching pieces that grouped around a circular coffee table and faced a handsome entertainment center.

"Sit, please. Can we get you something?" Abigail asked anxiously.

"No, no, I'm fine, thank you," Craig said, indicating that he couldn't sit until they did.

They perched, close together, on the sofa.

"This is so dreadful," Abigail said.

"I'm sorry. How well did you know Charles Mayhew?" Craig asked.

"Oh, not really at all," Lindsey said.

"We shared the elevator once," Abigail told him.

"I understand he did most of his business from his home," Lindsey added. "He'd go away sometimes, but we really only knew that because one of the doormen would mention he was gone. We always report our comings and goings — oh, and if we're going to have guests."

"We're so sorry, of course, to hear that . . . that he's dead," Lindsey said.

"Murdered," Abigail put in.

"But we're so scared now!"

"I think you're going to be okay. I don't think this killer will strike again here. He had a plan and it involved Mr. Mayhew. But . . . did you see or hear anything at all last night?" Craig asked.

"We were watching old Burt Reynolds movies," Abigail said.

"We were watching television and . . . we didn't hear anything. Anything at all. We were laughing at *Smokey and the Bandit* while that poor man was being killed," Abigail said.

"Which is why we didn't hear anything," Lindsey explained, as if he might not understand.

"Burt Reynolds was a very good-looking man," Abigail said.

"With a sense of humor about himself," Lindsey said, and then apologized with, "I'm so sorry. We're not helping you at all." They seemed to be in perfect unison with one another, each woman adding on to the other's words at every point. "No, no, you're fine," Craig assured them. "Did either of you misplace or lose a key?"

"No!" Abigail said.

"Oh, no!" Lindsey agreed. "But if we had, it wouldn't matter. Well, I mean it wouldn't have gotten anyone into Mayhew's apartment. Each key only goes to the floor where that particular resident lives. Did you know that?"

"Yes, I did."

"The only keys that go to every floor are those held by the security men," Abigail said thoughtfully. "I guess you knew that." She sat up straighter. "If a guard lost a key . . ."

"That would put us all in danger, wouldn't it?" Lindsey asked.

"Apparently there are only two master keys, one locked away, and one that is passed from guard to guard."

Lindsey looked at Abigail. "Do you believe that?" she asked. And before Abigail could answer, she looked at Craig. "Do you believe it?"

"Don't worry. I'll see to it the system is reset, whatever we discover," Craig assured her. He produced one of his cards. "If you think of anything — anything you might have seen earlier in the day, anything suspicious, or out of the ordinary — will you let me know?"

Both women nodded grimly.

Craig rose and thanked them, and they rose as well, walking him to the elevator.

"You will let us know . . . if you catch him," Abigail said.

"Of course," Craig assured her.

"Was it . . . was it the Fireman?" Lindsey asked.

"Why do you ask?" Craig asked in return.

"The smell of smoke," Lindsey said softly. "We didn't smell it right away . . . not until the policemen came in here."

"And we let them search. There are fire-escape stairs just outside the windows there . . . and a stairway by the elevators. That, however, is kept locked unless there's a power outage or an emergency. You have to keep them locked — oh, they open with the same key as the elevator. But for us, it's just one flight down, one flight up. For the people at the top? Eight flights up or down, and no chickening out once you're committed. Keys only open there, by the elevator. And only on the floor where a resident lives."

The killer could have taken the stairs, stopping anywhere, if he had a master key.

Maybe there were more than two keys. There had to be a way to duplicate the keys, and that seemed to be the only plausible explanation for what had happened.

Still, the security footage showed no one who didn't belong come in — or go out.

"We don't know much at this time, but please know that we'll be doing everything humanly possible to find this killer."

"The Fireman," Lindsey said gravely. "We did smell the smoke, and we saw on the news he had escaped."

"We don't know," he repeated. "Ladies, thank you."

He used the small walkie-talkie device

he'd been given to summon Joey Catalano.

The elevator arrived. Joey was grinning when Craig stepped in, looking a bit better than he'd looked before.

"What is it?"

"Special Agent Dalton said you're a slow-poke. He's already moved on to his second interview."

"That's because Special Agent Dalton drank too much coffee this morning — turned him into a speed demon and he's talking double-time."

"Bringing you to floor number three," Joey said, apparently far more at ease than he had been.

"Thank you."

Just as the women had been waiting in the vestibule right off the elevator, so were Julian and Bernadette Chalice.

They appeared to be in their early sixties. Bernadette was a very attractive woman with swinging, chin-length silver hair that was cute and smart. Her eyes were large and blue; she was slim and handsomely dressed in workout clothing she evidently really wore to work out. Julian was balding, with keen eyes, a medium build, and a slightly receding hairline.

Craig introduced himself and explained

that the FBI needed any help they could receive.

"We talked to the cops," Julian said. "We let them search our apartment."

"Thank you," Craig said. "I'm just doing a follow-up. We are still trying to figure out how Mr. Mayhew's killer got into his apartment."

"Nothing to do with us!" Julian said indignantly.

"I wasn't making such a suggestion," Craig assured him. "But we are trying to find out if maybe you noticed anyone watching the building, watching Mr. Mayhew . . . not just yesterday, but in the days or weeks before yesterday."

Bernadette let out a soft sigh. "That's so hard to say. People do stare at this building. It's an attractive building."

"Did you notice anyone in particular?"

"Oh, gosh . . . I don't know," Bernadette said, looking to her husband.

Julian shook his head. "I'm busy . . . I don't notice strangers, I'm afraid. I believe in a world in which we all do as we need to do — as long as we don't hurt other people."

"Julian is always preoccupied," Bernadette said, smiling and placing a hand on her husband's shoulder. "He wouldn't have noticed a large gorilla on the sidewalk when he was coming or going."

These people weren't killers, Craig thought. Nor did he believe they would harbor a killer. He also didn't think they had any useful information.

He handed them his card just in case, thanked them, and called for Joey Catalano.

As Craig stepped out on the fourth floor, Joey's walkie-talkie beeped.

"Paged by Special Agent Dalton," Joey said.

"Go get him," Craig advised lightly.

This time, there was no one there to greet him in the vestibule.

He called out, "Mr. Blom? Special Agent Frasier, FBI."

There was no reply. Frowning, Craig waited a minute. "Mr. Blom!" he called again. There was no reply. "Ruff?" The dog had to be there somewhere.

He headed through the apartment; it was the same layout as Mayhew's.

The little dog, Ruff, had his own bedroom. There was a dog bed in it, and the walls had been covered with pictures of dogs at play.

Ruff was one beloved pooch.

Craig had seen the dog and his owner return to the building on the security footage last night. Where could they be now?

How had they left the building without being noticed by the security guards? "Ruff?" Craig called loudly. "Here puppy, puppy!"

If Ruff was hiding somewhere, he might well come out and bite. Little dogs could be protective and in that, fierce and vicious.

But he wasn't worried about being bitten; he was worried about the fact he couldn't find the dog or his owner.

"Ruff, here Ruff. Are you hiding somewhere?"

He didn't hear the dog and couldn't find the dog, and he sure couldn't find Olav Blom. At least not in any obvious place.

He began a methodical search of the place, starting in the dining room and looking under the table and into the hutch. A man couldn't *be* in the hutch, he wouldn't fit in the hutch, but Craig meant to leave no stone unturned.

As he searched under and behind every piece of furniture in the living room, he called Joey Catalano.

"Joey, did Mr. Blom go out this morning?"

"No, sir. No one went out," Joey replied.

"I thought Simon Wrigley spoke with all the residents, telling them we would be here early to talk with them. Blom isn't here."

"Special Agent Frasier, you saw him come back in yesterday. None of the residents have left since last night. I don't think Mr. Wrigley spoke with them all. He sent messages."

"Well, Blom isn't here."

"I don't see how that's possible, sir. I saw him come back in last night. No one has left since then. I mean, I wasn't on the door, but I was here. I never left. Slept awhile on the couch."

"Where are you now?"

"By the elevator, waiting on Special Agent Dalton."

"When he's done, get him, and come on down to the fourth floor."

"Yes, sir."

Craig went through every cabinet in the kitchen.

He'd covered the entry, the dining room, living room, and kitchen.

There were three bedrooms. He started with Blom's bedroom, going through the closet and every drawer. He didn't see a wallet. Wherever the man was, he must have that on him. But there was no sign he had left for any amount of time. The closet was filled with clothing, as were the drawers.

The next room was a guestroom — neat, tidy, and ready for a guest.

The closet there was filled with sheets, towels, bath soap, shampoo, toilet paper, and paper towels.

Frustrated, he searched both bathrooms — no sign of a disruption anywhere, no sign of blood. Nothing ill had happened to the man here.

He headed back into the dog's room. He'd already opened the closet there, but he hadn't pried into the boxes.

He started pulling out boxes marked as having come from a gourmet pet shop.

He began to hear a whining sound, punctuated by a weak growl.

He dragged out a box; from the back of the closet, the fuzzy little terrier suddenly sprang at him, teeth bared.

Craig leaped back. "Hey, hey, it's all right," he said, backing away to hunker down and stretch out an arm. The terrier growled nervously, and then stepped forward to sniff his hand.

Apparently he passed inspection.

Craig heard the elevator arrive and Mike call out to him.

"Craig, where are you?"

The call frightened the dog. He couldn't have weighed more than fifteen pounds, but when Ruff catapulted himself into Craig's arms in fear, he almost knocked him over.

"Here, Mike, here. First bedroom on the left."

"You found Blom?" Mike called as he came down the hall.

"No. No Blom. But I did find Ruff." He hesitated, rising with the little dog in his arms as Mike entered the room.

The poor dog was shaking uncontrollably. As Mike entered the room, Ruff began his quiet, nervous growling once again.

"Careful!" Mike said. "The little guys can be fierce. You might get bitten."

"I'm not going to get bitten. He's fine. Just let him sniff you."

"Sniff me?" Mike repeated indignantly.

"Your hand, Mike," Craig said.

Mike slowly stretched out his arm, bringing his fingers close to Ruff's nose. The dog sniffed and edged closer to Craig's chest, no longer growling.

"Any suggestion where Blom might be? Under a bed or somewhere?" Mike asked.

"I looked everywhere. In and under everything. No Blom, no sign of disturbance, and no sign of him taking a trip anywhere. Besides, I don't think this guy would have left his dog. Hell, the dog has his own bedroom. I don't have a good feeling about this," he told Mike.

"You think this man, Blom, was the killer?"

"He either is the killer or he's dead somewhere. But either way, a question remains. How the hell did he get out of the building?"

CHAPTER FIVE

"He gave absolutely no sign he was planning an imminent escape," Kieran said.

The task force meeting would begin in less than an hour; Egan had just her, Mike, and Craig in his office, questioning her before they were to begin. Egan perched on the corner of his desk. Since Kieran had taken the visitor's chair, Craig and Mike stood to the side.

"If anything, he seemed entirely earnest, trying to convince me he had been justified in what he did. Which, naturally, makes me wonder. He was telling me his victims had been evil, and they would kill others. By the command of Satan. This is something that never came up in other interviews — to my knowledge at least. The first two women Nicholson killed were prostitutes. I didn't see anything in the reports, but after my conversation with Nicholson, I'm wondering if they were HIV positive."

Egan looked surprised at her deduction. But when he glanced over at Craig, Kieran knew it was true.

"We held tight to a lot of information. We didn't need vigilantes on the street, or prostitutes being punished by their pimps or a rash of johns killing sex workers," Egan said. "They've got it hard enough as it is."

Kieran stared at Craig. He hadn't even told her. But then her info about the case had come from the media and Drs. Fuller and Miro. Craig hadn't talked much about it. She'd known when the murders had been happening and known Craig was investigating. And she'd known when he had been the one to apprehend Raoul Nicholson.

"How would a man like Nicholson — in his church every day, fully committed to his wife, lest he burn in hell — know about a prostitute's health?" Egan murmured.

"Actually, cases have gone many ways, but people have been charged with murder for the conscious and malicious spread of AIDS," Kieran said.

"Gretchen Larson, the first victim, had quit the trade," Craig said. "She was cleaning toilets. She knew her diagnosis, and she stopped seeing men. A few of the women with whom she'd been friends told me she'd been to a clinic where they tried to trace the virus to no avail. But all that information is locked away."

"What about the second young woman?" Kieran asked.

"That was something we looked for right away, she was not infected," Mike told her.

"And the student from NYU — straight flyer, super grades, and an amazing future ahead for her most probably," Craig said.

Kieran sighed. "Okay, here's what I've wondered from my talk with Nicholson. The voice — he couldn't really pinpoint it. He said it came to him in different ways. I'm wondering if someone fed him information and, maybe, even turned him into a serial killer with one particular victim in mind. If you were cold-blooded yourself but didn't want to get caught, and you were totally careless of other lives, why not find someone gullible, already close to the edge — like Nicholson — to do your dirty work?"

"You're suggesting someone out there is really the voice that Nicholson hears?" Egan asked her.

"It's only an idea," Kieran said. She shrugged unhappily. *"He* believed what he was telling me, and I trust my judgment on that. He seemed to accept whatever fate came his way. He didn't want his defense to be that he was crazy. His attorney, Cliff

Watkins, was the one who kept pushing for him to be seen by psychiatrists. When he talked about Satan commanding people, Watkins got nervous. It was the only time he stopped him from saying more. I couldn't be sure — no one can ever be sure about another person's mind — but through training and experience, I'd have sworn Nicholson was telling the truth — *as he saw it.*"

"His attorney was pushing hard for insanity," Egan said.

Kieran felt almost as a prisoner might — being interrogated by the three.

She wasn't at any fault, she knew. But it was still an uncomfortable feeling. She wished Nicholson would have said or done something — the slightest thing — to suggest he intended to escape.

Egan looked over at Craig. "Who else was in to see Nicholson yesterday?" he asked.

"Just his attorney, and he was only there to watch over the proceedings with Kieran. And his wife. According to the records, she came every day," Craig said.

"What's your take on the wife?" Egan asked Craig.

"She stands by her man. She doesn't deny he did what he did, but she swears if he says he was commanded to kill by a higher power, then it was so," Craig said.

112

"You want to have a go at Amy Nicholson?" Egan asked Kieran.

"Me?" Kieran asked, surprised. "I'm sure either Dr. Fuller or Dr. Miro —"

"I'd like to hear what she says to you. I believe I can get her down here. She's afraid with him on the loose. She knows she's being watched, and she knows a score of officers would love to come upon her husband with a weapon, shoot first and ask questions later. I think she'll believe you're trying to help her — and her husband."

"I don't know —" Craig began.

"I don't know if he ever said anything to his wife," Kieran said, "but he didn't think I was a witch. That could give me some leeway with her. But what do you think I can find out?"

"If she helped him escape in any way, if she knew he intended to escape, and if she has any idea of where he's gone now, and . . ." Egan paused. "And if he killed Charles Mayhew. Will you talk to her, Kieran?"

"I, uh, of course. If you think I can be of any help."

"I'll see if I can get an agent to bring her in here after the task force meeting," Egan said.

"We should be on the street looking for

Blom," Craig said.

Egan looked at him. "Word is out. Anyone on patrol or on the streets is looking for him. If we don't find him in a matter of hours, we'll get an APB out on him. You think he might have been the one to copy Nicholson and kill Mayhew?"

"I think he's dead," Craig said.

"Mayhew is dead and Blom is missing," Egan said. "Doesn't that make him look suspicious? The method of killing may be the same, but it's still a stretch to believe Nicholson broke out of the infirmary, made it to the building on the Upper East Side, got in, killed Mayhew, and got out."

"I went back over the security footage," Craig told him. "You never see Blom's face."

"But you said the dog was terrified, hiding in a closet. In the security footage, you see the dog walking calmly on his leash," Egan said.

"The man who we assumed was Blom was wearing a hoodie. You never see his face in the images. He barely waves at the guard, who hardly looks up from his newspaper," Mike said.

"Wherever he is, we'll find him," Egan said with assurance. "Task force meeting first, then you can get back out there yourself. Kieran can interview Amy Nicholson and see what she discovers. And . . ." He lifted a hand before Craig could interrupt. "I will then escort Kieran to Finnegan's. I'm in the mood for a really excellent shepherd's pie tonight."

Craig nodded. "Did you get the blueprints for the building?" he asked.

"They're in tech now. Feel free to go take a look. We've pulled everything we could from city hall. There have been many changes throughout the years."

Craig turned toward the door; Mike followed.

Kieran didn't intend to be left behind, and she quickly rose.

Craig turned back to her. "Kieran, you're not really an agent on this case," he reminded her.

"I can still . . . look," she said.

He nodded, acknowledging he was being unreasonable. She knew he didn't want her involved with Nicholson, his family, or his case anymore. She understood.

"You're down to about forty minutes to study the plans," Egan said.

"Then we'd better see what we can get done in forty minutes," Craig said.

Kieran followed Craig and Mike to the elevator; they headed up to tech.

She could see the young man who had the

blueprints; he was taking pictures of the plans with a digital camera, muttering to himself as he did so.

"Marty, hey, are those the building plans for the Mayhew case?" Craig asked.

"Yes, and wow, what a building!" the man he'd called Marty said, looking at Kieran curiously.

"Kieran Finnegan, Marty Kim," Craig said.

"Ah, your reputation precedes you!" Marty said with a big grin.

"In a good way, I hope," Kieran said.

"Oh, the best," Marty assured her.

"We're here to take a look at the blueprints," Craig said. "Sorry, but the meeting is coming up, so we're in a rush. You're taking the pictures with a special lens?"

"Yes. There are several sets of blueprints, and I'm taking pictures to overlap. There was so much construction done on the building through the years. The Tower Building — completed in 1889 — was, in most opinions, our first skyscraper, and certainly the first built with a steel frame. The first high-rises, nonsteel construction, started going up a bit before. The design was taken from the concept of putting a bridge up vertically. Anyway, this building started out at four floors. The higher levels came at the turn of the century. But as you can imagine, any tall building needs a good foundation. The basement was shored up time and time again to assure, of course, that the upper floors would be strong. The most recent lift the building was given had to do with more cosmetics as every floor was designed with the same flow for weight management. Reworked plumbing and electric — and cable, of course."

"So," Craig asked, "how did our guy get into the building and then out?"

"He didn't," Marty told them.

"What do you mean, he didn't? There are fire codes."

"Yes, of course, but . . . well, even the stairs lead back to the lobby. There are stairs that go all the way to the basement, but there's no way I've found yet out of the basement. Now, there are fire escapes outside the building, but once released, they can only be reset through a main panel. If one goes down, they all go down."

"That would mean he was killed by someone in the building," Mike said.

Craig shook his head. "Blom was seen coming back into the building and never going back out. And he's nowhere to be found. If it was him who came back with the dog."

"You really think someone else came in as Blom? But the dog. The dog was in the apartment," Mike said.

"There's a way in and a way out that we have to find," Craig said. "Keep going, Marty. Put all your images together and see what you can find for me. There must be something we're not seeing, because whether it was or wasn't Blom, someone came in with the dog. And someone has entirely disappeared."

"I'll do my best, sir, I'll do my best. Miss Finnegan, a pleasure," Marty said.

"Thank you, Marty. You, too," Kieran said.

As they headed back up the elevator to the conference room, Kieran tried to get a better grip on all they had learned that morning.

"Blom has disappeared. The dog was there, though?" she asked.

"Hiding and terrified," Craig said.

"Where is the dog now?" she asked.

Mike grinned without answering. Kieran looked at Craig.

"In my office."

"I think you have a dog," Mike said.

"They were going to take him to animal control," Craig said. "I figured we'd find something, because I don't think we're going to find Blom. Not alive."

118

"But you also think Blom might be the killer?" Kieran asked.

"Right now I have no damned idea whatsoever," Craig said. "Everything is a contradiction. It could be Nicholson, it could be Blom. And this killing may be a complete copycat by a person unknown."

"If Nicholson is the killer, then Blom is alive somewhere," Kieran told them.

"Why is that?"

"It would be a sin for him to kill the innocent. In his mind, he only kills witches."

"Unless he's the best actor–con artist in the history of crime," Craig said quietly.

"You're asking my opinion — or at least Drs. Fuller and Miro wanted my opinion, or the courts wanted my opinion. I've gone over it all in my mind a million times. I don't think he was acting. He believes in witches and evil and people controlled by Satan, or possessed by Satan, who intend to hurt others."

"He did escape right after your interview," Craig reminded her.

"Yes, but he still wouldn't have killed an innocent man to kill another. He'd have found another way."

They stepped out of the elevator and headed for the conference room along with other agents, nodding in acknowledgment of one another, and greeting those from other agencies who were joining the investigation.

Kieran had been to several such meetings. They always began with Egan detailing the situation. He didn't tell agents or officers what to think, but he did provide possibilities.

Every law enforcement agency in or associated with the five NYC boroughs had known about the Fireman. They had seen Raoul Nicholson's face in the media dozens of time. There would likely be no mistaking the man if they were to find him.

Certain details regarding Nicholson's murder spree had initially been held back. Only those who were immediately involved were aware he'd removed the tongues from his victims. The removal of the eyes had been evident to any officer on scene when a victim had been discovered. Some knew or guessed, but any public information officer or agent speaking to the press knew not to give out any details. The public knew he claimed he executed witches — and he had burned the bodies. His belief was that they could not regenerate or create more havoc if they were destroyed by fire.

Egan gave them the details of the newest murder, and the time line for Nicholson's escape, and the possibility that he might have killed again.

He asked Craig to come to the front. Craig gave what information he had on the Mayhew murder, and what he knew of the building, informing them that one resident was missing. He acknowledged that they still had dozens of unanswered questions. How could a man have disappeared from such a building? And the fact he was missing — could that suggest that he was the killer? "Or else, we're going to find Olav Blom, I'm afraid," he went on, "but not alive. We can speculate that the killer caught him outside the building. He used Blom's clothing and took his dog as a way to get into the building without rousing any curiosity. And he knew how to get out of the building once he was in it. How he did that is something we have to discover."

Egan stepped forward to speak and summed up the briefing, and all those on the task force were given two directives — find Nicholson and find the missing tenant, Olav Blom. Special Agents Michael Dalton and Craig Frasier would be taking lead. Any information or anything deemed a clue should be reported and shared.

Egan always thanked his force. He did so now, reminding them the public was going to be anxious and fearful.

"Yeah, everyone is going to be all over this," Mike, standing by Kieran, said lowly. He looked at her and grimaced. "You know, it's sad to say, when two prostitutes were dead, the good people of New York could feel safe — as long as they were not prostitutes. Men could feel safe — only women had been killed. But then the Fireman moved on to a student, a designer, and an accountant. No one is safe. No one can know for sure they haven't been targeted as a witch."

"I'll be speaking with the media and suggesting, as much as possible, our populace should not go out alone, stay out of dark alleys, and make a point of remaining in crowds. Also, they should carefully monitor their locks, close windows, and so forth," Egan said.

"A boon for the locksmith and alarm companies of the city," an officer muttered dryly.

"Yes, well, I don't think we need to create a panic," Egan said, "but this killer managed to get to Charles Mayhew in a building that should have been impregnable — well, at least without leaving a dead armed guard lying around to be discovered."

"That's the thing," Kieran said. "If I'm

right, Nicholson wouldn't murder a guard, or anyone else who wasn't a witch. He didn't believe he was killing human beings. Killing a human being would be a sin. Killing witches was commanded to him by his voice."

Egan finished the meeting, sending the room of officers out to scour the city for Raoul Nicholson and Olav Blom.

Craig came over to join Kieran and Mike, and she said quickly, "I don't believe Nicholson did kill this man, even if he did escape just in time to do it. Someone saw to it he was released so he could be blamed for the murder. Or used his escape to cover their crime."

Craig nodded. "That is definitely a possibility, and we haven't ruled it out. But because of the method, we still need to consider that Nicholson is a suspect." He looked at Mike. "We need to get back to the apartment building and get on this thing, fast. Egan is doing a press conference in an hour. I'd like to give him more to talk about."

"I'll be leaving here with Egan and his driver and heading to Finnegan's," Kieran told them.

Craig smiled and stepped close to Kieran. "I'll talk to Egan on my way out, but there's one more thing."

"What's that?"

He took a deep breath. "Well, I guess you're in this one whether I like it or not. And I figure you're better off with agents than alone. I know you'll be safe with Egan, so . . . well, I surrender again. This is your work, too, and if you didn't have your streak of caring for humanity . . . well, you wouldn't be you."

"Thank you. Neither of us had much choice on this one," she said, smiling weakly.

"No," he agreed. "But whether he's guilty of this new murder or not, Nicholson is dangerous. I'm going to be as careful as I'm asking you to be."

"That's a good deal," she said. "So, is that it?"

"Uh, one more thing."

"Okay?"

"Can you drop the dog off at the apartment first? He's not a service dog, so I don't think he should go to the pub."

"Dog?" she asked, forgetting what Mike had said earlier.

But Craig was already quickly striding out.

Mike called over his shoulder as he followed Craig, grinning. "Ruff. Pup's name is Ruff!"

■ ■ ■ ■

When they returned to the building on the Upper East Side, Simon Wrigley was still there, along with Joey Catalano and the man guarding the door. There were also two NYPD officers out front.

"Today we've had anyone in and out signing a sheet, even the residents, and they've been good about it."

Craig realized Wrigley was likely feeling a bit defensive and shocked. He had cameras; he hired good men. He had probably thought such a thing as this couldn't happen.

Mike told Wrigley they were going to need a list of the security company's employees. Wrigley was, naturally, wary.

"I told you, my guys all had background checks and the key is handed straight from one man to another," Wrigley said.

"Still, there might have been a breach somewhere along the line. This took planning. We're not suggesting you hired a cold-blooded killer. We just have to find out anything that we can."

Craig cleared his throat and explained to Wrigley they wanted to get down to the basement.

"The elevator doesn't go to the basement. I don't know why. We're responsible for the key functions, but not the building arrangements," Wrigley said. "The stairway goes down, and Joey can open the door for you. But . . . there are no other exits. Tools and supplies are kept down there. But we haven't had anyone in for any kind of maintenance or repair in over three months. The basement is clean. The central heating and air-conditioning works are down there."

Wrigley and Catalano escorted Mike and Craig to the stairs to the basement and went down with them to see that the lights were all turned on. Foundation walls separated rooms in the tidy space, while the outer walls had stacks of boxes in front of them, most containing cleaning supplies, light bulbs, and other miscellanea that would be used for the building's upkeep.

One large area was given over to a new central heating and air-conditioning system. It was huge and covered about an eighth of the entire space.

"I'm not seeing anything," Mike said. "I mean anything that might be something."

"A man came in and never went out, but he's nowhere here to be found. That means he got out somehow," Craig said.

"There is no exit from the basement,"

Mike said. "So, what are we doing?"

"Finding the exit that doesn't exist," Craig said. "We'll go wall by wall . . . there had to be coal delivery here, at one time. We'll divide and conquer."

"You do realize the walls are concealed by boxes."

"Yep. That must be why they make us take physicals all the time," Craig said cheerfully.

Mike groaned.

"We're looking at another problem, you know."

"What is that?"

"Say there is an exit of some kind down here — an old ice or coal chute, a mail drop for giant packages . . . a tornado door, a doggy door for a giant German shepherd —"

"Mike."

"Sorry, getting carried away there. But here's the question."

"Yes?"

"How would he hide it after he got out?"

"If you know what you're looking for, it's easy enough. Move something aside in a way that allows you to draw it back in place. Mike, all I know is a killer got out of here somehow."

"Unless one of those nice people we interviewed today is really a killer," Mike suggested. "Or one of those nice people has a body stashed in a closet?"

"And that is possible, but . . ." Craig looked around. "But we're going to need search warrants to tear through apartments. And this space hasn't been properly searched yet."

"It's creepy down here," Mike said. It was clean, it was organized, brightly lit . . .

And still, somehow . . .

"There's something down here. An exit . . . or something."

"Yep, all right, so . . . let's get to it," Mike agreed.

CHAPTER SIX

Ruff was so scruffy looking he was cute.

Maybe fifteen or sixteen pounds, he had a little barrel body and short legs.

In the front he was a little bit bow-legged.

They hadn't talked about having a dog. They were both at work all the time, or so it seemed, but Kieran did love animals. When the little dog tried to leap into her arms and shower her with kisses, she knew that she couldn't argue much about him.

Perhaps they would find his master.

She just didn't think so.

She played with the dog while she waited for Egan to finish with his press conference. He must have spoken quickly and succinctly — and refused most questions politely, assuring people they would have more definitive information when he had it. It didn't seem to be that long before he came to Craig's office to tell her Amy Nicholson was there, deeply worried about her husband,

and happy to talk to Kieran, fully aware Raoul had seen the psychologist before his escape, too.

Kieran thought Egan was going to bring Amy in to Craig's office, and they would talk there, but she heard Amy and Egan talking, and then Egan told her they'd be in the small conference room down the hall.

Ruff heard them, too, and seemed agitated.

"Be good!" she told Ruff, setting him on the floor. "I'll be right back for you — just behave."

The terrier mix looked at her, cocking his head as if he really listened. He wasn't happy, but he seemed to be an obedient dog.

"I promise I won't be long. I'll come back for you," she said.

Ruff barked and wagged his tail, whined, sank down on all fours, and set his nose on his paws.

Kieran had no idea what a dog might really be thinking, but she left him there, closing the door firmly behind her.

Amy had been seated at the end of the long conference table, with Egan beside her, when Kieran entered the room. She stood nervously and apologized. "Sorry, I don't mean to be a pest, but I'm horribly allergic to dogs."

She was a tall woman, slender, with platinum hair becoming a true white. She wore a simple blue dress that extended past her knees, and a cotton denim jacket. She was in her mid-forties, and would have been attractive if her eyes weren't so puffy and red.

"Oh, it's fine," Kieran said. "It doesn't matter where we talk." She offered her hand to the woman. She had read many notes on her, but had never met her before.

Amy shook her hand with a firm, enthusiastic grip.

"And I'm happy to talk," Amy said. "I love my husband. I know what he's done, but you have to believe me — he's not a bad man. It's hard to understand. He does what he's commanded to do."

"Please, sit," Kieran said.

Amy sat. Egan waited for Kieran to do so as well before taking his chair again on one side of the long conference table.

"You saw your husband yesterday at Rikers," Kieran said.

"I know he's confessed to the killings, but again, I beg you to understand. I didn't know what he was doing, since he knew it was against the laws of man, but he is a dedicated man, a devout man."

"You haven't seen him, and you haven't heard from him?" Kieran asked.

Amy shook her head. "Well, I visited at Rikers."

"And you had no idea he was planning an escape?" Kieran asked.

"No. Did you?" Amy asked innocently, her eyes wide.

Kieran smiled. "No. But I just met him yesterday. You've known him for years and years."

"Yes, but as I said, my husband loves me. You must understand he wouldn't involve me. I keep telling you that."

"Of course. It's just . . . well, you do seem to have such an incredible marriage. I can't imagine there would be secrets between you."

"You don't understand — there aren't secrets between us."

"You're a good woman, right? You couldn't have approved of murder."

"It wouldn't be a matter of me approving. And what he did . . . wasn't like keeping a secret. You just don't understand the scope of his belief, the knowledge the voice that spoke to him came from a higher power."

"But you don't hear these voices."

She shook her head. No.

"That's just it. He's a good man. He is a better human being than I am. He did hear the voice. It was his calling. He would never involve me. He wants me to be there for our sons, and for their children, when they have them. Someone needs to be with them, Someone who can make them see the light of goodness and keep them from the sins of the flesh. Drugs, women, there's so much evil out there."

Not to mention knives and fire and maniacs like Raoul Nicholson, Kieran thought.

It was, however, somewhat unnerving to see this woman went beyond understanding what her husband had done — she seemed to condone it.

"Do you believe in witches, Mrs. Nicholson?" Kieran asked.

"I believe in evil, don't you?" the woman countered passionately. "Words — they're all just labels, aren't they? Witches, evil human beings. Ruled by Satan!"

"What would you have done *if* your husband had asked you for help in ridding the world of a witch?" Kieran asked.

Amy Nicholson shook her head, and her headful of soft white-and-platinum hair shook around her face. She let out a long sigh of exasperation and weary patience.

"You're just not listening to me. He wouldn't have asked me. It wasn't my calling. It was his. Would I kill anyone, or would I help in what you see as a murder? No. I have my place here on earth. I am to nurture another generation. I can't do that behind bars. I don't even think my husband is crazy. But if it will help his circumstances in the future, I will refuse to testify to my beliefs. I'm trying to help you now because I want my husband to live. If some of you people find him . . . well, I believe a lot of officers would love an excuse to shoot him. Even in prison, he could help others. Even in a mental facility, he could teach the goodness of the great provider . . . teach how our lives must be worthy."

Egan was watching Amy with steady eyes, giving no clue to his thoughts or opinions. It was one of the man's great strengths; he never gave anything away.

"Mrs. Nicholson —" Kieran began.

"Amy, please, just call me Amy. Raoul told me you were a good person. I'd like you to call me by my given name."

"Fine, and I'm just Kieran."

Amy leaned forward. "Kieran, Raoul didn't tell me he had a plan to escape. He did say he had talked to you. He believed you might even understand."

"I'm trying to understand his state of mind. But you must realize something, as well. The people he killed had loved ones."

Amy shrugged. "I'm sorry for that. Sorry

for anyone in pain. Mr. Watkins — our attorney — is the one fighting for him, you know. Raoul didn't really care what he was charged with. He was ready to answer to the State of New York. Wherever they chose to send him, he was ready to accept it even if the federal government stepped in to make it a capital crime. He is truly a believer, ready to die to obey commands from above. And, by the way, *Raoul* is worried for you, I know."

Kieran smiled, though she was determined not to let this turn around. "Right now, I'm very worried about Raoul. Who do you think helped him?"

"Helped him?" Amy asked, sitting back.

"I think he had help. He saw both of us and his attorney . . . and gave nothing away. I can't tell you how difficult it was for him to manage that escape. Someone helped him."

Amy smiled, looking up toward the ceiling. "Divine power!" she said.

"Oh, in human form, I'm pretty sure," Kieran said. "Amy, I'm sorry to ask this, but of course, I must. Was he seeing . . . someone else?"

"What?" Amy demanded, shocked.

"I'm sorry. Another . . . a secret companion. Perhaps not loved as you are loved, and therefore someone he might be willing to turn to for help."

"No."

"Please think."

The woman was irate and indignant. "He was not seeing another woman! My husband loves me. He cleaves to me, as ordained," Amy said.

"I wasn't necessarily suggesting a woman," Kieran said softly, surprised she had touched a nerve.

"What were you suggesting?"

"Perhaps a man."

That was too much for Amy. "Oh, no — no, no, no, no. A thousand times no!"

"Anyone might —"

"No! Oh, I'm sure you have lots of friends of a different persuasion —"

"I do. My higher power is all about love and caring," Kieran said. "Any gender expression, any sexual persuasion, any color, ethnicity . . . you name it."

"No wonder Raoul is so worried about you!"

"His escape was a very tricky accomplishment," Kieran said.

"No one helped him — no one, but his higher power," Amy said. "Listen to me and listen well. My husband loves me, he wasn't seeing anyone else during any time of our marriage, and it was his voice — the same voice that had led him all along — that led him to freedom!"

"You're sure of that?" Kieran asked very softly.

"Sure. Certain. Absolutely, positively certain," Amy said.

Kieran nodded. "Well, if you think of anything, you must tell us, and — since you want your husband to live — if you know of his whereabouts, if you have any clue as to where he might be, you have to tell us. Because we don't want him shot down by a nervous officer who might just come upon him."

"I want him to live," Amy whispered.

"Of course," Kieran said. She smiled then, abruptly changing her line of questioning. "What about your sons, Amy? Is there a wedding on the horizon? Grandchildren someday?"

Something changed again in the woman's mind. She had come in with a great deal of confidence; Kieran had shaken that.

Amy was finding it again.

"Not soon. They have been tainted. We should have moved years ago, out to the country somewhere, where sin and evil aren't available at every corner and mid-block, too. But I know my boys. They'll

137

come around. They will live the True Life."

"The True Life? Is that your . . . church?"

Amy looked away. "We are small, special. We don't need a building filled with craven images. We are the true chosen ones."

"Do others among you hear voices?" Kieran asked.

"Only Raoul — because he is truly special."

"But your children have strayed from the faith?"

"Yes. And children may stray, but they'll come back to the fold, for our children are as we are — chosen. We stayed here, thinking we might do the most good. I'm afraid it was at the peril of our sons' souls. But I know, as my husband knows, there is no greater glory than in the True Life. And my boys will come back, and I will do what is my mission — molding the next generation, letting them see. My calling, you see, just as my husband was moved to do what was his calling."

"I see," Kieran said.

"If only you did," Amy murmured.

"As I said, I'm trying very hard," Kieran assured her. "And, please, I have to ask this one more time, because you could be the key to saving his life. Think back. You had no clue — until he was caught — he was

138

killing witches. No clue at all, no suspicion he was killing? He must have smelled like gasoline or smoke at times."

"It is not a wife's position to question her husband."

"No matter what he's doing?"

Amy leaned forward. "If he is a good man. My husband is a good man. How many times must I say it? You can't see it, because you are not a believer. You're kind, Kieran — but so naive! I am sorry for you. You are susceptible to the evil that lurks in the world. You must always be on the lookout."

"That is rather what we do here," Egan said lowly, evidently unable to keep silent any longer. "We are the FBI."

"Initials on a badge mean nothing," Amy said.

Egan stood. "Mrs. Nicholson, I'll have an agent drive you home. Thank you so much for coming in. We appreciate the cooperation you've given us."

Amy Nicholson stood. She looked from Egan to Kieran. "If I knew something," she said passionately, "I would tell you. I love my husband. And I believe he can still do good in the world. Wherever he may wind up, as long as he's alive. I will call if I think of anything. Yes, it's frustrating to attempt to explain what others can't understand.

You are good people. Perhaps somewhere along the way, you'll realize that isn't enough, and you'll come to the True Life."

"Well, thank you again for your cooperation," Egan said. He smiled. It was a plastic smile; he still seemed to be in amazement that anyone could seem as passionate as she was in the position she was in. His smile slipped, but he still spoke in an even tone when he said, "We're the FBI, Mrs. Nicholson. We serve everyone — Christians, Buddhists, Muslims, those of the Jewish faith . . . atheists, and even Wiccans and more. Everyone." He didn't want an answer; he was already on his feet.

"An agent will take you home now," Egan told Amy Nicholson firmly.

"Thank you," she said, smiling and nodding in his direction. She looked at Kieran and offered her hand again.

She gave her a very strong shake and said ardently, "Be well, Miss Finnegan. Raoul said you were good. Be well and protect yourself from evil."

"I will do that. Thank you," Kieran told her, extricating her hand.

Egan walked Amy Nicholson to the door. Once the woman was out of earshot, he turned back to Kieran. "I'm sorry. I asked you to speak with her. I should have left the

140

room. I couldn't listen to any more. I might have kept you from discovering if there was anything to discover. I don't usually interfere when I've specifically asked for someone to take on a task."

"I don't think we would have found out anything other than what we did," Kieran said.

"What did we find out?"

Kieran was thoughtful. "I don't think she did know anything about her husband's plan to escape, and I don't think he's seen her. I'm pretty sure the escape took her entirely by surprise. And she does have a weakness."

"What is that?"

"Jealousy. She didn't want there to have been anyone involved, anyone helping him. Especially if it might be another woman."

"Do you think she has had a communication with him since he's escaped?"

"No, I don't think so, and that bothers her. She doesn't want him to die, but I'm not so sure she minded him being locked up. It made her something of a martyr to her cause. These are my impressions. All the training in the world will never make anyone completely understand the working of another person's mind."

"Of course. But I've seen you be right on

many occasions," Egan told her. "Well, then, want to go get that puppy you seem to be adopting?"

"Fostering," Kieran told him. She followed him down the hallway to Craig's small office.

Before they reached the office, Egan's phone rang, and he paused to answer it. After saying "yes" a number of times, he paused. "I need to see Nicholson's attorney for just a minute," he told Kieran.

He headed down to the floor's reception area. Kieran tagged along. Egan didn't object.

Cliff Watkins was standing waiting with a young female agent.

"Mr. Watkins. What can I do for you?" Egan asked him.

"I hear you were interrogating Amy Nicholson," Watkins said.

The man didn't appear to be angry, just tired.

"We weren't interrogating her."

"You should have asked me to come, too," Watkins said.

"Mrs. Nicholson wasn't under arrest, and she wasn't being interrogated. We were asking for her help."

"You have Miss Finnegan here," Watkins noted, nodding Kieran's way. "You were obviously trying to get something out of her."

"Yes," Kieran said, "we're hoping to get Mr. Nicholson back into custody before he kills again — or gets himself into trouble." She hesitated. "In a confrontation with officers or agents."

She wondered about the lawyer, and what it was like to defend a man who had admitted to such heinous crimes. She wondered why his firm had decided this was a case to take on pro bono — unless they wanted the media attention it drew.

Except Watkins seemed to try to avoid the press.

But everyone accused of a crime deserved a defense. And Watkins hadn't tried to say his client was innocent — a difficult task, certainly, when Nicholson had been caught just about red-handed and had confessed.

Watkins looked older than his years, and exhausted. His suit — usually impeccable — seemed a bit rumpled, and his head could have used a shave. Little sprouts were appearing on his customarily bald pate. Maybe it was just getting to be too much for the man.

It had probably been hell for him since Nicholson had escaped.

Watkins shook his head and let out a long

sigh. He looked around. "Off the record, they're crazy people. I mean, I'm begging him — and the courts — to force the mental health issue. Thing is, Amy is . . . well, she isn't a killer, but she's got a lot of issues, and I don't want . . ."

"We're not out to hurt your client. I have no problem believing he's delusional," Egan said. "We need him locked up. And we need to know if he killed again."

Watkins nodded. "If you need to speak to her again, I ask the courtesy of being present. And I'm to be informed immediately when you do find my client. At the moment — other than the fact he's on the loose — you have no evidence that suggests he killed again."

"Other than the method," Egan said softly.

"You need more than —" Watkins broke off, waving a hand in the air. "You already have him on enough. But I wouldn't guarantee it's the same man. Copycats are always out there. Look, I can't force anything legally, but . . . someone like Amy . . . who knows what she'll say? She needs an attorney."

Egan was noncommittal. He smiled and offered Watkins his hand. "We'll all hope Nicholson is apprehended as quickly as possible," he said.

"Thank you," Watkins said. He nodded to Kieran and she nodded in return. They waited as he headed back to the elevator.

Egan didn't speak again until he was gone.

"Good lord! Let's get the dog and get out of here!"

The dog had been very good; there were no messes.

"Leash is on the desk," Egan said.

She nodded, collecting the leash. "Nothing else for him, huh? No food, toys, or anything?"

"No, Craig just had the dog, said he couldn't figure out anything more expedient than to take him and . . . I think he just liked the dog."

"I see."

She attached the leash to Ruff's collar. As she stood, a thought occurred to her. "Craig and Mike are at the building where Mayhew was murdered, looking for Ruff's owner, Mr. Blom, right?"

"Yes," Egan said.

"I was just thinking . . . if there is a way to find Blom, Ruff just might be able to help. Who better to sniff out where his master went?"

"You might be right. Okay, Special Agent Jimenez planned on driving us on over to Finnegan's. We'll make a big detour and head to the Upper East Side, see if the dog does have anything to show us," Egan agreed.

Kieran scooped up the dog and they headed out. Jimenez — Jimmy Jimenez, a fairly new recruit, young, polite, and like-able — was waiting for them. Kieran knew him because Craig and Mike had brought him by Finnegan's a few times.

He greeted her warmly and listened to Egan's new directions, nodding at his new assignment. "Hopefully, traffic won't be too bad. Saturday afternoon isn't nearly so hor-rible as Friday."

Ruff gave a little yelp, as if he were in complete agreement.

On the way, she realized this was a case Egan was interested in, and he hadn't been to the building yet either. He was in his position because he was good at assigning the right men and women to their cases. He wasn't a micromanager, but this was a high-profile case. The building looked to Kieran to be about 1890s, well-maintained, with handsome architectural features with mold-ing and brick.

A doorman — or security guard — met them at the door. Egan showed his creden-tials, asking for the whereabouts of his agents. They were brought to another man,

Simon Wrigley, older and warier than the guard who had first greeted them. He called a third man he introduced as Joey Catalano, who had now been working nearly twenty-four hours, but was staying on because he had been on duty the night before, when Mayhew had been murdered.

At last the man named Catalano brought them to a door, unlocked it with a master key, and showed them the way down to the basement.

The first thing Kieran noticed was that Craig and Mike had both taken off their jackets. They were hanging over the rail at the foot of the stairway. But she didn't see either man.

Egan called out for them over the mechanical hum of the air heating and cooling system.

Mike came from one direction, Craig from another. They had their sleeves rolled up as well, as if they had been working for a long time.

Craig didn't appear at all pleased to see them, but as he got closer, Ruff let out an excited sound. Kieran set him down. The dog raced toward Craig.

"We thought the dog might help pick up a trail," Egan said.

Craig stooped down, apparently certain

147

the dog was coming to him.

But Ruff didn't go to Craig. He rushed past him, barking excitedly. Kieran couldn't see where he went because he raced behind a section of wall.

"What . . ." Craig muttered, following the dog.

Everyone trailed behind Craig.

Ruff had paused, as if confused, beyond the area where the massive heating and cooling system sat, in a middle area with a clean floor and space to see stacks of tools and products neatly kept against the walls.

One section of boxes had been completely shifted. It looked like someone was in the middle of reorganizing and the boxes might eventually be returned to a position against the wall, Kieran thought.

Ruff began to race in circles.

Barking.

"What is with him?" Egan asked. "Craig, maybe you'd better . . ."

"Sir, I think we should leave him be," Craig said. He approached the dog, hunkering down next to it, not trying to stop him when he ran in a circle again.

"What is it, boy?" Craig asked.

Ruff left the clear area where he'd been running in his circles; he darted to the piles that had evidently been recently moved.

He sniffed there for a minute and started barking again.

Craig followed the dog, frowning.

"Ruff, there's nothing there. I know that for certain."

Kieran wondered if the pup wasn't just looking for a place to lift his leg.

But Ruff moved on. He started sniffing around the whole floor. Craig ran after him and Mike did the same.

The floor space was sizable. Mike held up a hand and stood still. Only one of them needed to run in circles with the dog.

Ruff stopped and pawed at boxes filled with various cleaning products; mops and other housekeeping items poked out the top.

Craig looked at Mike and walked over to that pile. Together, they started pulling the boxes out of their positions by the walls, a hasty effort with Ruff barking and whining in the background.

Then, Craig froze, staring down.

Kieran instinctively ran over.

She gasped.

Ruff let out a horrible whine. It was just a pile of rags. But the rags were covered in something red, something that caused Ruff to next let out an, eerie, howling cry . . .

Blood.

CHAPTER SEVEN

"Ruff could stay in the office. No one would need to see him," Kieran told Craig. "Declan wouldn't mind, and the dog wouldn't actually be in the pub."

Craig didn't want her to go to Finnegan's, and he was pretty sure she could guess why: he didn't want to leave the dog, and therefore thought Kieran should just take the pup back to their apartment.

They'd bagged up the bloody rags and sent them on to the lab; thankfully, new procedures allowed for quick DNA testing. They'd have results by tomorrow, since it was easy enough to get DNA from Olav Blom's toothbrush for comparison.

Craig was positive, though, they'd find the blood belonged to Blom.

And, somewhere out there, they'd find his body. He was now certain there was a way into and out of the building through the basement. They still had to find it.

"I guess I could bring him to our place," Kieran said tentatively. "Or . . ."

"Wait. He doesn't look like a bloodhound or tracker, but Mike, we should keep him. He did find our next lead," Craig said.

"Loyal little bugger," Mike said. "But we have to keep him on his leash. He might take off and we won't be able to follow."

To his surprise, Kieran was frowning. He hadn't been entirely sure how she'd feel about him taking the dog. He just knew that something about the little pup had pulled at heartstrings he hadn't even known he possessed. He just couldn't give the mutt over to animal services.

"Bobby," Mike said. He grinned at Craig. "Surely you heard about Greyfriars Bobby, the little Skye terrier who guarded his master's grave in Edinburgh for fourteen years. There's a statue in his honor — loyal little dog."

"Yeah, I've seen the statue," Craig muttered, studying Ruff. He really did fall into the "so ugly he was cute" category with his spiky white fur with black and brown blotches here and there. He had great eyes, though, big and brown, in a terrier face. He wasn't sure how many terrier breeds were mixed in the little dog's makeup, but beyond a doubt, he was loyal — and smart. And

151

bloodhound or not, he had found the rags.

"Poor thing has been really traumatized," Kieran said. "Do you really think —"

"That we have to find out what happened and try to save lives? Yes." Craig spoke quietly. "Look, he's going to be okay. I have no intention of calling animal services," he reminded her.

She nodded. "Okay."

The dog was struggling in Kieran's arms. She set him down and he bounced away from her, racing then toward the large machines that controlled the building's cooling and heating.

Craig looked at Mike with raised eyebrows, and then the two of them walked after the dog. He'd disappeared behind what appeared to be a large, six-foot-high cylinder on its side, pressed straight back against the wall.

Craig caught hold of the cylinder; it was firmly in place, but he realized, by getting down on his hands and knees, he could follow the dog behind it along the floor, in the space between the wall and the curve of the equipment.

Ruff started barking wildly. With all the metal, the sound of his barks was amplified and seemed to echo sharply throughout the basement.

Behind the cylinder, Craig found a metal slide. It looked as if it had long rusted hard against the poured concrete of the building. At one time, he thought, ice had been delivered through that chute. More recently, it had been drywalled and plastered over.

No more. Someone had gotten behind the HVAC system, and had meticulously chipped away plaster and torn out drywall.

He pushed at the metal hatch.

And the chute opened, allowing plenty of space for an able-bodied person to crawl in — or out.

"Well, you knew what you were doing," Egan said, his face peering around the edge of the cylinder.

Craig backed out of the space. "We'll head up and around, join the troops looking for Olav Blom," Craig told Egan. "We have a Saturday crew in, working the computers for information, trying to see if we can find any relationship between Raoul Nicholson and Charles Mayhew or this building. And Nicholson is somewhere. We will find him."

"There are dozens of officers and agents searching," Egan said. "For Nicholson. And we'll get a likeness of Olav Blom out there now, but . . ." He broke off and pointed to the old ice door. "You may as well get started."

Craig nodded. "He has to show up — every law enforcement officer in the city will have him on radar. No one can hide forever." He looked to Mike. "Let's head out."

Craig pulled at the chute; plaster crumbled around him as he hiked himself up, lying flat once he reached the small space behind the building. He looked down at Mike.

"Uh, I'm taking the stairs. Meet you out there," Mike said.

"We'll inform Simon Wrigley that he has to get his people on this," Egan said. "Kieran, shall we head out? We're in the way now. Those two need to get moving. I can take you to Finnegan's. To be honest, I'm really hungry."

Kieran nodded.

"Hand Ruff up to me, first," Craig said.

"Hey, maybe the dog wants to take the stairs, too," Mike said, but he grinned and collected the dog.

Kieran was watching Craig. He gave her a grave smile.

"I'll watch out for Ruff," he said.

"And yourself," she said quietly.

"And myself," he promised. "And, of course, the dog and I will both watch out for Mike."

"Funny," Mike said, lifting Ruff to hand

him over through the opening to Craig.

Craig collected Ruff, making sure he had a good hold on the leash before setting him down. Then he stood, looking around at his environs.

There wasn't exactly an alley behind the building, but neither had the newer building to the side been built flush against it. The narrow strip of space led toward Central Park West in one direction, and to a small courtyard in the other, where two buildings had been erected about twenty feet apart, allowing for something rare in the city — outdoor space. He looked toward the courtyard and then toward Central Park West.

Central Park — one of the city's most amazing assets. Stretching from Fifty-Ninth Street to 110th Street, between Fifth Avenue and Central Park West. Over eight hundred acres of ball fields, picnic space, event locations, jogging paths and more — places where, in the dark, the unwary just might become prey . . .

He looked up. The sun was beginning its downward slant. The day remained bright, however, just a few puffy white clouds hovering between the blue.

Mike joined him, sauntering around the

corner of the little alley. "Which way?" he asked.

Ruff barked. He strained against the leash.

"I was thinking toward the park," Craig replied.

"To the park," Mike said. And added dryly, "I guess he's walking us."

Saturday afternoons at the pub tended to be filled with families.

Kieran knew that, once upon a time, men had filled the main room by the bar, and ladies and children had been escorted to the side. Now, while they were downtown — a bit of a trip for anyone who lived up past midtown — Finnegan's was still a popular destination, especially for those who enjoyed the casual tone of the place and easy atmosphere for children.

The pathway to the bar from the front double-doors, which were handsomely attired with cut glass on the upper half, was lined with small curved wooden booths, making cozy tables for duos or small groups.

Kieran recognized several of the families taking up the larger tables in the dining room. Brent Dunne and his two teenaged sons and ten-year-old daughter were at one table with his dad, a native of County Cork. Another group consisted of the Murphy cousins. The grandparents often brought whichever of their fourteen grandchildren happened to be with them that day.

Of course, it wasn't just the American Irish who came. Another table consisted of the D'Onofrio tribe, a family of Italian descent who also enjoyed the Saturday shepherd's pie special. The Alonso clan, who were regulars, originally immigrated from Ecuador. Kieran smiled, thinking she was proud of the welcoming way her parents had managed the pub — and equally proud of the way Declan had carried on the tradition.

Egan took a seat in one of the enclaves near the bar while Kieran went to check with Declan and see how his day was going.

He wasn't behind the bar; Mary Kathleen was working there and greeted Kieran with a friendly smile.

"Busy?" Kieran asked.

"The usual, and everyone showed up to work bright and early. We're doing fine. Declan is back in the office — apparently," she added with a grin. "I've been deemed competent to man the bar on my own."

Kieran laughed softly. Mary Kathleen had worked on the floor for several years, then risen to the status of daytime bartender. And then she had become part of the family: she and Declan had been married last year. Now she filled in wherever she was needed.

Kieran loved Mary Kathleen; she was the best sister-in-law one could ever hope to have.

Declan, being Declan, usually backed up the bartender, no matter who it was. But he wasn't there with Mary Kathleen.

"Congrats on being so competent!" Kieran told her with a smile. "Craig's boss is over there, if you'll make sure someone checks on him soon. I think he's come for the shepherd's pie."

"No Craig?" Mary Kathleen asked her.

"I think he'll show up — eventually. I'll go say hi to Declan," Kieran said.

"Soda with lime?" Mary Kathleen asked her.

"You got it."

Kieran left her and headed down the hallway to her brother's office. The door stood ajar and she pressed it forward, peeking in. Declan looked up at her; he'd been intently studying something on his computer.

"Hey! Accounting?" she asked, stepping in.

He sat back, arching his brows, and then he flushed.

Kieran frowned, curious — Declan didn't hide things.

"Porn?" she asked.

He laughed. "No." His expression was sheepish. "I, uh, I was looking up all kinds of things. I'm trying not to micromanage. Mary Kathleen knows what she's doing, and . . . my chefs are doing well and the floor is covered nicely, as well. So, I'm trying not to look over shoulders."

"You could take a day off."

"I do take days off," he said defensively.

"Okay, sure. So what were you doing?"

He let out a long sigh. "Looking up everything I can find out about Raoul Nicholson."

"Oh!" she said, surprised. She wasn't even sure why Declan's activity should surprise her so much. There had been times when the pub and every one of her brothers had become involved in various cases. One case concerned the deconsecrated church behind the pub, which had been connected through an underground system, something that none of them had had the least bit of knowledge or even suspicion about.

But Declan was usually inadvertently roped in to these kinds of things.

"Oh," she said again.

"He's on the loose. And there has been

another murder. I watched Egan's press conference." Declan sat back, his blue-gray eyes zeroed in hard on her. "And," he added softly, "no big surprise, but you are right in the middle of this."

She didn't dispute it or try to wave his words aside.

"And what did you find out? The man does belong in an institution. If he were out, and believed he was told to kill another 'witch,' he would. Without hesitation or remorse. He should never be let out — except he got out. And he planned an escape so well-executed it's almost impossible to believe he did it on his own."

"What about the murder of Mayhew?"

"At this moment, your guess is as good as mine."

"And after all those years in college!" Declan ribbed her.

"Hey!"

"Sorry — I know you're good at what you do."

"Well, what have you learned?"

"You know about his church, right?"

"The Church of True Life?"

Declan nodded grimly. "It isn't a recognized church. It's so fundamentalist that the fundamentalists want nothing to do with it."

160

"Yes, I do know that."

"Did you know that the membership is secret? The members are not known except to one another. It exists nowhere else on earth — Raoul Nicholson was the head of the church."

"I wonder who has taken over in his stead."

"That's what I was looking for. But I couldn't find anything. I'll bet it's on the dark web."

"Could be. I can ask Craig if any of his guys can check for us. They might already be on it. In fact, I would almost bet with the Mayhew murder, they're already trying to find out if Nicholson was grooming anyone to take over his position."

Declan leaned forward. "What if it was one of his sons?"

"I never met the sons, though they have been interviewed by Fuller and Miro. It must have been rough for them growing up. No parties, no sports, no — no anything! Both Fuller and Miro believe the boys knew nothing about their father's activities, and now they want to lead more normal lives. There are other restrictive religions, I know, but this 'True Life' thing appears to frown on anything but hard work."

"Could be a sham," Declan said.

"Yes, it could be. You mean, they're pretending to embrace wine, women, song, and fraternities while secretly planning to take over for the dad?"

Declan shrugged. "Just a layman's theory."

"Anything is possible at this moment. Someone may have just wanted Mayhew dead and used Nicholson's method of killing to get away with murder. Or Nicholson did manage an almost impossible escape. Maybe he managed this, too."

Declan stood. "Okay."

"Okay . . . what?"

"Enough of this. I've kept myself from micromanaging long enough. I've got to check on the pub, and you have to go out and be social and nice, and try to forget about Raoul Nicholson and his homicidal craziness for a while."

They joined Richard Egan at his table, and Mary Kathleen wandered over to see if they needed anything.

They chatted for a while, Egan asking Mary Kathleen and Declan how they were doing. Egan had been at the ceremony when Mary Kathleen had wed Declan in a beautiful ceremony at St. Grace just a few months back. She'd originally come from Ireland and had been at Finnegan's ever since, falling in love with Declan while working as their head server.

Married life was amazing, Declan assured him. And he was so happy to have his wife working with him. It was a family pub, family owned, and family operated, and she was amazing now as a comanager, bartender, cook, and bottle washer — as they all were.

Kieran made a face at Egan behind her brother's back. Egan smiled. It was obvious Declan had been the perfect Finnegan to take over when their dad had passed on.

As the two kept on about the state-of-affairs in the city, Kieran found herself looking idly around the pub.

An odd feeling swept over her, and she turned toward the door. A man was slipping into a trench coat, ready to leave.

There was something vaguely familiar about him — something disturbing — though she wasn't sure what. She could only see the back of his head. He had dark hair — a lot of it. He was straight-backed and moved with the ease and dexterity of a young man.

He'd obviously been in the pub, but she hadn't noticed him before at any of the tables. She hadn't seen any lone diners in the restaurant area. It didn't even seem that anyone at the bar had come in alone.

But he had to have been in there —

because he was now leaving.

She glanced quickly back at the dining room.

Families ate, laughed, and chatted.

Who had he been with? Someone, certainly. She hadn't studied everyone at every table when they'd come in — she'd just noted a few of their weekend regulars.

He adjusted the trench coat, opened the door, and stepped outside.

Kieran excused herself and slid from the booth, heading for the door. She moved quickly out onto the sidewalk.

For once, Broadway was not particularly busy. This close to the financial district and Wall Street, it was a zoo by weekday and nicely quieter on the weekends. Glancing right and left, she caught sight of the man moving around the north corner. She hurried after him, wondering what she was going to say if she caught up with him. Something like, *Hey, why did seeing you disturb me? Are you a criminal of some kind?*

No, she could just say she thought he'd left something at the pub . . .

And then hope he hadn't actually lost whatever item she might invent.

Better yet, she could say she thought he was a friend of Danny's or Kevin's, and she was just mistaken and so sorry.

None of her excuses mattered; when she reached the corner and turned, he was gone. Just gone. The street wasn't crowded; there weren't even many cars. The offices were closed.

But somehow, he'd vanished.

She hesitated for a minute. But even as she turned back, she had the eerie feeling that someone was watching her.

"You do know Central Park is larger than Monaco?" Mike asked as they walked.

"The dog is heading this way," Craig said. "Yes, I know the size of it. And I also know at the end of the 1800s, police found a runaway — who had lived in a cave in the park for a month. And dozens of rapes and several murders have taken place there. And the police work damned hard these days, but you've got darkness and trees and stretches where — especially at night — no one can hear you scream."

"Oh, people might *hear* you scream and think it's just kids playing or a loud TV. Or they just don't want to get involved," Mike said.

Craig looked up at the sky. The afternoon was disappearing, and where just thirty minutes ago the sky had been powdery blue and benign, it was now darkening, as if with the foreboding of a storm.

The park itself seemed to grow darker with shadows. They moved along a trail used by runners, who huffed past every now and then. Ruff didn't seem to notice anyone who passed them. He was on a mission, sniffing the ground, walking ahead, as if he led Craig and not vice versa.

"Since you're just a kid," Mike said, as they walked through the trails near the bridle path, "you won't appreciate just how great the park is today. Before the seventies, it was falling into decay. I mean, think about it. Central Park was the first such major development in any city. It helped shape NYC. Olmsted and Vaux won a competition back in the 1850s and created an amazing piece of geographical art. So much here — a lifeline for urban dwellers. But it was in decline. Structures molding and chipping . . . decaying. Paths dark and scary with lots of bad things happening. Efforts in the 1970s changed all that —"

"Mike, you have me by ten years," Craig reminded him dryly. "You were a kid back then."

"Ah, but I remember. I remember how thrilled my mom was, saying it was so great we'd have a place to go and play that would be safe. It was always a brilliant 'center' piece for the city of New York. But they went to work and made it a much safer place. I mean, it's a park — huge, and things can happen. But much better because people went to bat for change. I guess no place is really safe, though, huh?"

"Look at the dog," Craig said. He paused.

Ruff was standing dead still.

He began to whine.

They had been on a trail; now, Ruff pulled Craig up a little incline and through the trees and before he knew it, he was on the street again.

He had to pull Ruff back — the dog had been ready to rush out into traffic.

"What the hell?" Mike muttered, following, shaking off a few leaves that had stuck in his collar.

"Don't know. Just following the dog," Craig said. He hunkered down by Ruff. The dog barked excitedly, desperately wanting to cross the street.

"Okay, okay," Craig said. Watching the cars, he swept up the dog and streaked across the busy street. He received a half dozen angry honks for his efforts.

Mike made it across seconds later, vociferously swearing.

But when Craig reached the sidewalk, he saw the alley — Ruff's determined destination. It was a fairly broad alley, allowing for delivery vehicles and garbage trucks to pass through, bringing supplies to businesses and taking away the refuse. Craig saw the storefronts offered a chic wine bar, an Italian restaurant, a doughnut and coffee shop.

He set Ruff on the ground. The pup looked down the alley and barked.

Mike came up behind Craig, panting. "Death by Audi!" he complained. "We're going to have to teach this guy about crosswalks. With our luck, we might have been stopped by a beat cop for jaywalking, you know."

"Sorry. I, uh, should have gone to the crosswalk. It's just . . . damn. The dog knows something, I think. Instincts."

"Yeah, he knows something. I think the mutt knows this is where you come for the tastiest garbage in town," he said. "Instinctively."

Craig smiled grimly and shook his head. "I don't think so."

Mike was looking up; he did the same.

"Look at the night, will ya?"

The sun had all but fallen completely beneath the western horizon, but it wasn't night yet. The sky with its promise of a storm was making it appear it was so. The air swirled with a chilling dampness, a promise of rain to come. Distant thunder came like a threatening growl from the sky.

Ruff whined again; the little dog was shivering at Craig's feet.

"Well, hell, let's move on this, huh?" Mike said, starting forward along the alley. "I wish I knew what we were looking for. An apartment, a restaurant . . . a hole in the ground."

Ruff barked. Craig let him lead.

Behind the Italian restaurant, they saw a pretty, young, dark-haired waitress in an apron turning her face away and holding her nose with one hand while she used the other to maneuver the lid up and toss a garbage bag in a dumpster.

She managed to drop the bag as they arrived.

"Uh, hey!" she said. Seeing them she seemed to freeze — maybe her instincts kicking in when she was alone in an alley with two large men walking toward her.

Craig reached into his jacket and pulled out his credentials, and while he did so, Ruff began to howl.

The pained sound was loud and eerie, as if they'd entered into a horror movie and Ruff was about to go from ugly-cute pup to vicious, slobbering werewolf.

Nothing about the dog changed, but the sound he was making was high-pitched and horrible, blood-chilling in the darkening alley.

He raced to the dumpster, now barking in a fury.

The waitress screamed, thinking the little dog was after her. She leaped back — and Craig darted forward.

He threw open the lid of the dumpster and the odor she'd been trying to avoid by pinching her nose came flying at them all like an invisible tidal wave.

Decomposition.

Death.

Mike stepped back, swearing and already pulling out his phone.

Craig passed Ruff's leash to Mike's free hand, then he caught hold of the edge of the dumpster and hiked himself up. Balancing his weight on one hand, he used the other to toss aside half a dozen large, black garbage bags.

Spaghetti had oozed from one, decorated with marinara sauce, now appearing as if it might be a contingent of bloody worms.

No worms.

Just a dead man beneath.

Covered in filth now.

Eyes wide open, stunned and staring, even against the coming darkness of the night.

CHAPTER EIGHT

Kieran was glad her absence hadn't been noted. Running out on her own, for no apparent reason, had not been a bright choice of things to do, but she didn't want anyone becoming unduly concerned about her.

When she returned to the table, Declan was leaning back, arms crossed over his chest.

Egan was on his phone, tensely listening.

When he finished his call, he stood up, shaking his head. "Craig's thoughts on the dog were right on. Ruff took them on a bit of a winding course, but he found his master for us."

"And?" Kieran asked.

"Dead, I'm afraid. Craig says he believes Olav Blom took the dog out for his usual walk through the park. Then they came across the killer. The killer managed to get them out of the park and across the street, kept the dog, murdered Blom, stole his

171

hoodie and got into the building to murder Mayhew."

"Mayhew was the target, but . . . how was Blom killed? Had he been strangled, mutilated and burned?"

Egan shook his head. "Stabbed and dumped beneath a bunch of refuse from restaurants." He hesitated. "I'm still not able to rule out Nicholson."

"No," Kieran said softly, shaking her head.

"No? Kieran, he got out — impossibly. And this happened — impossibly, so one would think. But Mayhew died like Nicholson's other victims."

"But you just told me Olav Blom didn't."

"I have no idea how anyone could believe that anyone's God condones murder, but if Nicholson is so fixated on what he believes he has to do, killing one man to get to another would be collateral damage, acceptable in Nicholson's dark mind," Egan said.

"I'll play devil's advocate," Declan said quietly. "Why not, Kieran?"

She glanced at her brother; he was looking at her worriedly. He never liked it when she became too involved in dangerous cases, but then again, the pub itself had been involved before, her brothers had been involved before . . .

Just not Declan, not so much, or to any

extent, other than he'd been caught in the fray.

"Kieran," he prompted.

"No one was killed during Nicholson's escape," she said.

"No," Egan admitted.

"I just don't believe Nicholson would kill one man to get to another. That would be wrong. Right now he's a righteous angel, doing as commanded. To kill otherwise would be murder. I'm just telling you what I see, the way that his mind works." She shrugged and let out a breath. "Nicholson does need to be apprehended, one way or another. He will kill again — if he hasn't already."

Egan nodded. "We've had cops watching his wife and his sons. He hasn't come near them. Not yet. Not that they've managed to see, at any rate. The city's resources have been stretched pretty thin on this — marshals, cops, agents, you name it. They're all on alert. Beat cops have seen his face plastered everywhere. His pictures have been on the news time and time again. Unless he's living in a hole somewhere, they'll get him soon."

"Even if he's in a hole, he'll have to come up for air," Kieran said.

"Or to murder," Declan added.

"Well, I'm on to the site myself," Egan said quietly. "Guess that little dog is one smart little creature." Then he looked at Kieran. "Not sure when you'll see Craig, but —"

"I'll be here for a while, then I'll head straight to our apartment," Kieran assured him.

"I'll have an agent watching your building," Egan said.

She thought she should argue. Everyone available should be looking for Nicholson.

And as for this copycat killer, she was growing more and more convinced Mayhew had not been murdered by Raoul Nicholson.

Nor had Olav Blom.

She smiled. "Okay."

Egan nodded, well aware she'd been about to argue.

"Don't worry. They'll be watching the street, as well. Who knows? Maybe Nicholson will try to get in contact with you. He liked you — so you say."

"I said he didn't think I was a witch."

"Yes, but he told his wife you were good. So, we'll keep a watch over you — just in case."

Egan waved at them both and headed out.

"Let it go, Kieran. It's not a bad thing,"

Declan told her.

"No, not a bad thing at all. Okay, well, you don't need me here. I'm going to get some dinner to go for Craig and head home."

"I can always find something for you to do," Declan said. "Danny will probably be in after his last tour, and Kevin may pop in between shows and —"

"You just heard Egan. There will be an agent watching my house."

"I'll get you home then."

"Declan, you don't have to leave the pub on a Saturday evening."

"Sure. My employees will all thank you. I won't be looking over anyone's shoulder."

"Fine. Walk me home."

At least she would be in her own space. And she'd be there when Craig got home.

Craig was glad to see that Dr. Layton had been called to the scene of this crime, as well. Layton had only been with the Office of the Chief Medical Examiner for the City of New York for about eighteen months, but he was proving his mettle. Neither cops nor agents were supposed to touch the body until the medical examiner had arrived, and so, other than somewhat disturbing the body when he'd pulled the trash off it, Craig had gone no further.

Layton had no problem crawling into the horrible brew in the dumpster. Craig noted he had stopped to slide some peppermint oil under his nose and that he covered his mouth with a mask before climbing in.

"Dead at least twenty-four hours. If it weren't for the fact this is a dumpster, I believe someone would have noted there was a body here sooner," Layton told them. "I believe the cause of death was exsanguination. Method, a very sharp knife." He looked over the edge of the dumpster. "He was killed here or near here. Hard to tell, again, because this is a dumpster with a great deal of spaghetti sauce in it, as well."

"You can't mean the killer lured the man into a dumpster?" Mike asked, doubting the possibility.

"No, he might have gotten him just there, where you are standing. But there's no blood spray. So, he probably drew the blade slowly and precisely, causing the blood to drip down this man's throat and chest, rather than spurt."

"Like so?" Craig asked, sliding behind Mike and locking him into a hold before showing how a blade could then be drawn against his partner's neck.

Layton nodded. "Like so."

Mike drew away from Craig. "Next time, you're the victim. That felt damned creepy."

"After all these years," Craig muttered.

"Creepy never stops," Mike said softly, and Craig nodded. Mike was right. You could go out case after case and never stop being amazed by the cruelty man could inflict upon his fellow man.

Craig realized Layton was watching them.

"Hey, bodies are my business. Never stops bothering me, either. I do like to think I perform a justice for them, though. Well, sometimes, my bodies are okay. Ninety-year-olds who have had full lives, experiences, and leave behind families who are sad, but accepting we all come with a time stamp. Anyway," he said, waving a hand in the air. "If the photographer is done . . . I'm ready for them to remove the body. I can tell you more after autopsy, but not much more."

Craig reached up with gloved hands to help the man crawl back out of the dumpster.

The ME smelled to high hell.

Craig figured he did, too.

Crime scene technicians would go through everything in the alley and the dumpster, but he and Mike had already given it a once-over.

Nothing — nothing that seemed to be anything at any rate.

They had dozens of cigarette butts, but every smoking waiter, waitress, dishwasher, and patron of the surrounding places could have slipped out back for a cigarette.

There were disposable cups, plates, napkins, boxes, and more.

There was marinara sauce.

There was blood.

He wondered if the killer's blood might be in the mix, too. But an answer to that would take time and the lab.

He looked down the alley to see that Richard Egan had come to the scene, fully aware he'd be having to give another press conference the next day. Egan believed the public deserved to know what was going on.

But he believed in hiding details from the public because in any city were people who would confess to crimes they didn't commit or insist they knew something, simply for attention. In New York, those numbers were multiplied many times over. It was a mammoth city.

Right now, he'd be carefully weighing what he should say.

Craig strode over to him.

He knew how badly he smelled by the way his boss's face crinkled as he arrived.

"You found him," Egan said quietly.

"As I feared."

Egan shook his head. "I don't get it. If the killer knew about the old ice chute in the basement, why go after Blom and kill him to get in the building? Why didn't he just come in through the chute and leave Blom out of it?"

"Well, I don't really know, and I'm working on that. For one, if he didn't figure out a way to get a key, he wasn't going to get anywhere other than the lobby," Craig said.

"But according to the security firm, each resident could only get to his or her floor."

"We're going to have to go through phone records and email. Maybe once the killer was in the building, they could have called Mayhew and had him bring them up? Mayhew and Blom might have been friendly enough to stop by each other's places for a drink or cup of coffee. Then it would be easy enough for the killer to get out."

"Right. So, the killer sees Blom leave with the dog. He lures the man to a back alley and kills him and leaves him. Then how the hell did Blom's blood wind up in a pool on the basement floor?"

"I don't know," Craig said. He hesitated. "Part of the problem is that because he was wearing a hoodie and doesn't look up at the security camera, we can't say if it was Blom coming and going, or someone else, either time. Maybe the killer found Blom in the park, lured him to the ice chute somehow, brought him down to the basement — and killed him there. Then somehow dragged him back out and disposed of him here."

"Why not just leave him in the basement?"

"To make it all harder to figure. Cast suspicion on him and slow us down. It's working, after all. Have we confirmed if the blood in the basement did belong to Blom?"

"You haven't checked your email."

"I've been dumpster diving."

Egan nodded grimly. "It's Blom's blood," he said. "Lab rushed for us — yes. We have a match."

"Then that's the only scenario I can figure," Craig said. "And damned difficult to pull off. There would have had to be a reason that Blom would trust someone enough to follow them down the ice chute."

Egan didn't answer.

"You know, I don't think Nicholson committed these murders," Craig said.

"Neither does your fiancée. But with Nicholson on the loose, we don't know, do we?" Egan asked. He swore softly, something Craig didn't often hear him do.

"Every officer is on the prowl for the man

— and we've got nothing!" Egan said with disgust.

"Sir, it's barely been over twenty-four hours since he escaped," Craig reminded him.

Egan looked at the agent and said, "We had him. And we lost him. And he may be killing again — or he may have an apprentice. Anyway . . ." He stared at the dumpster.

Dr. Layton was directing his assistants as they moved the body from its position among the garbage.

"Go home," Egan said to Craig. "You and Mike go home. Start fresh in the morning. Maybe Layton will find something in the autopsy, something to help explain this bizarre business and how this killer is moving around with a body and not being seen!"

"I —"

"Go home. You found the route out of the basement. You found your man."

"Dead."

"Dead whether you'd found him or not. And yes, eventually, he would have been found. But we're a step ahead. You found him before he could wind up in the dump, mangled beyond description. Go home, and for the love of God, take a really long shower." He started to turn away, but he hesitated, frowning.

"Where is the dog?" he asked.

Craig pointed. Ruff had been lying at the foot of the dumpster. He seemed to believe someone was going to help his master. He made no attempt to growl or snap at the men and women from the coroner's office or from the crime scene department.

He just whined now and then, pressing his head between his paws.

Mike, still standing by the dumpster, looking for anything that might go amiss, paused now and then to pat the little dog on the head.

"Well, his owner is gone," Egan said quietly. "But I'm guessing he's not going to animal services?"

"I'm guessing he's not," Craig said.

"Then may I give you another suggestion?"

"Yes, of course. You may always suggest, sir."

Egan lowered his head for a minute and then looked at Craig, a grim smile on his face.

"Give the dog a bath, too. As quickly as possible."

Kieran had talked Declan into walking with her the short distance to her apartment, but once there he didn't want to leave.

It was nice to have her brothers care about her the way they did. But she was getting a bit irritated. It was growing later and later, and Declan was going through every room and into every closet. He looked under the beds, and behind the shower curtain in the master bath, and in the bath on the ground floor of the loft.

She walked along with him, trying to assure him.

"Declan, Egan said there's an agent watching the place."

"I didn't see an agent."

"Come to the windows." Opening the curtains in the master bedroom, she encouraged him to look down.

A black sedan was parked along the side of the road — where it really shouldn't be.

"Bureau car?" he asked her.

She nodded. "See? Egan's watching out. And I keep telling you all Nicholson doesn't think I'm wicked. I'm not in any danger from him."

"You're convinced you read him correctly?"

Kieran hesitated. "I'd never ask anyone else to believe me blindly, especially where personal safety is concerned. But I'm sure."

"All right. You'll call —"

"I have an agent outside," she said again.

And finally she was able to show Declan out. He hovered on the other side of the door. "Door's locked, alarm on?"

"Yes! Go back to work!"

And, finally, he went away.

He was gone only a few minutes, and she had barely set her laptop up on the kitchen counter when her cell rang. It was Craig, and she answered it quickly.

"You heard, right? You were with Egan when we called him about Blom?" he asked.

"Yes."

"We're done here. I'm heading home. I'm sorry. I'm not in a pub mood."

"I'm not at the pub. I'm home."

"Oh, uh, okay. Good. I'm on the Upper East Side but heading out now."

"I brought food home for you. I'll go ahead and heat it up."

"That's great." He was quiet a minute and then said. "Kieran?"

"Yes?"

"I can't leave him. I can't leave him here."

She frowned, for a moment having a horrible vision of Craig referring to a dead man in a dumpster.

Then, of course, she knew.

"I didn't think, if you didn't find Olav Blom alive, that you would leave him."

"Thanks. But you know, in the city, a dog . . ."

"It's fine. He's going to need people. He's an amazing little pup. Too bad his name is Ruff. I'd have called him Scruffy."

She could hear the smile in his voice. "Thanks."

"Hey, I get it. I like the dog, too, okay?"

"Yep. One more thing — I smell really bad."

"I'm pretty sure that's why God invented water and soap and all that."

"And the dog smells really, really bad."

"I'll be ready."

"I was going to suggest you lock yourself in a room. And get out the disinfectant spray."

"You take care of you. I'll take care of the dog. Just get home — please."

"Okay, okay, the stinking dog is all yours. See you soon."

Kieran smiled at the phone as she hit the end button.

She started to sit at her computer, but instead stood restlessly.

She had the notes Drs. Fuller and Miro had made while they were interviewing not just Nicholson, but those in his life.

His sons.

Were they really as removed from their

185

parents' beliefs as they purported to be?

She wandered to the window, thinking she'd like to talk to the two boys. Maybe their mother had suggested they not talk to her.

Even if they didn't believe in their father's voices, they might not be that removed from their insular church.

Pulling back the drape, she saw the moon was rising; the rain had come and gone.

The sky was dark, oddly deep blue with shadows of clouds still hovering, but the moon was breaking through.

Across the street, near the corner, she saw a man. He was tall, wearing a hat pulled low, and a trench coat that fell just past his knees.

She could see nothing of his face, despite the pool of multicolored light from the traffic signal.

He was doing nothing; just standing. But she thought he was looking toward her apartment building.

She found herself thinking of the man who had been in the pub — the one she had chased but had disappeared. The one who had also donned a trench coat.

It was spring in New York; certainly hundreds, if not thousands, of men were walking the streets in trench coats.

For a moment her heartbeat quickened. But at that same time, she noted the open driver's door of the sedan parked in the street, and she saw a man step out and lean against the car.

He was in a simple, dark blue suit. Dark, nondescript car, dark nondescript suit. Looking around — before lighting up a cigarette.

She smiled. She looked across the street again. For a minute she could still see the tall man in a trench coat.

Then a crowd of people walked around him, stopping for the light.

He seemed to meld into the group. When the signal changed, the man in the trench coat was gone.

Below her, the agent who had stepped from the sedan finished his cigarette, tossed the butt, and returned to the car.

"You don't want to touch me. Really, you don't want to touch me," Craig told Kieran as she walked toward the door, ready to greet him. She paused, surveying him, her lips tightened in a grimace.

"I got a whiff from here," she said. And then — his fault, as he didn't have a good hold on Ruff's leash — the dog took off, leaving his side and catapulting himself halfway up Kieran's body. She caught the dog and winced as he bestowed a trail of wet dog-kisses on her cheek.

"Oh, I see . . . he, ugh, reeks . . . anyway, I'll give the dog a bath downstairs. That leaves you the upstairs. Thankfully, we've got a bunch of antibacterial soaps around!"

She turned away from him, heading for the downstairs bathroom with Ruff in her arms.

She called back over her shoulder, "Don't forget the alarm."

"Never would," he promised.

"And Egan's been great. Did you see the man downstairs?" she called.

"I did. Special Agent Milo DeLuca. Good guy, young. But you missed his partner — old Andy Kane, another good guy — non-smoker, spends half the day chastising Milo. We're in good hands. They'll be here through the night."

Her voice was more distant — she'd evidently gone into the bathroom — when she called out, "Great!"

Craig double-checked the alarm and headed up the stairs. He was glad Kieran had been conscientious about the apartment's security.

So far all the victims, whether the last two had belonged to Nicholson or not, had been easy targets. From the prostitutes to the very wealthy Mayhew, none of them was in any kind of law enforcement and none had been military. They hadn't been enthusiasts of target shooting or martial arts. Easy prey.

He wondered if a man like Nicholson would have tried anything if any of his victims had been prepared to fight.

Egan was right; there was a time when you just had to bathe — and in bathing, shake it all off for a while.

His favorite thing about their new apartment — the one they'd now decided was really going to be a long-time home — was that the shower quickly produced hot water. It had a powerful spray, and it lasted long enough to really wash the day away.

He poured shampoo generously into his hands for his hair, lathered up, rinsed, and then did it all over again. He scrubbed his body — just about scoured it.

He was finally feeling clean — maybe he'd even scrubbed off a small layer of skin — when he heard the door to the bathroom open. The room was filled with so much steam he might have been in a dense fog, but he knew Kieran had come in.

She slipped into the shower behind him, arms encircling him, resting her head against the expanse of his back for a moment.

He closed his eyes, just feeling her there.

Then he turned, taking her into his arms. He just held her.

She lifted her head to his.

"Ruff?" he asked.

"Clean as a whistle. He doesn't mind a bath. Of course, he shook it off several times, apparently thinking I needed a bath as well, so . . . figured I might as well join you. We could all be squeaky clean."

"And Ruff now?"

"Well, I'm thinking he was a fairly pampered pooch, so I dried him all off. He didn't mind the blow-dryer, by the way. Seemed to expect it as his due after a bath, and I put him to bed."

"In our bed?" Craig asked, wincing.

"Oh, no. Ruff has the guest bedroom. I didn't put him *on* the bed. I made him a little bed. We'll have to see where we go from here."

He touched her chin, studying her eyes.

"You know his owner is dead."

"I do."

"But you should have seen that dog. His loyalty . . . I swear, when he was under the dumpster while the ME and the crime scene people were working . . ."

"Yes, it's all right."

"What's all right?"

"I've always wanted a dog. I was thinking of something more like a husky or a shepherd . . . something a bit bigger. But Ruff has a big heart. That's the best big, right?"

He nodded, pulled her closer, and gently kissed her lips.

It was a tender kiss, full of emotion. But they were both naked. Steaming hot, slick . . .

The kiss deepened. He felt her hands slip down his spine to his rear. His hands molded the perfect curves of her breasts. He pressed closer.

Kieran's feet suddenly slipped out from beneath her; Craig caught her, his heart racing.

She laughed. "How much soap did you use?"

"A lot," he admitted, grinning. He turned slightly to steady her, also starting to slip.

Kieran grabbed the shower door, threw it open and staggered out, reaching back for him — still beautifully naked.

He managed to twist the tap off, then catch her hand, and emerge without sliding on the slick tile.

The steamy fog remained all around them. Groping for a towel, he wrapped her in it.

Then he took her into his arms again.

"Like a fantasy," he whispered. He loved the way her eyes, a mix of sapphire and jade, looked up into his, ever so slightly mischievous and ever so slightly wary.

He swept her up into his arms, stepping out of the bathroom and into the bedroom. He laid her down on the bed, unwrapping the towel as if she were an amazing gift to be discovered.

Exactly what she was . . .

She gazed at him for a moment, then rose to meet him, casting her arms around his neck and meeting him in a kiss . . . a really delicious kiss, as sleekly wet and steaming as the shower. They were familiar lovers now, with four years of falling in love and figuring each other out behind them. Even with that kind of love, each touch was new again, savored afresh. He knew every inch of her body, the silk of her flesh, the sweep of her hair, the way she writhed, and what to do to make her move in just that way.

They kissed, teased, and played, fingertips sweeping over skin, followed by light kisses and then urgent caresses until they joined together.

And then bliss. The world gone for those moments, only the heat and the thudding of his heart.

After, they lay entwined, slowly coming down . . . still keeping the world at bay.

She snuggled against him, head resting on his chest, and she murmured, "Better?"

"Oh, dear."

"Oh, dear, what?"

"Don't you dare tell me that was . . . medicinal sex?"

She laughed and lightly smacked his shoulder.

"No, but I do like to hope I can make a day better."

He kissed the top of her head. "Just by *being,* my love, you make any day better."

"Ah, very well spoken. Great line, by the way."

He chuckled.

"Your nonbroken bones should be thanking me," she assured him, smiling. "That entire bathroom is a Slip 'N Slide."

He shrugged. "Ah, yeah, sorry." He pulled her close.

"I'm so sorry you had a bad day," she murmured. "I know you wanted to find Blom alive."

"I always want to find a victim alive," he said softly. "I didn't know Blom."

"But you know . . . Ruff."

She barely spoke the dog's name before the plaintive sound of a broken howl came to them.

"What is going on? Did the moon rise or something?" Craig muttered, rising and reaching down to the footboard bedpost for his robe.

"Hey!" She was up quicker than a wink. "You — back in bed. You had a really, really long day."

"But the dog —"

"He likes me best, anyway. I guess dogs go through a grieving process, too."

She was determined. Craig dropped his robe and lifted his hands in acquiescence. "The dog does like you best," he said simply.

"Go to sleep," she commanded, slipping into her own robe. She glanced back at him. "Tomorrow is Sunday, but I know you. You'll be working."

"Yeah, and I know you. You'll work at the pub."

"I can go in anytime I so desire," she said, reminding him she wasn't an employee, and if she didn't go in at all, it would be just fine. "I don't really work until Monday. So, you get some rest. I'm going to go down and bond with a bereaved dog. Besides," she added with a grimace, "I'm a trained psychologist. I often work with those who are going through a loss process."

"You've become a dog whisperer?" he asked.

"Whatever. Go to sleep!" she commanded, and then she was gone.

He smiled slowly; as he lay back down, he could still hear Ruff's mournful cries.

Then, the dog fell silent.

He shrugged to himself.

The dog did like Kieran better. Hey, he didn't blame the pooch. What was there not to like?

Craig was bone-tired; in moments, he was asleep.

By rote and an internal alarm clock, he woke at 7:30 a.m. He felt as though he had just shut his eyes mere seconds ago.

He rose and dressed in a hurry. Downstairs, peeking into the guest room, he saw Kieran had fallen asleep there. Ruff was curled to her side.

The dog looked up at him as he stood in the doorway.

Craig could swear the darned mutt smiled.

He shook his head with amusement and silently left the two of them there. In the kitchen he quickly grabbed a thermal mug and filled it with some coffee to go.

The beeps of the keypad as he reset the alarm sounded loud in the quiet apartment. He let himself out, double-checking that he'd locked up.

Yeah, it was Sunday.

And it was going to be another long day.

CHAPTER NINE

There were times when Kieran wished she could thank her parents.

She'd been young when the Finnegan siblings had lost their mother, and it had been some years ago now that their father had passed away. They had been great parents, she often thought. Sure, her brothers had gone a little wild when her mom had passed, but wild in the Robin Hood sense.

If they acted out and misbehaved, it was always in defense of someone being bullied, someone being put upon, or some other misdeed that needed righting. And now they were all respectable citizens with Declan being the ultimate tavern keeper, Kevin doing well with his acting career, and Danny gaining recognition as one of the best historians and tour guides in the city.

But it was the pub that made her want to sincerely thank them that day. The place her parents had created was an amazing legacy, but more so in that it kept Kieran's world grounded. They had so many regulars. It had become a place where people came in good times and also times of trouble. When they wanted to share good news, or just wanted to share the day-to-day ebb and flow of their lives.

That Sunday morning, brunch was hopping. Kevin and Danny were both in, helping to rearrange tables to fit small groups, families, and duos. Servers were running ragged, and busboys and bus-girls were picking up just as fast as their hands would work and their legs would carry them.

It felt natural for Kieran to pitch in — good to hear Mrs. Mullaly, a spry octogenarian, would have her six children and fourteen grandchildren all visiting that summer to celebrate her eighty-fifth birthday with her.

The Smiths — newlyweds — were happy to announce that they'd be bringing a new little Smith into the world, a little boy.

Harry Rogers stopped to give Kieran a kiss on the cheek and tell her he'd gotten a promotion.

Of course, customers were also talking about the news among themselves. While many of them knew Craig, they didn't know

Kieran's bosses had been involved in the psychiatric evaluation of a serial killer or that she had been asked to interview Nicholson herself.

Harry didn't mention a thing about the news to her; he just chatted about his new job from his seat at the bar with Julie Oslo, who was listening to Harry and also talking about the fact she was getting ready to head off on a Caribbean cruise.

Life.

Life going on, and today, in the pub at least, going on well.

Kieran ran hard until 2:00 p.m., when the Sunday brunch hours were over. A lull followed, and she took a break, sitting at one of the little enclave-like tables with her brother Danny — the baby — one year younger than she and Kevin.

"So, how are you holding up, sister mine?" Danny asked.

"Fine."

"Yep, I'm sure you're fine. When you snap at me for a casual question."

"There was nothing casual about it."

Danny swept an arm around the room. "Oh, come on, Kieran, every New Yorker is talking about it. In between work, Little League games, sports events, baby showers . . . it's happening."

"Yeah."

A serial killer was on the loose in New York. The entire city was on edge. "So, truthfully, what's up? We're your brothers. It's our job to worry about you."

"I'm holding up fine — just tired of hearing about it, the same questions over and over again."

"Sorry. Um, I could tell you about my latest research into the original inhabitants of the island of Manhattan? Talk about the weather? Or, how about those Yankees this season?"

Kieran cast him a dire look and he smiled.

"Sorry," he said, leaning close to her. "But it is *the* topic today."

"It's just rehashed and rehashed. And . . ."

"And?"

"It's driving me crazy because I *think* I'm right, but I don't *know* I'm right, and it just seems to get worse and worse."

"You mean the body found in the dumpster? It wasn't burned but may still be a victim of that killer?" She nodded.

"But you believe it is a different killer. That Nicholson had nothing to do with Mayhew or Mr. Olav Blom."

She nodded.

"Nicholson is still dangerous and on the loose," he reminded her.

She nodded. "Of course. The police are watching his family and friends . . . members of his church."

"It is pretty interesting. Man's got a wife, kids, spends lots of time with his strange sect or whatever. Makes me think of what Dad used to say."

"What's that?"

"Oh, that most religions are good. They teach us to be kind to one another, to respect life, to be simply good people. He respected everyone's beliefs — unless they were fanatics. Like he said, it's what men can do with religion that can be bad. And I can't really begin to understand what Nicholson swears he believed, but that's sure one of those twists Dad meant."

"But that is what's driving me crazy," Kieran said. "Nicholson believed he was ridding the world of witches, those who would hurt others. And —" She broke off, aware the knowledge she had was not for the general public.

"You know I'd never say anything, share with anyone," Danny prompted.

She trusted Danny completely. "Okay, Nicholson's first victim was HIV positive. That was never made public. When he talked to me, Nicholson said he knew his victims would kill others. Now, she had

201

stopped practicing the trade, but being a sex worker with HIV . . . she might have infected others. That can mean death. But she didn't act with malice."

"What about the other woman?"

"I don't know. But what perceived danger could there be from a stellar college student, a fashion designer, and an accountant?"

"Say there *was* something. Does that make a difference? The man committed murder. Because of a voice he heard in his head. How would the voice know something like that about a very diverse group of people?"

"Maybe that's what we need to discover . . .

"The whole thing . . . it's frustrating. The other thing we're having a hard time with is the killer's movements with regards to Olav Blom. From what I understand through Craig and Richard Egan, the blood in the basement was . . . plentiful."

"And they know it's the victim's blood."

"They do. But we're almost positive it was the killer who walked back through the lobby with the dog. Oh!" she said suddenly. "Wait!"

"What?"

"The killer knew there was an old ice chute in the basement, covered up with drywall and plaster. What if he initially got in that way, somehow got Blom to the basement and killed him for his key, *then* the killer pretended to be Blom so that he could get up to see Charles Mayhew. He escaped the way he got in — through the chute."

"Left a pool of blood and dragged or carried the body to the dumpster? Across a busy street. In the middle of Manhattan."

"Can you figure anything else?"

"No. Not from evidence," Danny said thoughtfully. He hesitated. "Maybe there were two killers."

"Only one man came through the lobby."

"Yes, but now you know about the old ice chute. It's how he got out. What's to say someone else didn't come in that way?"

"I'll call Craig, tell him what we think," Kieran said. Her phone was in her jacket pocket and she started to pull it out.

She paused, frowning as a man who seemed to be in a hurry walked past them. He had a gleaming, clean-shaven head and moved with confident purpose, focused on the bar.

"What is it?" Danny asked her.

"The man who just came in . . . who just walked past us . . . I know him."

"We know lots of people here, Kieran. It's our pub."

"No, he's — he's Nicholson's attorney," she said. "Cliff Watkins."

"You met him? I mean, I guess his name has been in the papers — is still in the papers. Of course, a zillion outlets tried to interview him after Nicholson's escape, but he sent out a statement saying he was as eager as everyone else to have his client back in custody."

"He was with Nicholson when I interviewed him," Kieran said. She stood up. "I think I'll see how he's doing."

"Or *what* he's doing. He's not a regular. And if you're not a regular and you haven't got business in the neighborhood or aren't out for a fantastic Irish brunch, what would you be doing this far downtown?"

Kieran wove through the tables to the bar.

Watkins had already been served. A whiskey, neat.

She slid into the space next to him. "Mr. Watkins."

He turned to her. "Ah, Miss Finnegan!" He studied her for a minute and then smiled and shook his head. "I was about to say, how interesting, seeing you here. But your family owns the place, of course. I wasn't thinking when I came in. Finnegan. Finnegan's."

"Yes, we do own the pub," Kieran said.

She cast her head lightly to the side. "I was surprised to see you here. I don't believe you've been before?"

"Oh, I have, once or twice. My firm isn't that far away. We're just over on Church Street. I'm not usually around on a Sunday, but . . ."

"With everything going on?" she asked.

He nodded grimly. "I'm sure you know my firm took this case on pro bono. I was given one of the most lucrative cases we had this year, and, to be fair, I was given this, as well. I had no idea it would turn into more murders and a manhunt." He swallowed his drink and shook his head. "I was doing my job — to get the best possible outcome for my client. Thank goodness he never wanted to enter an innocent plea, but I was begging him to go with an insanity plea. There is no question, really. You've interviewed him. I've never seen a better candidate for that kind of defense. Now . . . well, it seems he fooled all of us, used all of us . . . and I can't get off the damned case."

"I'm sorry."

"I'm sorry, too," he said. "And, of course, for you. I understand you're engaged to the agent who brought him in — and you interviewed Nicholson yourself."

She nodded.

"No sign of him, eh?"

"None I've heard about. You?"

"I'm afraid not."

He looked gloomily at his empty glass. "I'll take care of that for you — on the house," Kieran said, slipping behind the bar to give the man another shot.

He nodded his thanks. "Well, I've got to get back to work. This has . . . well, it's made a major change in all the tons of paperwork we've been doing. Nice to see you, Kieran. Thanks again," he said, swallowing half of the second shot. He winced, offering her a grim smile.

"Of course," she said, and before he could move away, she asked, "He really did play both of us, didn't he? I think of all the work I've done and the studies and . . . I just had no idea whatsoever he intended to escape. I feel like a fool."

He nodded. She thought he would agree with her.

He just pursed his lips. "Paperwork!" he said, shaking his head. "My firm just had to take this on . . . such a high profile case, an obviously very sick man, and what could a good defense attorney do except try to ensure he received psychiatric help. Lord, the trade-off wasn't worth it."

He finished his drink and set his glass down.

"Mr. Watkins, you would bring Nicholson right in — if you were to find him?"

He grinned. "I'm basically a coward. Client or not, I would call the cops immediately if I were to see him. After getting myself a safe distance away."

"Mr. Watkins —"

"Please. Just call me Cliff. We're not in a courtroom here. We're in a family-run pub, right? All friends and at ease here."

"Cliff," she said. Despite his appearance, his clean-shaven pate didn't exactly make him look like a tough biker, but he was tall, well-built, and confident in his manner. Right now, though, he appeared worn down and extremely weary. Nicholson's escape was taking its toll on the attorney.

"Cliff," she repeated. "You know Amy, of course, and the boys —"

"I met both of his sons just once, and not with their mother," he said. "They weren't concerned about whether their father went to a psychiatric institute for help or to a prison filled with hard-boiled criminals. They both think their father is crazy, and while they say they love their parents, they're both somehow — well, God help us all with the term — *normal.* Feel free to call them and talk to them. Maybe you can get an insight from them that I couldn't. And I suppose I'd appreciate it if you'd let me know what you uncover."

"I don't actually call the shots," Kieran said. "I work for two of the best people in the field. And I'm sure if Nicholson isn't apprehended by tomorrow, there will be a new round of questioning and interviews with anyone and everyone close to the man."

"I'm sure. And I'd be happy to help you, but I'm not sure where to start." He shook his head sadly, looking at her.

"I can see how hard it's been on you. I appreciate you talking about it."

He nodded and stood off his barstool. "Anytime. Thank you again for the drink. You have my card, right, from the other day?"

"I do." He lifted a hand to her, turned, and left the pub, moving with as much assurance as when he had entered.

Danny was waiting for Kieran to return to the table.

"Must be a bitch to be him," he said.

"I guess. He really is in a thankless position," Kieran said.

Danny shrugged and turned to her. "You know, I've looked up everything I can about witchcraft cases in the United States, back to when we were colonies. But I can't find a single incident of someone being accused of witchcraft here — not in the colonies, not in the US — and being burned."

"But people were burned all over Europe and other places," Kieran said.

Danny nodded. "Witchcraft most often went along with heresy in Europe. Heretics burned. Thousands in one day, more than once, if history counts correctly."

"But we're not in Europe."

Danny shrugged and took a swig of his coffee. "I'd say, if you believe your man does hear voices, he is a purist — he didn't kill the other guy. The man who was just stabbed."

"That's what I say. And explain this to me. How did Nicholson break out at the same time these other murders occurred?"

"How, or why?" Danny asked her.

She stared at him, then suddenly leaned over and kissed him on the cheek.

"What was that for?"

"Not a what or a how — but a why!" she said. She jumped up, ready to run back to the apartment, her computer, and her notes — just as quickly as possible.

"Hold on," Danny said, and she stopped. "I'll walk you to your place."

She smiled at him. "No argument."

"My sister, Kieran Finnegan, being agreeable?"

"Let's get going. Tell Declan we're heading out," Kieran said.

"All right. You're really going to stand there and wait?"

"I really am."

She watched as Danny went back to their older brother's office. She waited for him near the door and grinned when he returned. His features were puckered into a wary frown, as if he'd been suspicious he would find she'd gone off without him.

"You waited for me," he said.

"I did. I'm not causing a bit of trouble," she promised him. When he still looked surprised, she said, "Look, I know you all worry. I intend to toe the line, okay? But right now, I really have to get back to my notes. I was thinking at first that . . ."

"That?"

"I was thinking Nicholson might have somehow been helped to escape by an apprentice, by someone who believed in him, who wanted to help him, who maybe even wanted to be him."

"That would make sense."

"Yes, except for the death of Mr. Blom."

"Oh . . ."

"There's another possibility. The killer is

210

not someone who likes or admires Nicholson, rather, it's someone who despises him — and wants only to use him!"

Danny looked at her, an odd smile on his lips while he gave her a perplexed look at the same time. "Okay. There's someone out there who wanted to murder Mayhew and blame it on Nicholson. But that means the same person helped figure out Nicholson's escape, how to get into a secure apartment building, and commit a double murder?"

"Someone could have had a goal that we're not seeing."

"As in someone specifically wanted Mayhew dead, but also wanted Nicholson blamed."

"Yes."

"How does that explain Blom?"

"A means to an end," Kieran said.

"So, who did it?"

"I haven't the least idea. Hey, do you feel like pie?"

"Pie?" Danny demanded, shaking his head, clearly taken aback by the question.

"Often comes in apple, blueberry, pecan?"

"We just left an excellent pub with excellent food, including pie!" Danny said.

"Yes, but we need different pie."

He groaned. "Where are we going and why?"

"Annie's Sunrise!" Kieran said. "Raoul Nicholson's breakfast location of choice."

Danny let out a sigh. "Sure. I love pie. I take it you know the way?"

"Just pulled it up on my GPS. Walking, four minutes from where we stand now. Cheer up. It's a one of a kind. Not a chain. Could be our new place for pie."

"I didn't know we had an old place for pie."

"So there you go — we need a place for pie!"

Danny groaned and started walking. Kieran led the way.

There were no surprises to be found in the autopsy results on Mr. Olav Blom.

Craig had been to too many autopsies. It was often better for an officer to use the time to search out friends, family, and witnesses of the deceased and then later study the medical examiner's report. But Mike had suggested that with Blom, it was going to be important to find out every factor regarding his death.

They stood by while Dr. Layton went through the routine of the steps of the autopsy as the body was photographed.

Right at the beginning they learned something: there were no bruises or any signs

212

that Blom had been involved in a struggle for his life, that he had fought off his killer, or that he had been restrained in any way.

He had been stabbed straight through the chest and had bled to death. The blade had nicked the heart, causing the pool of blood in the basement and the mess of dried and sticky blood in the dumpster.

Olav Blom had been forty-eight years old, in good physical condition. He had not been drugged. The lab was still working on his clothing and the items found with him in the dumpster, and they were still going through the contents of the basement.

Dr. Layton promised to call them immediately if there were any further discoveries.

"I'm just sad to say that . . . that I don't have more to say," Layton told them. "I thought we might find he had been drugged, or he'd been tasered. It would be good to have an explanation of how he met his death, and then wound up in a dumpster a few blocks away." He flushed suddenly. "Sorry — I'm the medical examiner. You two are the investigators."

"With us, your opinion is always welcome," Craig said.

"Do you think . . ." Layton began, and then fell silent.

"Do we think what?" Mike asked.

"Well, whoever killed him might have been his friend? Someone he trusted."

Craig nodded. "Quite possible," he said.

As they left, his phone rang. It was Egan. The assistant director had gotten search warrants for every apartment in the building, the guard station, and any vehicles associated with the apartment.

A massive search was being carried out as they spoke.

"Are Simon Wrigley, Joey Catalano, and the entire roster of the security personnel there?" Craig asked. "Despite the killer going after Olav Blom, one of the guards might have been involved — down to 'losing' their master key for a while and making sure not to mention it."

"We're going through everything and everyone. Simon Wrigley's roster looks clean enough to send his employees off to work for the Pope. But we're still looking for what might not be on someone's records. We have a man going through computer data on social platforms, so if there's something off, they'll report. We're also cross-referencing any associates of Charles Mayhew and Olav Blom."

Craig asked, "Anything interesting yet?"

"Still working it. On your end, now. Any

autopsy results?"

"By supposed friend, stranger, or foe. Blom was taken by surprise. Nothing that even begins to resemble a defensive wound on him."

"So where are you going from here?" Egan asked.

"I think Mike and I should drop in on Nicholson's sons, and then maybe his wife. Kieran recently interviewed her. She didn't know her husband was killing, but even if she had known, she wouldn't have come forward. Her husband was like a prophet in her mind. Holier than regular men, and only acting on what was dictated from . . . from whatever his 'higher power' might be."

"I'll keep you advised of any connections we can discover, and, of course, if anything is found at the apartments."

Craig ended the call. Mike was looking at him.

"Onward to see the sons?" Craig asked.

"We have to start somewhere. Sounds as good as any place. I'll drive."

"You hate driving," Craig reminded him.

"Yes, but you're too preoccupied. I'm a New Yorker. I hate driving in the city, but that doesn't mean I don't know how."

"We're both preoccupied."

"You more than me. I can see your mind

215

working."

"How can you see a mind working?" Craig demanded as they got to their FBI issued sedan. It was true that he did most of the driving. If Mike wanted a turn behind the wheel, fine. They weren't heading into a car chase. They were heading to an apartment in the East Village.

Thomas Nicholson's home was a second-floor apartment in a small building. The first floor of apartments — the ground floor — was home to a florist's, a bodega, and a children's shoe shop.

They called up; Thomas Nicholson answered his buzzer with a cautious voice. Once Craig announced who they were, they heard a sigh, and then the door buzzed.

The older Nicholson boy, at twenty-four years old, was lean and cut a good appearance; he met them in a shirt that advertised an eighties rock band and a pair of jeans. He was neat and clean, hair cut moderately short, clean-shaven, and possessed dark, keen eyes and an easy manner.

He offered a hand to each of them, saying, "Would God — any god — allow that I could change my name and disappear. Thank God I do have some good friends. I'm a pariah to most people. Anyway, how can I help you?"

216

He indicated they should sit on the sofa. His living space, like his appearance, was contemporary, neat, and clean. He had prints of paintings by famous artists on the walls, with a penchant, it seemed, for the medieval, and posters put out by rock bands for New York performances. He had a computer at a desk by the far wall, a wide-screen TV, and certainly seemed to have the taste of just about anyone his age getting by in the city.

"Please, sit down. I don't know what I can do for you. I swear I had nothing to do with my father's escape, and I sure as hell didn't kill anyone. I wish there was something I could do. I was serious — I'd give about anything to change my name and start life somewhere I wasn't known as the son of a crazy serial killer. And feared," he added softly.

"We're hoping maybe you can point us to someone who might have helped your father. Friends from the past, from his church perhaps, who might have taken what he saw as your father's mission to heart," Craig said.

Thomas had taken a seat in a chair at an angle to the sofa. Mike and Craig waited across from him. He appeared to be thoughtful, and he finally shook his head, upper teeth biting into his lower lip.

"I've been no-contact with my family for a long time," he said quietly. "The day I turned eighteen, I was out of my house. They say any minister's or pastor's children go through some kind of rebellion at some point, and then they might return to their church and their parents' religion. Not me. Not John. You can't imagine what it was like growing up in that house. Once, in high school, my mother found out I'd bought roses for a girl I had a crush on for Christmas. She whipped me with the roses — thorns and all. I think my back still bears a few scars. No presents for anyone ever. I know there are other religions that don't recognize holidays, that don't allow for dancing, singing, or any form of enjoyment or entertainment, but my parents took it to extremes that were unendurable."

He took a deep breath then continued, "John and I were in public schools, and it was hard for me to believe my friend Micah Kaufmann, following the Jewish faith, was going to go to hell. He was the guy who stood up for the weak kids, who helped anyone disabled. In fact, he's one of the best human beings I've ever met. The more I looked at the world around me, the more I turned against my father's fanaticism. Dad and I had a huge fight. I told him he had the right to believe whatever he wanted, but so did everyone else in the country." He paused. "I wonder if I should have known then. I wonder if I could have done something."

"What could you have done?" Craig asked him gently. "You didn't know what he was doing. Your mother didn't know what he was doing."

"I was out of the house by the time he was . . . killing people," Thomas said. "But . . . when we had that fight, he told me only a few were chosen, and sinners could see the light if they opened their eyes, and that . . . that they should burn for all eternity. They were blind, and they had no truth to speak. If I would have begged someone for help . . ."

"Nothing could have been done. There's nothing illegal about being a religious fanatic," Mike said.

"But it was illegal for your mother to beat you so that you bled," Craig said. "I'm sorry you went through that."

"Ah, my mother! She's just . . . she was normal, once. I think. But then she embraced everything my father said and did. She thought he was a great leader. A prophet, even. On a par with Christ or

Mohammed. I don't know. I left home and I didn't look back. And the day my brother turned eighteen, I knew he'd show up — and he sure did. He arrived at my dorm. I'd been smart enough to skip classes that day, so I could wait for him. He showed up — and he cried for hours. John was more torn up than I was. He hated being disloyal, but he couldn't bear living so harshly anymore either. I've been gone six years now. John has been gone four years, give or take."

"How did you get through school? I believe you went to an expensive university, and John is at a prestigious college right now," Craig said.

"Scholarships and working," Thomas told him. He grinned self-consciously. "I won a scholarship that paid my entire tuition by writing a paper and entering it in a contest. I worked as a dishwasher to pay for my dorm, and I was then able to get a job through the school as a reading and writing tutor. You'd be amazed how many kids get into college — even a place like NYU — with the reading level of a grade school kid. All you need to do is finagle some grades and test well. I have friends who got through some of the tests simply by randomly picking answers A, B, C, D, or E. After that, I was able to help John. Now, I have a job with an online newspaper. I'm getting by, and I'm helping John. We honestly didn't know what my father was doing, but learning he was the Fireman wasn't a complete shock." He stopped speaking, assessing the agents' reactions. "I'll be honest. My father is such a fanatic he could come after John or me. Neither of us is going anywhere alone or walking by ourselves at night. I'm worried about Johnny. I thought he should pull out for the semester. He doesn't want to, and I've warned him, but . . . I can't make him do anything." He hesitated. "You . . . you really have nothing on getting my father back into custody?"

Craig could have misled Thomas, to reassure him. He didn't.

"Not a damned thing to go on. We know how he managed his escape, and we believe he had help. And now two more related murders have taken place," he said.

"Yeah. I read the news." He leaned toward them, folding his hands together. "Well, I'm afraid. As I said, God knows if my father hasn't fingered me or John as a witch. But we know him, and we're on the lookout for him. He's not a big guy in the least. He's tricky — that's how he gets around people. I'm sure he made those prostitutes think he was a john. He probably had the student thinking he was a visiting teacher — he would have given the fashion designer the belief that he was an incredibly rich man, wanting to create a fantastic new line. He's a chameleon, when he chooses to be. But . . ."

"But what?" Mike encouraged gently.

"It's as crazy as can be, but even when I lived with my parents . . . he would point people out. Say they were evil. I was supposed to avoid them, but never, never, never, harm an innocent person. He believes these things. If he killed Charles Mayhew, he thought the man was a witch, someone who would hurt the innocent. Ordered to do so by demons, or something. Or even living with a demon inside him." He shook his head. "Again, I haven't spoken to my mother or father since the day I turned eighteen. Those two guys working for him, they'd know my father better than me at this point."

"You remember them — they worked for your father a long time?" Mike asked.

They already had that information, of course. It was in the copious file they had on Nicholson. Though neither Mike nor Craig had interviewed the men personally.

"Bart, great guy. He must be close to seventy now. He used to slip me candy or cookies. We weren't allowed treats of any kind at home, right? He lost his wife to cancer and spent his free time visiting his grandkids. He knew how to entertain young ones, as my father never did. Mark was quieter, but nice enough. Both of them would try to keep my brother and me free from our father's wrath anytime we were down in the shop. Good men. They weren't part of my father's flock, but yeah, you should talk to them. They saw him five days a week every week."

"Anything else you can tell us?" Mike asked.

"Anyone else you think we should see?" Craig added.

"Axel Cunningham. Reverend Axel Cunningham. He got my dad going — until my dad turned on him. He left our old church about six years ago to form his True Life sect when he left his 'mainstream' house of worship. Reverend Cunningham was wishy-washy, in dad's mind. He wasn't saving his people. He was easy on them, and because of that, they might all go to hell."

Thomas Nicholson frowned. "And he went into that coffee shop every day. Every single day. The rest of us could go without indulgences like that, but he was the bread-winner. Dad deserved the best every morning. Good coffee and a full meal. I think, when we were little kids, it had a different name. An uncle owned it or something. For the last eight years or so, it's been owned by the niece, and she calls it Annie's Sunshine or —"

"Annie's Sunrise?" Craig suggested.

"Yeah. I think he kind of knew people in there — and Annie herself, of course. I guess he was a good customer. We got stale, no-name cereal. We weren't breadwinners. We didn't work. Even my mom got stale cereal. Well, she never did get fat — she stayed in great shape. Half-starving will do that for you, I guess. Anyway, sure, see my brother. Maybe he remembers something that I don't. But definitely talk to his coworkers, Pastor Axel, and Annie and her crew. Maybe, just maybe, one of them will be able to help you. Would God that I could."

Craig and Mike stood, ready to leave.

Thomas Nicholson followed them to the door.

Craig turned to thank him. Thomas nodded bleakly. "Think I'll ever get to live a normal life? Do the kids of serial killers ever have happy lives? Is it even possible?" he asked, his tone all but dead.

"Maybe you can get a legal name change,

move somewhere else," Mike suggested.

"Yeah, well . . . at least here, I have a job. Though maybe, since it's an online publication, I could keep it and go remote . . . my employers don't mind who I am. I go by a different byline, anyway. Nick Thomas. Started that long before the world knew my father was a serial killer." He was quiet a minute. And then he grinned weakly. "I've encouraged John to switch things up, too. He could become John Thomas, and that way, we could still be brothers."

"If you see or hear anything about your father, anything at all . . ." Craig said, handing him one of his cards.

Thomas accepted the card. "Oh, I will. You can bet I will," he swore.

Craig and Mike took the stairs down to the street.

Once there, Mike looked at Craig. "Okay, out to Princeton, New Jersey, next? Or a hop on over to Broadway, near the pub and your place? Shall we take a break to get it all together on a Sunday afternoon?"

Craig hesitated; if Thomas Nicholson was right, his brother wouldn't have much to give them.

But he might also be in danger.

"I'm going to call Egan. Get him to talk to the cops here and in New Jersey. I think

225

we should be watching these young men — Nicholson's sons. They might be in real danger. We'll get someone on it, and then . . ."

"Annie's Sunrise," Mike said.

Craig agreed. "Now, finally, we've got a plan I like."

Moving briskly, Mike headed for the car. He'd apparently done all the driving he wanted to do. He walked straight to the passenger's side.

Grinning, Craig headed to the driver's side.

He paused, looking back at Thomas Nicholson's building.

Before getting into the car, he pulled his phone out to make his call to Egan.

If the kid was telling the truth, he could well now be at the top of his father's hit list.

CHAPTER TEN

"I'm kind of surprised we've never been here before," Danny said, looking around the little coffee shop and appreciating the bright cleanliness of the place.

Picture windows looked out to the street and let sunlight pour in. The tables were clean, most in a line against the windows. Little jukebox machines on each table allowed patrons to pick out tunes for a quarter. Behind the counter, two servers hurried along the expanse of swivel stools, catching orders from the gleaming metal shelves that connected to the kitchen.

The place was cheerful in shades of red and yellow; Broadway posters were set at angles about the walls. Kieran did like it — she thought she had been in, years before sometime, when she'd been a child. Her dad, she thought, might have been friends with the old owner.

But she knew, too, why they probably

hadn't been in the coffee shop forever — or why Danny might never have been in it at all.

"We own a pub," she told her brother.

"And that means we never eat anywhere else?" Danny demanded.

She laughed. "No, it means when we're in this area, we're usually heading in to meet up or work, and so we wouldn't be thinking, wow, let me grab something to eat quickly before I go into the pub."

Danny shrugged at that. "I like this place, though."

"I do, too. Very cute. And clean. Declan would approve."

"So, is one of those people Annie?" he asked, pointing to the servers behind the counter.

Annie wasn't their server, for sure. They were being helped by a young man of about twenty-two or twenty-three.

A college student, Kieran thought. And if they asked him, she was sure he'd tell them he was an actor. New York was filled with actors. Luckily it was also filled with eateries where actors could earn a living while they attended auditions and vied for roles.

Kieran studied the two people behind the counter. One woman — round, dark-haired, with a great smile — looked to be about fifty. The other woman — tiny, lean, and wiry — might have been about ten years younger.

"I don't think so," Kieran said. "I think Annie's closer to our ages . . . maybe she's thirty-two or thirty-three, in there somewhere."

"So, if we don't see her, how do we talk to her?"

"We ask for her?"

Their server arrived with two glasses of water and two cups of coffee, smiling as he set them down. "There you go. Have you had a chance to look at the menu yet?" he asked.

Danny looked at him very seriously and said, "Pie."

Their waiter smiled. "Pie . . . okay. Um, which pie?"

"Which do you recommend?" Danny asked him. "It's our first time here."

"Oh, well, we're known for everything, not just pie!" their server said enthusiastically.

"They say this place has always been good, but that it's even better since Annie took over — and renamed it, I guess," Kieran said, following her brother's lead.

"Annie is amazing. And the place was always wonderful! But Annie has added more desserts, and made in-house is even

229

better. And she does things like making sure our entrées are easy to fix to taste." He made a face. "I personally hate, loathe, and despise cilantro. And I can get guacamole here without cilantro — we make it to order!"

"Wonderful!" Danny said, wrinkling his nose. "I'm an anticilantro person myself. I hear you either love it or hate it. But seriously, you don't have cilantro in any of your fruit pies, do you?"

As he spoke, Kieran gave him a light kick beneath the table. She'd seen a woman come around to the front from the kitchen.

Annie.

She was tall, probably about an inch or so taller than Kieran, who hovered somewhere between five-nine and five-ten. She was a redhead, but with a much lighter shade of the color, with curling waves that fell around her shoulders. She was wearing a waitress's uniform, just like the two women behind the counter, but she headed straight to the cash register, ready to accept a bill and credit card being presented by a departing customer.

She was pretty and vivacious.

Danny, with his camaraderie over cilantro going on with the server, grinned suddenly. "That's Annie now, right?"

"It is!" the server said. "Oh, and I'm Blake. Blake Hunter." He leaned in. "I used to be Angus Hunter, but in grade school the kids liked to call me Anus Hunter. So, thinking as how I want my name to be in lights one day, I went with my middle name — Blake — and I think it's a lot better. Anyway, you want to meet Annie? I'll ask her to come over."

"That would be great. Oh, and what's your suggestion for pie?"

"Blueberry, with a dollop of vanilla ice cream."

"We'll take it — two orders, please. Right, Kieran?" he asked.

"If *Blake* suggests it, I'm all in," Kieran said. "And we'd love to talk to Annie."

Blake went off to fill their order.

"I knew he was an actor," Kieran said.

"It's New York. Everyone is an actor — in one way or another. And as our talented brother would tell you, every actor should work waiting tables and learning about people, and how to be polite and decent and all that. Because sometimes, actors get rich and famous, and they should remember what it was like not to be rich and famous."

"I'm not sure we can call Kevin rich and famous yet," Kieran said. "Immensely talented, of course," she added. "Then again, you're also a bit of an actor."

"I'm a storyteller these days. I just tell real stories about the city."

Kieran laughed. "And you get a little carried away and really emote sometimes."

"Sometimes I do, but I never bore people!"

"She's coming," Kieran said softly.

Annie Sullivan was heading their way, smiling at people at other tables as she came along, checking to make sure they were all doing well.

When she reached their table, she looked at the two of them and frowned slightly, her gaze lighting on Kieran last.

"Hello, welcome to Annie's. Do I know you?"

"I don't think we've ever met," Kieran said. "Actually, we might have passed in the street. We're two of the Finnegan siblings who own Finnegan's on Broadway, just a few blocks from here."

"Oh." Annie's face changed immediately. She slid into the booth beside Danny, somewhat pushing him over as she did so, but entirely oblivious to it. "You're Kieran Finnegan. I saw you on the news a few years back when you kept that girl from being killed in the subway."

"Oh, I, uh . . . yeah." Honesty seemed the

best course now. "We did come here to speak with you specifically."

"Raoul Nicholson," she said grimly.

Kieran nodded.

"He came in every morning — well, every weekday morning — at least. He was bright, friendly, cheerful, and nice to all of the staff all of the time. I was stunned to hear what he'd done. I mean, I knew he was a bit of a fanatic . . . he'd bless people and sometimes make weird signs as they walked by, or as they were leaving. But he was always smiling. When he was arrested, and it came out that he was the Fireman, I was shocked."

"He talked to you a lot?" Kieran asked.

"Sure. But he talked about the seasons, the weather . . . nothing . . . nothing at all about people being evil, or . . . he certainly never said he believed in witches, except . . ."

She paused, frowning. Blake had come up with their blueberry pie and ice cream orders. He had apparently heard the last.

"Oh my gosh!" Blake said. "This one day, there was an article in the newspaper on the amount of people involved in the Wiccan religion in the United States. And a man at the counter here was saying it shouldn't be allowed. Raoul Nicholson was in, and he said they didn't hurt anybody. They were misguided, and might never get to heaven, but they didn't hurt people."

Kieran, Danny, and Annie were all staring at him. He blushed and apologized quickly. "Sorry, I couldn't help but hear what you were saying, Annie."

"It's okay," Annie said quickly. "I knew there was something. I couldn't quite remember. He did say that. So, the fact he thought people were witches . . . there's a difference, right? Between being a Wiccan and being a cauldron-stirring evildoer, right? Or, I guess, at least in Raoul Nicholson's mind?"

"I imagine," Kieran murmured.

"He's still on the loose!" Blake said.

Annie nodded and said gently, "Blake, we have customers."

"Yes, yes, of course!" he said, and moved on.

Annie turned to Kieran and Danny. "You didn't come for the pie."

"The pie is absolutely delicious — really. The second I saw it, I had to take a bite," Danny told her.

She offered him a half smile. "I'm sorry. I can't tell you anything more about Raoul Nicholson. I never saw him outside this shop. He was always nice. He was great with other customers, too. This is Sunday, so . . .

our usual weekday crowd isn't sitting up at the counter. I'm not sure anyone, other than the employees here, would have seen him or talked to him. We try to forget he used to be a regular here. It's so creepy — but you must understand I bought this business from my uncle and everything I have is in it. So I have to get past the fact the Fireman hung out here, and I keep it low-key because . . . some people would come here specifically because Nicholson was a customer. But many, probably many more, would not."

"We don't want to cause any problems for you," Kieran assured her. "We're just trying to find out who his friends might have been — if there was anyone he seemed to bond with particularly."

Annie studied her. "You think he needed help to escape, right?"

"The way he escaped . . . he knew the way the infirmary worked, the way the guards worked, how to get out and off Rikers Island. Inmates have escaped before, but usually they're found right on the island, and it's not often at all," Kieran told her.

"I wish I could help. But as far as I know, he wasn't close to anyone here. People saw him and talked to him and he talked to people, but . . . you know, it was all just

235

pleasantries. 'Good morning, how are you doing,' that kind of thing," Annie said. She drummed her fingers on the table. "He had a wife. He'd say she was the best now and then. And he had sons, but he didn't talk about them. And, of course, he had two guys who worked for him at his business. Have you talked to them?" she asked, and then she frowned. "Um . . . you know, cops and FBI agents were by after Raoul Nicholson was captured and they came by again when he escaped. I'm not sure why you two are asking me this kind of question."

She had grown wary of them. While Kieran debated what to say, Danny answered.

"Kieran is engaged to the FBI agent who brought him in."

"Oh. Oh! He must be really bummed!" Annie said.

Danny bent low suddenly and murmured, "Speak of the devil . . ."

Kieran looked up. She should have been the first one to see Craig and Mike had arrived at the coffee shop — she was the one in the booth seat facing the door.

Craig spotted her right away. She sat straight, watching as he politely informed the dark-haired woman behind the counter he and his friend were meeting others who were already seated.

He and Mike walked to the table.

"The devil?" Annie murmured, looking from them to Danny.

Craig reached the table. He had his credentials out, as did Mike. He smiled pleasantly though. "Special Agent Craig Frasier, Miss Sullivan, and my partner, Special Agent Mike Dalton."

"Oh!" Annie said, surprised.

She started to rise. "Please, stay," Craig said. "I'm willing to guess these two have already been quizzing you about Raoul Nicholson."

He kept his voice low so other diners could not hear.

Annie obviously appreciated that.

Danny scooted to the far side of the booth. Annie moved closer to him, and Mike joined the duo while Craig slid in next to Kieran.

He didn't look her way. He kept his eyes on Annie.

"I've been telling them everything I know. Which is nothing," Annie said. But she was in a rush to repeat everything, down to the information Raoul had once told a customer that Wiccans should just be left alone — they didn't hurt anyone.

"Annie, can you think of anyone he might have actually been friends with, anyone he might have talked to more, or talked to outside of the restaurant?" Craig asked.

"Not that I know about," Annie said. "I suggested your friends here talk to his coworkers. I mean, I know he went to work every day. Or rather, when he left here, we all assumed he was on his way to work. He had a shop and two fellows who worked for him."

"Did they ever come in here?" Mike asked.

She shook her head. "No. I just know about them because sometimes, when I'd made special doughnuts, he'd buy a box and say he was taking it to the boys at work. If he was close to anyone, I'd say it was them. I'm so sorry for them. I imagine they're out of work now." She inhaled a deep breath. "I also told your friends I'd been questioned already by cops and by agents."

"We're truly sorry to bother you again," Craig said. "We just really need to find him and get him back into custody."

"You do!" Annie said, nodding a strong agreement.

Craig produced a card. "If you see or hear anything . . ."

"Of course. I, uh, did suggest if you're looking for people who might have a greater insight into his mind or activities, a morning would be a better time to come in. He

238

was a regular right around 8:00 a.m. every day. That might be the time to come."

"Thank you. We'll do that," Craig told her.

Kieran's blueberry pie sat untouched, the vanilla ice cream well-melted over it.

Craig helped himself and took a bite of it. "Wow — wonderful!" he said.

Annie smiled. "Thank you. I can get you a fresh piece with solid ice cream —"

"No, no, thanks. I love it melted into the blueberries." He looked at Kieran then. "You love it this way, too, right?"

"Yep, just yummy," Kieran said.

Annie looked uncomfortable. Of course, she was wedged between Danny and Mike, and the booths just weren't that big.

Mike rose, allowing her to stand.

Annie was holding Craig's card. "I'll keep this," she said. "And if I think of anything — if any of the staff think of anything — I'll call you right away. Oh, and the pie is on the house!"

"No, no, Annie, thank you, we can't do that," Kieran protested.

"Leave Blake a big tip. He's going to be out a lot on auditions next week," Annie said, and before any of them could protest, she hurried away.

She strode to the cash register, taking over for the dark-haired counter waitress and greeting the next customer with a bill to pay with a sweet and genuine smile.

For a moment everyone at the table was silent.

"Kieran, I can't help that you are involved with this, but . . . pursuing it? We're the agents — yeah, me and Mike. We do this. Danny, I can't believe you're helping her get deeper and deeper into the mire here," Craig said at last.

"Hey," Danny protested. "You're the fool who is marrying her!"

"Hey, yourself!" Kieran protested, giving him a good kick beneath the table.

She missed. Mike let out a startled howl.

Danny leaned in and lowered his voice. "I could have let her come alone. You know Kieran. If she's got something on her mind . . ."

Craig let out an aggravated sigh, looking at Kieran. "Yep," he said. "But this man is the worst kind of dangerous, and we don't even know if he has an accomplice or a copycat of some kind. Your wisdom on the working of the mind is deeply appreciated, but Kieran, please . . ."

She dug into her bag and set two tens on the table for Blake Hunter, the budding actor.

"We just came for the pie," she said.

240

"I can see that — by the way you ate it all." He stood. "Let's all call it a day. Kieran, Danny?"

She was aggravated to feel like a chastised child, but she didn't feel like getting into it with him at the coffee shop or in front of Mike and Danny.

"Sometimes," she said with dignity standing dead in front of him, "knowledge can be — safe. The more we know, the safer everyone can be."

She walked by him, not sure if she'd made any sense or not.

Craig was starting to think that maybe it was a great thing to have a dog.

Danny had left them at the restaurant, saying he was heading back to Finnegan's on Broadway just in case Sunday night got busy at the pub, though it seldom did. Sunday was a laidback time.

Mike was keeping the car, with a plan to pick Craig up at 8:00 the next morning.

Kieran hadn't spoken since they'd left Annie's Sunrise. She was pointedly quiet as they entered their building and went up to their floor. The moment they opened the door, they both heard Ruff yapping with excitement. He came flying out at them, jumping on Craig at first, and then catapulting himself against Kieran.

She captured him in her arms and laughed, looking at Craig. "I guess he likes us."

"Are we keeping him?" he asked. "I mean, really keeping him?"

"You mean as in give him a 'forever home'? Of course, what else would we do? If we brought him to a shelter, he might well wind up being put to sleep. Why do we use that term, huh? Put to sleep! Well, he's not a puppy, and he's not a purebred, and . . . he could be described as scruffy and even ugly by some people. Of course, we need to keep him. He . . . he lost his owner badly. He helped you. He's a great dog. Yes, he's our dog now. Neither of us ever knew Olav Blom, but . . . it's the least we can do for him."

Craig leaned in and kissed her lips.

He hadn't meant to offend her by being overprotective. In this case he'd been put out because she and Danny had beat him to a witness who had already been questioned, but who might just know something to help the investigation. Maybe there was nothing new to discover, but they were leaving no stones unturned. He felt justified in his annoyance because Kieran should know better than to get overly involved. It had led to trouble and danger in the past.

The search of the apartments in Mayhew's building had yielded nothing. If his neighbors were homicidal maniacs, they were hiding it well. The building security guards were clean as a whistle.

But someone had to know something — answers existed.

They had to be found.

Kieran was walking toward the guest room, Ruff still in her arms. "Hey! You used the puppy pads. You are a good, good dog." She chatted to the pup in a silly, cheerful voice. "No messes. But then you're used to apartment living, aren't you? Still, we're going to take you for walks. Just like your old master. Just like you're used to. The neighborhood will be a bit different, but trust me, it's fun, and you're going to like it."

She looked over at Craig. "I think I should take him out."

"I think we should take him for a walk," he said.

She paused, lowering her head, a slight smile curving her lips. "Fine. I think *we* should take him for a walk. I'll get his leash."

They went out together, running into Mr. Asher from apartment 607 in the elevator. Asher was a dog lover apparently, and was happy to see Ruff.

"Dogs and kids — they make for real living," he assured them.

Ruff wagged his tail wildly when Asher bent down to pet him.

They walked along the street. At the bodega, Mrs. Dimitri was standing in the doorway. She clucked over Ruff and told them she had just put out a fresh leg of lamb on the buffet and had a few scraps she'd love to give the pup — if that was okay.

"The heck with the dog!" Craig said, realizing that he hadn't eaten all day. "That sounds incredible."

Mrs. Dimitri frowned. She spoke English well, having come from Greece with her husband about ten years ago. But sometimes she didn't quite understand the words that were being said.

"Oh, dear, Mr. Agent. If you wish, of course, I believe I could give you the scraps instead."

He smiled. "No, no, I'm so sorry. The pup would love the scraps. I'll hit the buffet," he assured her.

As she went in to get the scraps, Kieran arched a brow to him.

"I haven't eaten all day," he said.

"Well, that's sad, but you and Mike are adults," Kieran reminded him.

"We'd originally planned to come to the

pub," he said. "But . . ."

"You ate my blueberry pie instead," Kieran said faux sweetly.

"You weren't touching it. Oh, that's because you didn't really go there for pie." He gave her a stern look.

Kieran let out a sound of aggravation. "Well, Ruff is not a service dog. We can't take him into the bodega. I should be able to watch him while you go to the buffet and make yourself a meal, since your guys in the blue suits and black cars are never far away. A sedan is back in front of our place, and I'm pretty sure one followed Danny and me from the pub to Annie's Sunrise."

Craig smiled; Egan was true to his word. He narrowed his eyes, trying to see who was in the car. Someone new, he thought, fresh out of the Academy. Egan liked to put young agents on surveillance duty while they learned the ropes. But they would be expected to give a report at the end of shift every day, and every agent wanted to follow through on their first assignments if they wished to rise within the Bureau. "I'll go in and fix a to-go box," Craig said. "Shall I get anything for you?"

She smiled. "I'm fine. I'm just going to wait here . . . in full view of that black sedan."

He smiled, nodded, and went in. As he headed to grab his food from the bodega's buffet bar, Mrs. Dimitri was on her way out with a little wrapped package for the dog.

There was no way to keep Kieran out of something once she was determined she had to see it through to the end, he thought to himself. There were only two things to do: be there if she did get herself into trouble, and catch Nicholson and a second killer if there was one — fast.

He selected food, weighed his box, and paid his bill to Mr. Dimitri at the cash register while his wife chatted with Kieran.

"Good women are not easy to find, my friend," Mr. Dimitri told him.

"I know."

Mr. Dimitri leaned over his counter. "You keep that one, yes?"

"Doing my best," Craig assured him.

Mr. Dimitri smiled. "Good men are not so easy to find either. She knows she has a good man. Kiss and make up."

Grinning, Craig headed out. He thanked Mrs. Dimitri again for the dog's scraps, set an arm around Kieran, and waved goodbye.

"You're smiling," she told him.

"Why not?"

She didn't answer. They started walking back, Ruff apparently aware treats awaited him in the bag that was being carried.

"So, anything else new today?" he asked her.

"Oh, yes, actually. Cliff Watkins was in the pub. His office is downtown, and apparently this case has caused all kinds of new work for him and his law clerks."

"What did he have to say? Any insight into Nicholson's escape?"

"Nope. We didn't talk long. He took two shots in two swallows and headed out."

"He's in a bad place, I imagine," Craig said. After a few seconds he went on, "Mike and I had a chat with Raoul Nicholson's older son."

"And how was that?" she demanded.

He smiled at her. Tell her everything? *She was in it full throttle. No way out.*

"He says he hasn't had contact with his father since he left home when he was eighteen. He thinks his own father would kill him, and basically his mother is obsessed with his father and would never say he had done anything wrong. Seems honest. He's a journalist for an internet paper. We'll study a lot of what he's written and try to see if there is something between the lines."

"What about the younger boy?"

"He's in school down in Princeton. We'll drive there tomorrow and see if he supports everything his brother had to say. First, we're going to check on the two men who worked with Nicholson at his shop."

"Bart Washington and Mark Givens," Kieran said.

"What, you've already been to see them, too?" he demanded.

"No. I just know the case." She hesitated. "There's his old pastor, too," Kieran reminded him. "Axel Cunningham."

"From everything I've heard, that was a parting of the ways because of Nicholson. The way it sounds to me, Nicholson's old church — with Axel Cunningham the pastor — was on the fundamentalist side, but nothing compared to what Nicholson thought should be the tenor of the church. I got that from his son Thomas. Thing is, how could he have just disappeared? I'm referring to Nicholson, of course. If you're right, someone helped get him escape. Then . . . say that someone lured Blom, got the key, killed Blom and Charles Mayhew, and is still on the loose out there somewhere. So, what did he do with Nicholson? Unless it was all Nicholson. Damn, but we need answers!"

She touched his face gently. "He just escaped, you know."

"And you've heard about the first forty-eight hours being the most important, right?" He shook his head. "We're running out of time. Getting nowhere."

"But you are getting somewhere. You're getting the pieces. A few more, and you will put it all together. I know you."

He smiled at that, pausing on the street and turning toward her.

"You know what I think we should do?"

"What?"

He nodded gravely. "Sex. Lots of it. Lots of hot, dirty, wild, wicked sex . . ."

"Always the romantic," she said.

He laughed softly. "I try."

"Well," she murmured, stooping to pick up Ruff, "it sounds fine to me. We'll head back, you eat, I'll feed junior here and put him to bed — in his bed, downstairs — and fall for your every romantic word."

"Deal," he told her, walking faster.

And faster.

She laughed and kept up.

He lifted a hand to the agent in the sedan as they reached their building.

Egan always said a man should clear out his mind, then set to a problem again.

Well, he was going to clear his mind. And he had a hell of way to do it.

Monday morning Craig had gone with Mike to conduct their various interviews. He'd left in a good mood after checking to see if a dark sedan, with an agent within, was still parked down the street.

"If he's going to follow me anyway, he can give me a ride downtown to my office," Kieran had suggested. She still had an hour after Craig left before she needed to report in. She decided to give Ruff a little tug-of-war time. After a bit, she became tired of it, and just patted the dog, who loved and craved the attention. He'd learned to take a flying leap up into her arms, and when she rose to get prepared to head out for the day, he jumped up to her.

She laughed, catching him, and walked over to the living room windows. She gazed out at the street below.

The FBI sedan was there, the agent waiting to drive her to work.

Once again, though, she noted she was being watched from another quarter.

He was there again: the man in the trench coat.

CHAPTER ELEVEN

Bart Washington sat on his porch at a pleasant little house in Brooklyn. It was a two-story home, in an area where the lot sizes were very small, but he had a small front yard with nicely mowed grass, a narrow strip of land on the left and on the right, and probably a little patch of grass in the back.

He was an older man, dark and wizened, with graying hair and a lean physique. His wrinkled face was somber as he shook hands with Craig and Mike, asking if they'd like to talk inside or out, and could he get them anything?

They demurred, and since Mr. Washington seemed to enjoy his porch, Craig and Mike drew up plastic all-weather chairs by him to talk.

"I know what's happened. And I'm reckoning you know the police already spoke to me and Mark when Raoul was arrested, and

251

then again on Saturday," Washington said.

"Yes, and thank you for speaking with us again," Craig told him.

Washington shook his head in thought. "We knew he was a religious man. Didn't know his religion, didn't understand his religion, but hey, it's America still, isn't it? I mean, we couldn't believe it when we found out that he . . . that he *murdered* people. That he *burned* them. I mean, that's like, well, medieval!"

"Did anyone come to see him specifically when you were working, anyone who might have agreed with his thought pattern? Did you ever see him behave oddly?"

"This is New York," Washington said wearily. "You're going to have to be more specific when you ask that kind of a question."

Craig offered him a rueful smile. "I'm sure you've heard he claimed a voice, some kind of higher power, told him certain people were witches. He told a psychologist the people he killed were evil and would have killed others."

"You think that might have been true? I mean, that he knew something about those people maybe no one else did?" Washington asked, and then he answered himself. "That is ridiculous. He murdered people. He was a holier-than-thou, cold-blooded killer."

"Did you ever see him talking to himself?" Craig asked.

Washington frowned suddenly. "You know . . . I always thought he had earphones on, or maybe he had his phone on speaker when he was in his office. We'd see him often . . . talking on the phone, or so we thought. I mean, maybe he was on the phone . . ." He trailed off, shaking his head again. "I still don't know. I can tell you this — he was often in his office while Mark and I were working. I mean, that meant nothing. He was the boss. Figured he was talking to accounts or whatever. Sometimes though, now that you ask, I did see him just sitting there, staring ahead, as if he was listening to someone. I guess maybe that was kind of odd, but I don't think it occurred to me until now. And then again, like I said, maybe he was listening to someone rant about the way they wanted a certain job done or something like that."

"We caught him on a workday. Do you remember hearing the Fireman had been apprehended? Were you still at work then, and if so, can you remember anything about that day?" Mike asked.

"Was he in his office a lot that day?" Craig prompted quietly when Washington was silent, thinking back. "Listening, as you say, or maybe on the phone?"

Washington looked at him, frowning. "Yeah," he said. "He was in his office . . . and then came out and asked me and Mark to keep working on a project we were doing for a guy in Williamsburg. Mark and I were fine with it. He was leaving early, but he paid us for our work. We weren't paying him." He cast his head to angle curiously. "Do you think he heard a voice because someone called him?"

"We don't know," Craig said.

"You haven't seen or heard anything from him, right, Mr. Washington?" Mike asked.

"What do you think?" Washington asked roughly. He shook his head. "Sorry — no. I'm scared of that guy. I don't think he'd come near me. I have a permit for a hunting rifle. And I promise you, right now I have it loaded and ready to go. Wife died last year, but I got grandkids, and I want to be around for them. I'm ready if he does come anywhere near here. I'm sixty-seven. I like doing stuff with my hands — didn't mind working in the shop. But after this . . . well, I'm retired now. I want my life to be nice and easy here in my golden years."

"What about Mark Givens?" Craig asked.

"I don't know why you're asking me. I'm

sure you've checked up on him, and you're gonna to speak with him, too."

"We will," Craig agreed.

"We know he took a job at a deli in Tribeca. We're meeting him at noon, right before he starts his shift," Mike said.

"So, what about him?" Washington leaned back in his chair.

"Was he closer to Raoul Nicholson by any chance? Maybe he heard him talking to whoever he was talking to — or listening to," Craig said.

"Mark is in his fifties — has a kid in college. He had to keep working," Washington said. "Was he closer to Raoul? No. Were we close? Yeah, just the two of us, day in, day out. We got along real well, although . . . ." He paused, frowning again.

"What is it?" Mike asked, pressing him.

"On my birthday Mark came in with a present for me. Not much, just a big insulated coffee mug. Nicholson had a fit. We were welcome to be pagans on our own time, but birthdays were not to be celebrated at his place of business. He couldn't make us understand we were sinners, but there would be no presents, no holidays, and no partying at his business. It was a sin, he said. Satan instigated that kind of dangerous foolery. Well, I was mighty pissed. So was Mark. But like I said, Mark has a kid in college. Can't rock the boat too much. We tossed the mug in a dumpster as he watched." Washington grinned. "I went back and got it, of course, but . . . like I said, he just acted as if he was so holy all the time. Me, I'm a Baptist, but I've never seen anything like the way Nicholson wanted to be. Shouldn't have been so surprised when we found out he killed people he thought were sinners." He shivered suddenly. "When you boys leave, I'm going to be sitting back inside my house, holding on to that shotgun for dear life."

Craig nodded. He knew that seeing this man had been important. Elimination of suspects was crucial to narrowing down who could be the guilty party. And one of Nicholson's coworkers could know a lot about what made the man tick. In fact, he was making Craig wonder more and more if Nicholson's "voice" had somehow been a real one, playing on the man's extreme religious practice and his belief in himself as a messiah.

But Bart Washington had never been in any kind of legal trouble in his life, nor did anything in his background suggest that he would know about the security measures in an elegant building on the Upper East Side.

"Hey, listen, if anything scares you — if you think you're facing a real threat — you dial 911 right away," Mike told him as the agents stood.

"And if something is just making you suspicious, call us," Craig said, offering one of his cards.

Washington took the card and slid it into the pocket on his T-shirt. "You bet I will. I'm even keeping my distance from my family right now, staying here all locked in, or keeping watch on the porch. He's not getting close to me, I promise."

"Thank you again for your time."

They waved to him, walking down the street to the car. Craig slid into the driver's seat.

"Do you really think Nicholson heard the voice because someone pulling his strings actually called him on his cell phone to tell him about witches?"

"I'm calling Egan. We'll get a list of his calls. I know he hadn't called any of his victims. We looked into that right away. But if someone was calling him . . ."

"If someone called him to tell him to kill, it will have been on a burner phone. If there is someone out there who helped engineer his escape and either helped him into Mayhew's building or got in and killed the man

257

himself . . . well, they'd have been smart enough to not be traceable."

"I agree. But it will help to know if he did receive several calls from a burner phone. We'll know that maybe he was hearing a real voice. And," he said, looking over at Mike, "we'll know there is another killer out there, a killer with an agenda, rather than a religious calling."

Traffic seemed to be especially heavy, but Milo DeLuca, the FBI agent on Kieran watch duty, was an able and competent driver — not losing patience and not prone to sit on his horn.

He was from Ohio, he told her as he drove; Cincinnati specifically, a fine city, in spite of the fact people loved to tease people about being from Ohio. He'd graduated from the Academy about a year and a half ago, loved his job, and wanted to stay with the FBI forever.

Monday traffic was intense, but the agent kept up an easy flow of conversation. He wasn't obnoxious about it, just pleasant.

They reached the office building in Midtown where Drs. Fuller and Miro kept their offices. Milo left the car in a spot where he shouldn't have parked, but that seemed to be okay with their Bureau cars.

He insisted on walking her up to her office, where Jake, their young receptionist, greeted her — and eyed her escort. But Milo DeLuca was a friendly guy, and he started chatting with Jake, who wasn't much older, and the two had moved on to sports before Kieran even went down the hallway. She found that Dr. Fuller was in Dr. Miro's office, and the two of them were discussing the events of the weekend.

They both looked up, falling silent as she tapped on the door frame, since the door was ajar, and they knew she had heard them discussing Raoul Nicholson.

"Kieran!" Dr. Miro said. She stood from the chair behind her desk. Dr. Miro was a tiny ball of energy. Where Bentley Fuller stood several inches over six feet and could have played a heartthrob on any soap opera, Allison Miro was eight or so years older, plainer in her look and attire, but arresting with her energy and her simple love for humanity — and the determination she would find the best of it.

"Morning," Kieran said.

"We were just talking about you," Fuller said.

"You must have had a dreadful weekend. Not that you're not accustomed to dealing with hard and dangerous situations," Miro reflected.

"We're just so sorry. We should have never asked you to see Raoul Nicholson," Fuller said apologetically.

"Why not? I do work here," Kieran said.

"Yes, but . . ." Fuller began.

"Nicholson escaped," Miro concluded.

"And he was at it again!" Fuller said with a sigh.

"We don't want you to be in danger, dear," Miro said. "Bentley and I . . . well, we chose our practice. And you do such incredible work, helping those who have been abused, those who need help to live on their own, or to become good parents, put together a life after tragedy or trauma . . ." Her voice trailed off.

"She does get into enough trouble on her own," Fuller murmured, winking at Kieran. Miro didn't see the wink.

"Bentley!" she chastised. "We might have put her into danger."

Kieran inhaled on a deep breath. "I'm not in any danger. Nicholson said as much. And you know Craig. I came up here with an FBI escort."

"Yes, well, we knew you would be with your family or Craig over the weekend, but then . . . oh, actually, he must have been quite busy," Miro said.

"You know, Nicholson pulled off that escape not more than three hours after we left," Fuller noted.

"Yes," Kieran said.

"And murdered again," Miro murmured.

Kieran paused for a moment and then said quietly, "No, I don't think so."

"You don't? But I understand the method of Charles Mayhew's murder was Raoul Nicholson's method . . . exactly," Fuller said. "I spoke to Assistant Director Egan yesterday."

"And I'm sure he told you another man was also killed," Kieran reminded him.

Fuller and Miro exchanged significant glances. "We did have you speak with Mr. Nicholson because, quite frankly, for all our experience, neither of us was sure we'd read him well enough. He seems so real, so passionate. But I have seen psychotics who can pull off amazing acts, and sociopaths who have learned to pretend they have emotion. They can even fake regret. With Nicholson . . ."

"I am ninety percent sure he really hears a voice. I asked him about that voice . . ." They both looked at her, waiting. She plunged in. "It's just a theory," she said, and they both nodded. "Law enforcement thinks he had help — with knowledge of the guards, the layout of the prison, and other factors — to escape. A voice in his head? Maybe. But maybe a real voice. Mayhew's apartment was impossible to get into, but the killer there used another resident to get into the building initially. He killed that resident he had made use of and got in with his key card, and probably used that man's friendship or acquaintance to get Mayhew to bring him to his apartment level. I believe there is another killer — someone who wanted Mayhew dead, and wanted Raoul Nicholson blamed for the murder. Maybe that same person has been Nicholson's 'voice.'"

"Then you're talking about someone Nicholson was close to before his arrest," Fuller said. He looked at Kieran. "You've given Craig this theory, right?"

"Yes, more or less. He questions it all himself. And he is very thorough."

Fuller looked at his watch. "I have to be in court. The Bellamy case. Thankfully, that little girl is going to live. Her mother is one of the most blaring cases of Munchausen's syndrome by proxy I have ever seen. I'm afraid the girl will be looking for foster care. The father isn't in the picture. I hope they find the right someone for that child. She's going to need a lot of help. Kieran, can you . . . ?"

"She's adorable, and it broke my heart to find out she was being continually poisoned by her own mother," Kieran said softly. "I do very well with her. I'm happy to give her all the time we can, and work with trying to find her the right fit while her mom . . . winds up wherever she's going to wind up."

"I have to be at the local precinct," Miro murmured. "Kieran, you have Lynda Semple in about thirty minutes, and right after lunch, the Nottingham teenager, Shelly. You're . . . all right?"

Kieran smiled. "I am just fine, thank you," she said. She gave them a firm smile. "Go — go forth and conquer. I have Jake and an FBI agent here with me. I'm in good hands."

She had barely taken a seat in her own office before her phone rang. It was Egan, just checking to see if she was comfortable, if Special Agent Milo DeLuca was discreet enough for her to function well.

"He's great," Kieran assured him. "Though, I admit, I feel quite guilty, you putting a man on duty to protect me."

"Don't feel guilty. He's not just protecting you," Egan said.

"Oh?"

"If Nicholson did like you, you're a person

263

he might try to contact."

"Oh. Well, then . . . anyway, thanks. You have work. I have work . . ."

"Hanging up now," Egan said, and the call cut off.

Kieran set her phone down and logged on to her computer, glancing at the clock. Her first appointment that day was a young woman named Lynda Semple. She had been the victim of an abusive husband, and the police had been called regarding their arguments several times.

She had refused to press charges, as so many women did.

But eventually the husband attacked their young son. Lynda had pressed charges, and she was now going through intense therapy. Prosecutors feared she would recant; there were other witnesses, but it was important Lynda not hesitate on the stand — for herself and for her child. Kieran believed she was getting stronger each time they had a session. As always, she could only hope she was right. Lynda wouldn't be alone; she was being given protection by the NYPD. She had a restraining order against her husband, though he was out on bail.

Kieran had thirty minutes, though, before Lynda arrived. She found herself looking up killers who heard voices, along with fanatics who had killed by inciting mass suicide. Certainly, the worst case seemed to have been Jim Jones, who had ordered the suicide of 909 of his followers in Guyana and the shooting death of Congressman Leo Ryan as well as others when they had tried to defect. He'd killed himself, too, but . . .

She thought of the babies and little children, given cyanide by their own parents.

Survivors and those who had managed to escape Jones's hold at various times claimed it was not any god he had worshipped — it was power.

She shook her head. Nicholson wasn't about power.

He was an earnest man, an everyman, not particularly charming, like a Ted Bundy who had smiled and coerced his victims into his clutches, claiming injury with a sweet smile. He hadn't slowly lured them into his hold like a Jim Jones, preaching to his flock.

He had simply watched them and taken them by surprise, strangling them until they were dead, removing their eyes and tongue and then burning them, but at least killing them before the torture of mauling and burning their bodies.

But Olav Blom had somehow been talked into going to the basement of his building, possibly even by crawling down an old ice delivery system.

His killer had known about the building — down to looking through old blueprints until he had found the one chink in the armor, the old ice chute that had just been drywalled and plastered over.

She shook her head. That just wasn't Raoul Nicholson's MO. His learning had to do with the oldest and most severe religious texts he had come across. He knew how to design furniture that was unique and gave him a survival income while he created his True Life religion.

Kieran sat back, thinking, idly thumping a pencil on her desk. So far, the one kind of witness they had really needed had eluded them.

Nicholson hadn't given away any members of his True Life flock.

Amy Nicholson had told Dr. Fuller after their first interview she didn't know the names of the church members. They were like an AA club and only first names were given, not for anonymity, but because that was all that was needed. They were chosen, one true family, and if they had a surname, that name would be *Chosen.*

Raoul Nicholson had been ready to pay his dues. His "higher power" would have rewarded him for eternity.

She jumped when her intercom went off. It was Jake in reception. Her first appointment had arrived.

"Send her back, please," Kieran said.

She slammed her computer closed, decided not to think of anything but the person she was charged to help at this moment. She loved what she did, which was usually helping people get by tough times in their lives, helping with the legal system at the same time. She wasn't an agent; Craig was the agent. These hours, she owed to her work.

But later she'd get back on it. Because pieces were coming together. It didn't look like it, but there was something there, something she was just missing in her thoughts.

And she knew she had to figure out what it was, agent or not, for her own peace of mind.

Mark Givens had a headful of graying hair and was almost as lean as Bart Washington, evidently a man accustomed to moving all day, to working manually and enjoying it.

When they met, just inside Mona's Deli and Café on Canal Street, he was wearing an apron, though the café had yet to open. Mark Givens might have constructed furniture before, but apparently he was already manager of the café, and it was no problem for him to sit with them at the back of the café to talk.

He shook hands with them and didn't seem to begrudge them his time, though like Washington, he let Craig and Mike know he'd talked to police and agents already.

"Raoul was pretty good to us, except when it came to a holiday. He didn't believe in holidays. Only the legal status of holidays allowed for me and Bart to keep our jobs, and celebrate like the rest of the country. He didn't like to micromanage. He'd give us his designs and orders, and expect Bart and me to get it all done. He worked himself — all day in the office. He did the billing, he acquired our supplies. He was regular about everything — even brought in muffins or special doughnuts or whatever from that place he went to every morning. He was polite, decent, all that stuff. I know Bart was surprised when he was arrested. I'm not so sure that I was. I mean, looking back on the guy, he'd sit in his office and seem to be working, but sometimes I'd see him looking up. He didn't drop down on his knees or anything, but . . . it was like he was talking to someone. Or listening. Imaginary friend, you know. But I guess his imaginary friend was telling him who to kill when. I mean, I don't get it. He was a family man, always heading home to his wife and, in the past few years, really bummed out his kids had moved on. Me, if my kids didn't want anything to do with me at all anymore, and they weren't junkies or criminals, but cool college types, I'd have taken a step back to worry about what I was doing that caused the situation. Never got to go to college myself, but the guy didn't help those two out. They did it on their own. Seems like his kids are okay."

"Did you have any communication with him after he went to jail?" Craig asked.

"No, just his attorney, that Cliff Watkins. Decent guy, trying to do what was right for Amy and for us. He got a good deal on the business for Amy and severance pay for me and Bart. Bart was ready to quit. I couldn't quite go that route yet. I live in the Bronx. Life is not cheap. And honestly? I like working, like meeting people, like keeping busy and . . . well, frankly, the few weeks I was home with my wife, we kind of drove one another crazy. Working is good."

"Let's ask you this, though. I mean, Nicholson isn't a stupid guy, but did you think he was a particularly smart guy, like one who might know all about buildings or the way that jails work?" Mike asked.

"He was a smart enough guy where figures were concerned," Givens said. "He knew what we were going to make on every piece we worked on. He knew his overhead, that's for sure. But I remember one day he got his key stuck in the lock. He called me, frustrated, thinking he was going to have to pay a locksmith. But I'd phoned to tell him I was going to be a few minutes late — there was a problem with the A-train. I told him just to go have a cup of coffee or something and wait. I'd get a pincer and we'd get his key unstuck. It was easy enough. Ran into the little hardware store near the shop, bought a five-dollar tool, and got the door open, and we were good to go. I guess, after that, it is a little mind-boggling to think the guy got himself out of jail and off the island."

"He hasn't tried to contact you? He hasn't come in here?" Craig asked.

Givens shook his head. "No. I don't think I'd be the one he'd try to contact. I am careful when I leave here, though. And you'll never guess what I got the day the man was arrested."

"A large dog?" Mike suggested.

Givens nodded gravely. "Damn straight.

Older guy. He'd worked a K-9 unit, and his owner had passed away. He was up for adoption. Massive shepherd. Love the guy. No one is coming near my place without me knowing it. And here's the thing. I don't think Nicholson is a brave guy. He went after three young women and then that fashion designer, a little guy, maybe five-five and a hundred twenty pounds, and then from what I read, the accountant he killed was pretty small, too. Larry Armistice. I remember his name, because I thought, what a bitch. The guy was due to retire from his firm in less than a month. His golden years were just starting, and they were cut short before they started. But looked like he was a small guy. I mean, maybe some higher power was telling Nicholson who to kill, but he sure wasn't told to kill anyone who might have fought back. No big, tall women, no bulky males, no one he couldn't take. Like I said, the guy wouldn't call on me as a friend, and I stand a good six-three, spend a few nights a week at the gym, and now I have a big dog."

"Can you think of anyone who might help us figure out who did help him?" Mike asked.

Givens frowned. "You believe someone helped him?"

"You just said it yourself. He couldn't get a broken key out of a lock," Craig reminded him.

Givens paused thoughtfully. "I know he loved his wife, and he was estranged from his sons. I never heard about him being social or anything. He wasn't the kind of guy who was going to meet friends on a Saturday to tour the Met. Nor did he ever mention saving up to go to the theater. The only thing he did that was remotely social, that I know about, was stop by the coffee shop every morning. I guess he liked someone there, the wait staff, regular customers — I don't know. He'd bring things in now and then, and he often made comments like, 'That Annie. She knows how to run a good business and have plenty of good customer service. That's what we're aiming for boys, a tightly run ship, good service, and customers who come back for more.' "

"We've stopped by Annie's. Haven't found anyone yet who knew him, but we've talked to you and Bart now, and between you, all we've got is the coffee shop. So we'll head in for some breakfast nice and early tomorrow," Mike said, rising.

"Breakfast!" Givens said. "How rude of me. Can I offer you anything? On the house?"

"Thank you, but we have to get moving," Craig said. As usual, he handed out a card. "If you think of anything, if you suspect you might be in any danger —"

"I'll call you."

"Well, if you're in immediate danger, dial 911. But if you think you're being watched, or he's been by this place or your home, call us," Craig said. They headed out.

"You know, we could have paused long enough for lunch," Mike said.

"Yeah, I know — we'll go through some lousy drive-through on the way down to Princeton. You made sure we're going down there for a reason, right?

"I didn't really want John Nicholson to know we're coming, but I called the school and got through to a counselor. He should be in class until six this evening. We'll catch him coming out."

Mike glanced at his watch. "We could have had lunch," he said.

Craig grinned and glanced his way. "Not to worry. Tonight, for sure, we'll head straight to the pub. There's plenty of good food there."

"Yeah . . . I'm already tasting the bangers and mash. Or maybe corned beef or . . ." He broke off and looked at Craig, pained. "We are going to have to get something, though. Promises just aren't going to work for my stomach right now. You might have noticed — it is lunchtime."

"We'll hit a drive-through as soon as we see one. Will that do?"

Mike nodded. Craig thought that he was thinking about food.

He wasn't.

"Nicholson didn't kill Charles Mayhew or Olav Blom," Mike said. "Mayhew was a pretty big man. And Blom was no small fry, either. Not that you can fight back much once your throat is slashed, but . . ." He turned and stared at Craig. "I am thinking, more and more, we are looking at two killers."

"Yeah. And one of them knows locks, keys, jails, and buildings," Craig said. "We still have to get Nicholson. If we can get him, well, then, we just might have our ticket to finding his accomplice — Mayhew's killer."

It was a long day but a good one. Kieran had given her attention to Lynda Semple and then Shelly Nottingham. She really liked them both. Despite the hardships life had cast their way, both realized there were good things out there to be had as well, and were slowly gaining the strength to know they deserved them too.

Lynda had been a hard sell at first. She had long ago accepted her role as a punching bag; her husband had been the one who supported the family. That had, in her mind, made her a servant.

Lynda had joined a support group at Kieran's suggestion. She was now amazed at herself, and not just willing to testify against her husband, but anxious to do so — and to see him locked up and herself divorced.

Of course, Kieran reflected, closing her files for the day, it wasn't just women or children who might wind up abused. It was less common, but she had dealt with a few men during her time with Drs. Fuller and Miro, and some of them had accepted their fates, as well. Today, though, work-wise, had been productive, and she felt good when she walked out to the reception area.

Special Agent Milo DeLuca was waiting for her, serenely playing a game on his phone.

"Ready to go home?"

"To the pub. Craig is meeting me there. We'll head home together after, and you'll be off for the night, right?"

He smiled. "I'm off when the new agent replaces me at eight," he said. "This is an assignment I'm not minding at all." Despite the time and the Monday traffic, the ride went quickly. The good thing was there was more traffic heading north out of downtown than there was traffic heading south.

When they arrived, Special Agent DeLuca said he'd wait in the car, keeping an eye on the door; she convinced him it was fine that he come in.

"I'm really not supposed to take advantage," he said.

"You can watch me better from inside, and we have soft drinks, tea, and all kinds of juices. Come inside, sit and watch. It will be fine."

He brightened at that. "I can guard you better when I can actually see you."

He followed her in. Mary Kathleen, Declan's bride, lovely with her dark hair and bright eyes, greeted them first, telling Milo DeLuca she was delighted to meet another one of Richard Egan's agents, and he must make himself comfortable.

She would personally see to it he received a real pot of tea. None of that dangling a tea bag in a cup of hot water!

DeLuca took a seat at the booth closest to the door. Kieran went on to check with Declan, who was back behind the bar.

"My lovely wife is on the floor, and we're

276

moving along fine for a Monday night. But you want to run down to the basement and grab me another bottle of Jameson's?" he asked Kieran.

"Sure."

"I see you brought your bodyguard in."

"I hate seeing them just have to sit out in their cars."

"I agree. Hope he likes the place," Declan said.

Kieran grinned. "What's not to like?"

A bodyguard was in the restaurant; her brother was behind the bar. Mondays weren't their busiest night, but there was a fair number of clientele in the restaurant.

Kieran didn't give a second thought to running down to the basement. The stairs were lit; the basement was lit. Declan didn't keep service areas dark.

There was simply no reason whatsoever for her to hesitate.

Not until she got there.

Not until she saw the man she'd been seeing on her corner . . . who she'd first seen leaving the pub.

Just standing there, still in his trench coat, watching and waiting . . .

For her.

CHAPTER TWELVE

"What do you mean, he's not here?" Mike
demanded.

The counselor, Anita Smith, according to
the plaque on her desk, flushed with misery.
"I'm so sorry. I had no idea. I checked
John Nicholson's schedule . . . he, um, apparently hasn't been here all day. We just
came in from a weekend, you know, but I've
checked with his frat brothers, and apparently he cut out for Manhattan on Friday
after his last class. They assumed, as I did,
he'd be back for classes on Monday morning. I mean, it isn't like him. He's truly a
fine student. He's going through a lot, of
course, but you won't find a friend, teacher,
or anyone who doesn't support him to the
fullest. I mean, trust me, I've spent hours
with the young man. He's worked hard
to . . . to create a life for himself. To distance
himself from his family, from the horrible
things . . ." Her voice trailed off. She was a

278

slim woman, her passionate voice belying her tiny stature.

Craig and Mike had waited outside the advanced calculus class where John Nicholson should have been. When he hadn't appeared, they'd headed to speak with the counselor who had given Craig the young man's schedule.

"I am so sorry!" Anita Smith said. That was easy enough to see. She was almost crying.

"Is there anyone close to him we could talk to?" Craig asked.

"Me," she whispered.

"But you knew nothing about him taking off for the weekend and staying out of classes?" Mike asked. "I don't mean to be disparaging, but . . . what about his friends?"

"Yes, yes, of course. He's in a fraternity. A top-notch fraternity, where grade point averages count, where the boys are boys of course, but . . . I'll find someone. Please, um, sit down and I'll be right back!"

They sat. Mike gave Craig a dour look.

Craig guessed he deserved it; he was the one who had called ahead and determined to talk to a counselor rather than John Nicholson himself.

"I'm sorry too — and worried," Craig said.

Mike nodded. "His brother hasn't seen him, or else he lied to us."

"I don't think Thomas was lying."

"Someone is lying."

"Maybe, and maybe we just haven't gotten to the right person yet."

Mike shook his head. "Nicholson should have shown up by now. Not that it's all that hard to hole up somewhere and not be seen, but we're talking about a man who every cop across the nation has heard about, and seen his face plastered on the most wanted list."

"He should have shown up by now, yes — if he's been out in public, if he's made any kind of a movement," Craig said. "But if he's holed up inside somewhere, maybe even in another state, we could be looking for a really long time. I imagine he's lying really low. I never thought he was the brightest man in the world, but he's not stupid. He knows every law enforcement officer out there is looking for him, and his face has been all over every form of media. I think he has a hideout and he's staying put, getting help from someone."

"That is possible and probable. Feels like we've been on this forever. But remember, it's only been three days since we lost him."

They had taken seats in front of the counselor's desk. Mike started to speak again but fell silent as Anita Smith came back into the room, trailed by a lanky young man with long light brown hair, light eyes, and a worried look.

"This is Frank Austin, Agents, and he's good friends with John."

Austin didn't offer his hand. He looked at them as if they were the enemy.

"I'm hoping you're not here after John. He's one of the best people I know," Austin said.

"We're not here 'after him,' " Craig said. "We just came to talk. But if you don't know where he is, then, we're actually worried about his welfare."

Austin swallowed at that and set his book bag down.

"He's one of the best people I know," he repeated.

"Do you know where he is?" Mike persisted.

Frank Austin nodded. "Yeah," he said on a weak breath. "Manhattan."

Mike glanced over at Craig.

"Could you possibly be any more specific?" Craig asked.

Austin didn't look quite so hostile anymore; he shook his head with misery. "I told him not to go. I told him he was with a group of people who cared about him and would stand by him. I asked if he was going to his mother's place or his brother's. He said neither. He said his mother . . . he said his mother belonged to his father, heart and soul. And he didn't want to cause his brother any pain. I wanted to know why he was going. He said his father might be crazy, but that . . . well, he was afraid if cops caught his dad before he could safely turn himself back in, they'd just shoot him down. He didn't hate his dad. He told me his dad was messed up as all hell, but he really believed he was some kind of prophet . . . He just didn't want to see his dad shot down, and I . . . None of us could stop him."

"No, you can't stop someone when they're determined," Craig said. He pulled out a card and offered it to the young man. "Please — for John's safety. We're not after him to hurt him in any way. We could just use his insight, his help. If you even hear from him, can you let us know?"

Austin took the card. "Yeah. Totally. But believe me, he's one of the good guys. John just wanted to . . . live. Be . . . normal."

"We believe you," Craig said quietly. "And I swear, we just want to help him."

282

"I am so, so sorry!" Anita Smith said again.

Mike turned to her. "If you hear from him, let us know."

"I will!" she promised.

"And so will I," Austin vowed.

Craig and Mike left. "You can definitely drive back to Manhattan in rush hour," Mike said, heading to the passenger's side.

They both slid into the car and started out on the road.

"A good kid, like his brother," Mike muttered. "How do you come from a home like that — and wind up being a good kid?"

"Everyone swore Raoul Nicholson was a good man — until they found out he'd murdered people."

"Yeah," Mike said. "That's true, too. So, what do you think? Two really good kids who somehow not only survived their upbringing but came out of it soaring, or . . ."

"Or one of the two is a killer," Craig said.

"Two good kids, or one killer, one good kid, or . . ." He paused and looked over at Craig. "Or two killers — very clever chips off the old block?"

Craig kept one hand on the wheel and started to pull his cell phone from his pocket.

"You know, that is majorly illegal in the

state of New Jersey. They were among the first to ban improper use of cell phones, you know."

Craig cast Mike a glance, hit a button on the steering wheel, and spoke to the car's phone system. "Call Kieran," he said.

"Thought she knew we were coming to the pub."

"She does. I'm just checking to see if she's on her way."

The system called Kieran. Her number rang. It went to voice mail.

"You know, she might be at the pub by now, maybe running around, helping out, carrying on a conversation with some of the regulars," Mike said.

Craig ignored him and asked the system to call the pub.

After a minute Declan answered. "Hey, it's Craig. I'm trying to reach Kieran. Is she there, at the pub, with you?"

"Yes, she's here. Your guy is at a table. Kieran just ran down to the basement for me. I'll have her give you a call."

A scream nearly ripped from Kieran's throat.

Somehow, the man with the trench coat managed to speak first. "Please! Please! I don't want to hurt you, I swear. I just need your help, please, please . . ."

There was some distance between them. Kieran was only halfway down the stairs.

Or, halfway back up them, if the need arose. She paused, not saying anything.

He kept his distance and spoke quickly. "I'm John. John . . . Nicholson. Not a name that's a great one to have, but . . . anyway, I talked to my dad. Not since he escaped! I talked to him on the phone. And he said he'd spoken to a psychiatrist named Kieran Finnegan."

"Psychologist," Kieran corrected by rote.

"Sorry, psychologist, and he said you had been really decent to him. He's sorry as hell about you going to hell for not being part of True Life, but then, he's sorry as hell my brother and I will be going to hell if we don't come around." He lifted a hand as if warding off an accusation before one could come his way. "I knew nothing about the fact he was going to escape. He just happened to mention how decent you were, and he'd gotten to have a visit from my mother, and his attorney, that Mr. Walford —"

"Watkins, Cliff Watkins," Kieran interrupted.

"Yes, sorry. I'm nervous here — slipping into a pub's basement. Guess I could be arrested just for being down here. I just felt like I needed to hide and figure out some way to talk to you alone. But anyway, when I heard what had happened . . . I had to find someone. I just don't believe . . . well, my dad only killed people he believed to be witches. And he wrote them notes, warning them. And he said they would know why and understand when they got the notes. Well, you talked to my father. I know the public believes him to be a monster. He's not a monster. He's just really, really sick. And I thought if I could get to you . . . maybe you could make all the cops and agents and marshals and whoever else out there know if they corner him, they don't need to shoot him. He won't hurt them. They can take him back into custody. They . . . they don't have to kill him."

"You were in here before — in the pub before," Kieran said.

"Yes, but there were so many tough looking people around you."

"And you've been watching my apartment."

"I just needed to speak with you alone. I — I'll go now. Or you can have me arrested for wandering into a basement, trying to steal booze, whatever. But please, my dad said you were really decent. I can only pray you'll understand me." He flushed suddenly. "Yeah, I pray. I just have a really different concept of what a higher power should be."

Kieran was quiet for a minute.

"It's all right. You can call your bodyguard now, whoever he is. You can call the FBI guy you live with. You can take me in."

Kieran let out a long breath and smiled. "Or you can come up and have a seat, and I'll get you something to eat. We'll both wait for Craig, and I'll introduce you. He's the one who first brought your father in. He didn't hurt him," she added softly.

John Nicholson stood there for a minute, as if doubting her words.

"Come on. Oh, grab me one of those bottles of Jameson's off the shelf over there first," she told him.

He looked at her for a minute.

"Please."

He turned and reached to the shelf where the whiskeys were kept, finding a Jameson's and taking it down, then slowly walking toward her.

She turned her back on him and started up the stairs, hoping she wouldn't regret doing so.

He followed her, keeping a certain distance, clearly aware there was really no reason she should trust him. When she reached the ground level of the pub, she hurried along the hallway to the bar, and there she waited for John Nicholson, taking the Jameson's from him to hand over to Declan.

Her brother stared at her, frowning, but she gave him a quick nod, indicating that everything was all right.

"This is John," she told Declan.

"Hi, John," Declan said. He didn't add more. He understood Kieran was all right; he knew how to read her expressions.

"I'm taking him over to sit with Milo."

"Okay. John, can I get you anything? You are twenty-one, right? Sorry, but I card."

"I'm twenty-two, but I don't want any alcohol. A soda would be great."

"You got it," Declan said. "Kieran?"

"Soda — great," she said.

"Oh, by the way, Craig called. He wants you to call him. I told him you were here, just down in the basement."

"Thanks. I'll give him a call in a minute."

Then she turned to John and said, "For now, come with me, we'll join my 'bodyguard' at that little table. Craig and Mike — Special Agents Frasier and Dalton — will be here soon."

"Thank you," he told her. "Will they arrest me?"

"For what?"

"For being . . . Nicholson's son?"

"No, they don't arrest people unless they do something illegal themselves. You know that. I know that you know that — you're a bright college kid."

He flushed. "I don't know. Maybe they think I'm aiding or abetting my father somehow."

"Are you?"

He shook his head strenuously. "I don't know what's wrong with his mind. He was always a fanatic, but not lethal. He was ridiculously strict, but he never raised a hand against my brother or me."

Kieran nodded. "Come on."

She led the way to the little enclave table near the door where Milo was sitting, a cup of tea and an order of one of their appetizers, Shillelagh O'Shannon Sticks, in front of him.

He stood and immediately frowned.

"John, Milo. Milo, John," she said, sliding into the curved booth as John took the other side, offering Milo his hand.

The agent looked at him, worried. "John is waiting to see Craig and Mike."

"Oh," Milo said. His eyes widened. "John . . ."

"Nicholson," John said glumly.

"Oh," Milo said, staring at Kieran.

She smiled sweetly. "It's all good," she told him. "He wants to help get his dad back into custody."

"I see. But . . . I didn't see you come here," Milo said.

John looked at Kieran.

"He's been hanging out at the pub, hoping to find one of us to talk to," Kieran said.

Her phone rang, and she excused herself to talk to Craig.

He sounded anxious. "You didn't call me back."

"Craig, I'm fine. You're on your way."

"As fast as the road — and the thousands of cars on it — will allow," he said dryly. "Declan said Special Agent DeLuca was in there with you."

"He is, and someone else who is anxious to see you."

"Who?"

"John Nicholson."

"He's . . . there?"

"Yep, waiting to see you."

"Don't let him leave. Tell DeLuca. Under no circumstances do you let him leave."

John was watching her across the table.

"Nothing to worry about. He's here, waiting, and he'll help any way he can," she told Craig.

290

"Be careful anyway. Okay?"

"Always," she promised, and hung up.

Both John and Milo were quiet, staring at her. She placed her phone down and picked up one of the menus Mary Kathleen had left.

"Might as well get some real dinner," she said. "They're on the way. But traffic, you know. We're really well-known for our shepherd's pie. Fish and chips — oh, and bangers and mash are great, too, all depending on what you like."

John stared at her worriedly for another few seconds.

Then he managed a smile at last and picked up a menu.

"I would like to arrive alive," Mike said, his voice calm, slightly amused.

Craig was driving fast, and weaving to move as quickly as possible. He glanced over at Mike.

"Just sayin'," his partner said.

"Yeah. Not to worry. I intend to get there alive."

"Kieran is at the pub with her family, a host of other people, and an FBI agent."

"But why there? Why the hell did the kid go there?" Craig asked.

"They have good shepherd's pie?" Mike

suggested, and then groaned slightly at the look Craig gave him. "You've heard from his counselor, from his friends, that John Nicholson is a good kid — no threat. And we thought we were going to have to look for him. Go figure! Kieran found him for us."

"You're right," Craig said, swerving around a slow-moving Cadillac.

"Okay, then," Mike said.

Craig managed a smile; he was still anxious.

"Right, and we were just discussing the fact everyone had thought Raoul Nicholson was a pillar of the community, just as everyone thinks his kids are amazing, especially coming from the home they came from. One homicidal kid, two homicidal kids . . ."

"And Kieran won't leave the pub. Come on, give her some credit."

He did. He gave her all the credit in the world.

"Poor dog," Mike muttered suddenly.

"What?"

"You're at work all day, she's at work all day . . . better bring him some shepherd's pie when you do go home tonight."

"Mike —"

"Shut up, yeah, I know. Hey, remember, I'm the one who taught you the ropes!"

"Yes, and that's why I'm not letting an old man drive," Craig murmured.

He moved fast until they got to the tunnel. Then he chaffed all the way through.

Neither he nor Mike talked any more.

Eventually they arrived. He barely had the car in Park before he was exiting the vehicle and hurrying for the entrance to the pub.

When he entered, Mike on his tail, he saw Kieran almost immediately.

And Milo DeLuca.

And John Nicholson.

Kieran saw him and stood quickly, pointing his way. John, across from her in the little curved booth, rose as well, turning to look.

He was a handsome kid, better looking than his mother or his father. He stood at about six foot one, tall and straight, and while he looked a little uneasy, his eyes were steady on Craig when Kieran suggested they might want to sit down alone somewhere together.

The table where they'd been sitting showed the remnants of their dinner. He thanked Kieran and asked her if she'd order meals for him and Mike.

Then, he looked around and saw another table at the back of the restaurant area that was empty. He lifted a hand to John Nicholson, indicating the way.

At first John kept trying to explain why he'd tried to see Kieran first. "My father said she was a truly decent human being. Of course, with my father, that might have meant she simply wasn't evil. But I'm concerned for others, and concerned for my father. I didn't just walk into a police station because I figured you had to be suspicious of me, my brother, or my mother. I want to help, but I really don't know how. If you spoke to Thomas, you know we both came of age and got the hell out. Don't get me wrong. I left home, but I did talk to my parents, and I do care about my dad. In my mind, he should have been locked up a long time ago. And my mother . . . well, you know, her wedding vows are sacred, a wife's duty is to protect her husband. I know he believed there was a real voice from someplace he considered to be on high that spoke to him."

"Do you know how the voice spoke to him?" Craig asked. "He had to have had some kind of help. There is no way your father could have escaped without help."

"We didn't know he heard voices telling him to kill witches until he was arrested. I asked him . . . after he'd been arrested. His lawyer has tried so hard to be helpful, convincing him he needs to make the jury understand the voices were in his head. But Dad's giving that man a really hard time. Or was. Didn't want an insanity defense. He's not insane, he's justified, trying to save humanity, and if that means he goes to prison, and they throw away the key, so be it." He paused for a minute. "And my father, in general population . . . well, I doubt he'd last a week."

"What we need to know is if there's anyplace your father might be hiding out," Craig said.

"You've checked my mother's house?" John asked.

"We'll pay her a visit again tomorrow, but our boss had her come into the office," Craig said. "She swears she knew nothing about him trying to escape, even though she had seen him that day. There has been an agent watching her building since this all happened."

"My mother wouldn't know. She's like a 1950s housewife, or a pre–WWII stay-at-home mother, do whatever the husband, the breadwinner, says," John told them. He took a deep breath. "I don't know how she would have survived if our attorney wasn't so great. He got my father's business sold, and he set up a trust so she'd be okay with the money from the sale."

"Are you going to go and stay with her?" Mike asked. "Where have you been staying?" he asked, frowning. "They said you left after your last classes Friday."

"There's a hostel in Hell's Kitchen. Gives me a bed and a shower as cheaply as one could ever hope for in New York," John said.

"Why didn't you tell your brother? Do you think he'd be helping your father?" Craig asked.

John shook his head. "No, if someone helped my dad, it wasn't my brother, me, or my mother."

"What about the other church members?" Craig asked. "No one knows who they are."

"Because they probably ran under rocks like scared rodents," John said.

"You've only been gone from home for four years. Don't you remember anyone?" Mike persisted.

John shook his head. "You had to be an adult to be a member of True Life. Able to swear yourself that you believed in all the tenets. Children were kept at home — with the women, by the way — while the men decided the doctrine and everything else. Women had church, but it was separate. There is no Sunday as in Christianity, or a Saturday as in Judaism. Every day could be a church day. Anyplace could be a church. Children were to learn to be obedient, and when they were ready, they could join the church."

"But by eighteen?" Mike asked.

"I was never ready to swear to the tenets," John said. "I fought with my parents through high school. I had to come home, do homework, do chores — never go out with friends, never go to a school dance, never socialize . . . but they couldn't make me say what I didn't believe. They knew I would take off, just like Thomas. But in my father's misguided mind, my brother and I would one day see the light and come back." He winced. "That's the thing. This is all real to him."

"Did he tell you how his voices came to him?" Craig asked.

John nodded. "Sometimes, the higher power would use a cell phone. Sometimes, he'd just hear the voice in his head while taking a shower or something. Or he'd see clues."

"He'd see clues?" Craig said, surprised. This was the first he was hearing about visual clues.

"He told me one time there was an arrow in the dirt right outside the apartment building. It pointed to a park. He went to the park." He hesitated, obviously pained by what he was about to say. "That's where he saw Sally Hendriks, the second woman he killed. He always knew what the voices and the clues meant. He was . . . on a mission."

Food came for Craig and Mike, and they took turns eating and asking questions. Over coffee they learned John Nicholson was convinced his father had been hiding out since he'd escaped. He hadn't killed again.

"You had to really know my father and how deeply he believed. He wouldn't have killed a man as he did. When he first heard the voice, the voice told him there was no reason to inflict pain on the flesh. The voice told him exactly how to kill. My father wasn't into blood and gore, just ridding the evil soul of the human vestment. That's exactly how he described the human body. It was a vestment, nothing more. And if an evil soul was going to be purged, it had to be by fire."

"What about the eyes and the tongue?" Mike asked.

John shrugged. "See no evil, speak no evil."

"What about hear no evil?" Craig asked.

John shook his head. "The ears burned, I guess. My father's method of killing was part of his mission, and while the news hasn't had many details about the second man killed on Saturday, he wasn't killed in the same manner. I know that from what no one is saying, and of course, reporters got wind of a body quickly — and there was no fire. I'm not saying my father wouldn't kill again and that it isn't a very real and desperate thing he needs to be locked up again, I'm just saying he would only kill someone as part of his mission. He would never kill someone who was presumed innocent."

Craig looked over at Mike; they had heard that many times now.

Most likely, it was true.

But who the hell was helping him, and who had killed Mayhew and Blom?

A member of the church?

Maybe.

Or maybe just someone who knew Raoul Nicholson was a man who could be used.

Before the evening was over, Craig convinced John to call his brother, Thomas. And Thomas convinced John to come and stay with him.

Mike would drive John to his brother's, and Milo would drop off Craig and Kieran.

Not even Milo spoke much in the car. When they reached the apartment, late as it was, Kieran started out by insisting they take Ruff for a walk.

Craig felt guilty then about keeping the dog. Maybe it was wrong if the only life they could give him meant he'd be shut in the apartment a lot of the time. But Ruff was happy to see them both, running in circles, jumping up and into his arms and then into Kieran's arms.

"Sure, we'll take him for a walk," he said, gathering the little blue bags they'd gotten for cleaning up after their pet. Kieran had the leash. They went downstairs.

Even the Dimitri family bodega was closed for the night.

They said good-night to Milo, who was being replaced by Special Agent Lena Gulden, who would be watching the apartment building through the night.

As they continued with the dog, Kieran asked, "Isn't it a waste, to have an agent watching the building when you're home?"

He shook his head. "I wasn't lying to you. They're not just watching out for you — or us — as a protective detail. Nicholson could try to reach you just as his son did tonight." She didn't reply, and he asked, "John Nicholson was just at the pub tonight when you got there?"

"Exactly," she said. "He was at the pub when Milo and I got there."

He didn't know why he sensed she was holding something back. She was telling the truth; Milo had said as much to him.

"So, there are two killers," she said.

"It would seem so."

"Someone close to Nicholson, someone who could . . . know him well and get to him when he was being held pending trial."

"That's not so terribly hard. Innocent until proven guilty."

"Then . . . someone he saw when he was in jail. Of course, that would include me, his attorney, and his wife."

"He talked to John on the phone. We don't know who else he might have spoken to. And it's frustrating. His church had to be the most secretive secret society I've ever heard about."

"I wonder if I should talk to Amy again."

"Maybe. The apartment was searched the night Raoul Nicholson was brought in, and nothing was found other than his stash of gasoline cans, lighters, and knives. The knives had been cleaned, but he hadn't used enough bleach. We know exactly what he used to cut out tongues."

"And the eyes?"

Craig winced slightly. "A grapefruit spoon."

"Oh," she said. "I kind of wish I hadn't

asked. And was it the same with Charles Mayhew?"

"Dr. Layton said the method of death was the same, but . . . I wonder. The body had burned. Thanks to the security guard, Joey Catalano, the fire was put out quickly. I don't know if he's been able to determine if there were any details at all different. I'll have a talk with him sometime tomorrow. It's going to be a long day for me. Mike and I want to go for breakfast at Annie's Sunrise, and see if we can figure if any of the weekday regulars knew him better than to say only, 'Good morning, how are you?' Monday to Friday. We want to get back over to Amy Nicholson's apartment. She just might be helping him somehow. What else is that kind of good, obedient, and loyal wife to do? And check in on any task force notes, and see if Layton or the crime scene techs can give us anything more."

"What about that apartment building?" she queried.

He smiled. "Oh, don't worry. Egan has people watching that building, as well."

"Is that what the FBI does — watch?" she teased.

"Surveillance is tedious. But we all do it, all pay our dues. Speaking of which, let me have a little baggie. Ruff has just paid a few 'dues.' "

She laughed softly; he picked up after Ruff, and they turned back, both tired and ready for bed.

"What I was getting at," he said, "is I'm probably going to be late, and even with a man on the door —"

"You don't want me to be at the apartment by myself. Some shifty-eyed person might drop from the sky and come in on the fire escape. But you don't want me to have to spend the evening at the pub, either, where everything is always perfectly managed whether I'm there or not. Not to worry. Danny was off tonight. I think he slept all day. So Danny can hang with me tomorrow night. He has all kinds of theories anyway, and he can enlighten me on serial killers the world over while we wait for you to get home. It will be great."

He smiled and nodded. "Go figure. I didn't ask to speak with John Nicholson when I called down to the school because I didn't want to forewarn him and have him disappear. And he just walks into the pub to talk to you."

"Yep, he just walked into the pub to talk to me."

"Still, suspicious."

"Suspicious? Why?"

"Oh, I'm not suspicious of him. I'm suspicious of you."

She smiled and went on her toes to briefly kiss his lips. "He was in the pub when I came in. And that, my love, is the absolute truth. He was already there when we arrived."

"You would tell me if anything made you uneasy, right?"

"I would," she promised. "I told you, Raoul Nicholson is not out to get me."

"I believe you," he said. "Not that any of us really knows his mind, but . . ."

"I didn't meet the older boy, but from what I understand, he just wanted out — big time. He got out. But even so, even knowing what he knows, he doesn't hate his father. He hates what he's done, but he — and John — believe their father is really sick."

"I'm not so afraid of Raoul Nicholson."

"Then, who are you afraid of?"

"Whoever killed Charles Mayhew and Olav Blom," he said quietly.

"Well, I have my bodyguards," she said, and added, "and I have you." She reached up, running her fingers along his collar, her fingertips just touching the flesh at his throat. She smiled, moving on to run her knuckles against his cheek. Her voice was husky when she said, "Let's put junior here to bed and head on up ourselves, huh?"

He caught her hand and kissed her fingers lightly.

"At least we can agree on something," he said.

She stooped, scratching Ruff on the top of his head and promising the dog, "I'll come home for you first tomorrow and spirit you right into Declan's office. But no leaving Declan any presents, okay?"

Ruff let out a little woof, as if in agreement, wagged his tail, and leaped back up into Kieran's arms.

"I guess I'm walking him home this way!" she said. "Lazy boy!"

Kieran wasn't sure why she woke early, but she did. She was comfortably curled against Craig.

He woke at the drop of a dime, because of his training, or just his personality, she wasn't sure. She eased away from him as carefully as she could. He could sleep at least another forty-five minutes or so before getting up to start his day.

She was drawn to the window and walked to it, carefully pulling the curtain back to peek her face around.

The morning was not promising as far as

suggesting it would become a beautiful spring day. The sun was struggling to come through dark clouds that hovered over the city, casting a dismal gray over buildings and streets alike. Ah, well, rain. It did do that now and then.

Her eyes were drawn to the corner, and it seemed her heart skipped a beat.

There was a man on the corner again. A man in a trench coat and a low-brimmed hat.

John Nicholson . . . John had admitted to trying to reach her. Had she asked him if he'd been standing on her corner, watching the apartment? Surely she had. And she knew that he'd been dropped off at his brother's apartment last night.

So?

Was this John again? Or was everything about him a lie?

Or was this a different man . . . someone else watching her, someone . . .

The rain began with a sudden, blinding onslaught against the glass.

Peering through the downpour, she saw that the man was gone. And as she looked out the window, she wondered if she had just seen him there because she'd expected someone to be there, or was someone else watching her, trying to reach her?

CHAPTER THIRTEEN

Annie's Sunrise was a busy place, and Craig figured it probably had a lot to do with Annie Sullivan herself. She was cheerful and charming behind the register, she helped her servers, and she walked along the booths that sat by the plate-glass windows to the street, seeing if her customers wanted more coffee, and if everything was all right.

Craig and Mike had been there about twenty minutes, and they'd watched her chat enthusiastically, pour coffee and help serve, and then she joined them at their table. She kept her face animated, as if they were discussing a sports team or a new play on Broadway. "The older woman by the cash register with the white-blond hair and the nurse's uniform. She's Candy Dryer, and she talked to Raoul Nicholson almost every day. He'd sit next to her and eat at least three times a week. Other people who came in ahead of him seemed to know that was his seat. Next to her is Xavier Green, and he talked to Raoul Nicholson on a regular basis, as well. The other person I see here today who spoke with him frequently is Bethany Sears, and she's next to Xavier at the counter now. They're all nice people. I don't know whether to introduce you, or . . ."

"Sure, introduce us," Craig said. "We'll have to say who we are anyway."

Annie rose and walked over to the counter, approaching Candy Dryer first. The woman stiffened, frowning for a moment as she looked over at the booth where Craig and Mike were sitting. Then she rose and picked up her mug of coffee, bringing it with her as she approached the table.

She was a no-nonsense woman, probably extremely beautiful when she'd been young, and still attractive, her wrinkles just seeming to add something that was dignified and serene to her look. "I hear you want to chat, that you're FBI."

Craig and Mike both stood politely as she joined them, introducing themselves.

She slid into the booth. "I wish I could help. Raoul was . . . polite, courteous, and dedicated. I just had no idea of just how dedicated," she said.

Mike glanced at Craig. He doubted they

had found the person who had aided Raoul Nicholson in his escape.

"I was a member once."

Mike had been taking a sip of his coffee. He choked, coughed, sputtered, and caught up a napkin just in time to cover his mouth.

Candy Dryer smiled at that. "True Life. I thought it was what I needed. I'm a nurse in a ward where most of my patients are terminal, dying of lung disease, kidney disease, liver failure . . . dying. I'm good with people, taking blood, you name it. And I always managed well. Then my husband — who was a nonsmoker, nondrinker, jogger — dropped dead of a heart attack. We never had children. Suffice it to say we couldn't, and while we talked about adopting, our jobs took over. We were incredibly happy." She smiled, perhaps trying a little joke. "Maybe we were so happy because we didn't have children. I do have friends who lose their minds over theirs. Anyway, what I'm getting to is that without Mel, I was lost. Completely lost. I picked up cigarettes — dropped them quickly. I guess we're meant to be smokers or not. I'd tried drinking at night, and it just depressed me worse. Raoul told me about True Life. I was ready to try anything to get over the pain."

"So . . . ?" Craig asked.

"Well, they are a bit archaic. I guess it was okay for me to be a nurse, and I think if I'd been a teacher that would have been okay. Pink collar jobs, you know? But I found out that me joining the church meant I didn't really go to any services. I prayed with Amy and a few other women, meeting at their apartment a few times a week. And while we were there, we knit or we sewed, always something constructive. I guess that part wasn't so bad. Raoul saw to it we sent our work to areas that needed help, you know. We gave to cities when hurricanes hit, when fires destroyed a place."

"Are you still a member of the church, or how long did you stay?" Mike asked.

Candy smiled sadly at them. "I guess I'm one of those people who is just more traditional. I certainly didn't mind knitting sweaters for those in disaster zones, but . . . I wasn't feeling any closer to God by listening to Amy Nicholson talk about a 'woman's place' in the world." She made a little face. "I'm one good nurse, have a half dozen degrees, and feel very much that my place in the world is — for so many hours per week, at the least — helping those in the hospital."

"How did Raoul behave when you quit?" Craig asked.

"Well, I never told him that I quit, per se. I didn't want to lie, so I changed my hours at the hospital so I was working nights. That was just a few months back. Raoul never challenged me, and I still asked him about his family and the other women when he came in and hoped that all was going well. He'd smile and tell me yes. I guess at that time his murders were progressing well," she said, irony in her voice.

"What about the other members of the church?" Mike asked.

She shook her head. "Men and women didn't mingle. Supposedly, there were certain occasions when they did, but I wasn't around for any of them. But . . . well, the good things the man did were for real. I went to the post office often enough, sending off care packages."

"Do you know any of the other women through any other ways? Did anyone work at your hospital? Were there any other nurses or women you saw here?" Mike asked her.

She shook her head. "At most there were ten of us. I can give you first names, but . . . not sure how that would help. I can describe them, but I think they were mostly moms, and their husbands were the breadwinners. One, Millie, worked at a day care center. I never saw any of the men — other than Raoul himself. I knew he had sons, but he said they were at the age when they found themselves, and learned the church gave them what they really needed." She glanced at her watch. "My shift starts soon. I have to go."

"If you can think of anything else —" Mike began.

"Oh, I've been thinking. And thinking and thinking!" Candy said. "I've thought of little else, especially since he escaped. But yeah, I'll get in touch with you. And if you think there's anything else I might answer, well, I am here every morning, or you can find me at the hospital."

"Just one more thing. Annie told us he often talked to Bethany Sears, the young woman at the counter now. Was she a member as well?"

"No, but I think Raoul suggested to her she should be. Her parents died about a year ago, and she got mixed up with the wrong crowd. She was seeing a man who was bad news — a dealer. She almost went down with him, but . . . she would have joined, I think. Raoul made her feel better. But that's all I know."

They both stood as she left. When she was gone, Craig saw that the man, Xavier Green, was standing just behind Bethany Sears. He nodded to them, and both rose to come join him and Mike. Introductions went around, and the two of them slid into the booth, taking seats.

Xavier Green cleared his throat. "I knew Raoul because I liked to play devil's advocate with him."

"How so?" Craig asked.

"I'd challenge his beliefs, and he'd put me down every time. Nicholson believed this life was meant for us all to be in service. The body was like a suit we wore whether we liked the design or not. I talked to him about simple morality, about being the best human beings we could be. I loved to argue there were wonderful things to be found in traditional religions, like the Ten Commandments, loving thy brother as thyself, the peace tenet of the Buddhists. And I liked to argue I knew a bunch of atheists who were good people, too — who happened to live well in their earthly suits, and simply because it was the right thing to do, they were good to others. He never minded debating with me, but he was absolutely convinced some people weren't people at all, they were demons in human suits and there was no saving them. There was only stopping them."

"Raoul was good in an argument," Bethany said. She was in her midtwenties, Craig thought, with a freckled nose, a slim face, and amber eyes. She was plain in her manner and dress, and spoke quietly, without the electric enthusiasm that made Annie such an appealing person. "I would listen when he would argue with Xavier, and I loved the sound of his voice. He was hypnotic, and he was so kind to me. He knew I almost went to jail, big-time. But I was innocent of everything except for hanging on to the wrong guy because he actually paid attention to me. I — I don't really date. I'm horribly awkward, and . . . well, I was going to join his church. I needed . . ."

"Friends, but real friends," Xavier said. He was closer to forty, his denim shirt and jeans suggesting he worked in one of the construction trades. He seemed protective of Bethany.

She probably had no idea he really liked her, Craig thought. Maybe, because she'd had that bad relationship and in her mind only a drug dealer could love her, she didn't realize someone else might care about her, too. "You never joined the church, though?" Craig asked.

"No, but I thanked him often. I thanked him for talking to me, and I told him I was

314

thinking about it, seriously. The only thing was . . ."

"Was?"

"I'm in banking — trust — and I just became an associate. That's really not an acceptable job, not for a woman in True Life. Though I bet with him out of the picture, there won't be a True Life anymore. He was the power of speech and belief behind it all. I guess he believed in it all too much."

"There could still be a church," Xavier said. "When he talked, he talked of his lieutenant, or his 'right-hand man.' Maybe he's taking over. I'm thinking Nicholson's wife, Amy, might know about that."

"She just might," Craig said.

"I have to get to work," Bethany said.

"Yeah, me, too," Xavier told them.

Craig and Mike stood so the two could leave, thanking them, and handing out contact cards. When they were gone, Mike sank back into the booth, looking at Craig.

"Still no idea of where the man could be now," he grumbled.

"No, but we'll have a nice talk with Amy now, and . . ." His phone dinged with an incoming message. He paused, checking to see what he'd received. It was an email from the prosecutor on the Nicholson case. "We just got our search warrant."

Mike nodded. "Great." He lifted his hand, smiling over at their server. He motioned the drawing up of a check.

"Interesting that Nicholson liked Kieran so much," Mike said, standing to take the check as it arrived.

"How's that?" Craig asked, as they headed to the cash register to pay.

"She's hardly Miss Domestic. I don't mean she's a mess, or anything, but I don't see her in any little basic ladies' group, chatting away meekly while doing her obligatory knitting. I mean, knitting is great. I know a ton of professional women who knit. And a few guys. What I meant is, she's not . . ."

"Meek or mild," Craig said. "I understand what you're saying. And come to think of it, I never have seen her knit anything. She tends to be on the computer or have her head in a book during off-hours . . . or working at the pub." He frowned and shook his head. "She definitely wouldn't be a good candidate for Nicholson's recruitment."

"So what about this lieutenant guy of his?" Mike asked.

Craig shrugged. "There has to be a chink in all this church armor somewhere. Come on, let's get over to Amy's. Even if women are in the background in her world, she'd have to know more than the others. She was his wife. And if they went anywhere, on retreats, to pray . . . I have a feeling she knows where her husband might be, even if she doesn't know it herself. We have to get through to her. Nicholson is out there somewhere, and we need to find him."

Kieran had barely gotten into her office and logged on to her computer before the telephone rang.

Her cell phone, not the work phone.

When she picked up, all she heard was breathing.

"Buddy, get a life!" she said, and hung up.

The phone rang again. She glanced at the caller ID. The number wasn't blocked; it was just a number she didn't recognize.

She answered.

Again, the breathing.

She was about to hang up when a man's voice, low, husky, all but whispered, "I didn't do it."

She frowned, and then bit her lip, knowing her next words were critical. "Raoul? I know you didn't kill Olav Blom and Charles Mayhew. You're not . . . you're not really a killer. It would be against . . . against what you believe."

"Oh, thank you," he said. "I'm . . . I was

317

never afraid of meeting man's justice, but now . . ."

"Raoul, who did kill him?" she asked.

There was silence on the other end. She heard strange scuffling noises, as if, perhaps, he had covered the phone with his hand.

"Raoul, please . . . it's important we get you get back into custody. Someone is killing people, trying to make it appear that it is you. Raoul?"

"Kieran." She heard his voice, and then he was gone again.

She didn't want to hang up; she wished she'd been at a police station or at FBI headquarters, somewhere a call could be traced.

She knew even if the call ended, experts might get an idea of where he had called from. But by the time she could get that information, he might be long gone.

"Raoul? Please, where are you? I want to help you."

"An —"

His voice went away.

What had he been trying to tell her?

She thought about the man she'd seen standing on the corner watching her apartment building that morning.

Not John Nicholson.

Maybe, just maybe . . . Raoul?

"I have to go . . . can you . . . help me. I need to . . ."

He went away again. She heard a tone and glanced at the screen. The call had ended. It had been Raoul Nicholson, and he was gone.

She stared at her phone; he'd called her. He wanted help. He wanted it proved he killed only those he saw as witches. He must feel outraged, of course. Others might not understand, but he had made himself clear enough — he killed only evil.

And it sounded as if he was afraid.

She hesitated just a minute, in case Raoul called back, but when the phone stayed silent she called Craig.

"Hey, Kieran. I'm with Mike. I'm doing the driving — thank God — but you're on speakerphone."

"No R-rated conversation," she heard Mike say. "And definitely nothing rated X!"

"You okay?" Craig asked.

"I'm fine. I'm in my office, and Special Agent DeLuca is out in the lobby with Jake. The doctors are in, and I'm nice and safe. But Craig . . . Mike, I just heard from Raoul Nicholson."

"What?" Craig said sharply.

She hoped he hadn't driven off the road.

"Nicholson — he called me. He sounds

319

scared. He told me he didn't do it. I mean, we've all thought as much. He didn't kill Mayhew and he didn't kill Olav Blom. I believe him, because he was ready to confess when it came to those he did kill. He doesn't want to be blamed."

"Where is he?"

"I don't know. He started to say something, but I don't know where he was. I don't know if he was with someone who scared him . . . I just don't know."

"Get your phone to the lab at headquarters. Marty Kim is a whiz with computers, phones, getting whatever data is possible. You said Milo DeLuca is with you, right?"

"Yes. Let me just check with the doctors. I don't think I have a session until this afternoon, but I can just give the phone to Milo and he can —"

"No. See if you can both go. Let me know."

"Okay. Where are you going?"

"Amy Nicholson's apartment. She has to know something. I'm not hanging up now because I'd rather not answer while we're there. Find out now and get right back to me."

Kieran ran out of her office, headed to see the doctors; they were together, going through court cases, new, closed, and those instances in which therapy had been court ordered.

"I — I got a call from Raoul Nicholson. Craig wants me to get my phone down to his office where the techs can trace the area the call came from," she said. "May I —"

"Yes!" Fuller said.

"By all means," Miro told her.

"I'll be back before my next patient to look over her chart again before she comes in," Kieran promised. She was counseling a woman named Jennie Peterson, who had started stripping as a way to pay for college. She hadn't worked in the nicest place. She'd started on drugs to endure what she was doing, then she'd been booted out of school and life had gone downhill. She'd stolen from a mom-and-pop jewelry store — with cameras. Since the owners were good people, they had come to court and asked for probation, that Jennie work, do community service, and go to therapy.

Jennie was likable, and really trying. Not just paying lip service. Kieran had also dealt with those who were only saying what they believed she wanted to hear. She wanted to see Jennie come through this with the tools to help herself. "Hey, plenty of time to drop off that phone and have lunch out of the office," Fuller said. "I see you with your tuna sandwiches often enough."

"Chicken salad," Kieran said, grinning.

"Pardon?" Fuller said.

"My sandwiches. I do like tuna, but they're usually chicken salad."

She left them and turned her attention to her cell, assuring Craig that she could get the phone to the FBI right away.

Hanging up, she headed to the reception area to tell Milo they were on the road again.

As they drove, she kept thinking about the call.

An. *What the hell had* An *meant?* An *what?*

And then, in a flash, she thought she knew.

"Amy, we know you love your husband. And we need your help."

Amy Nicholson had let Craig and Mike into her apartment with no argument at all. She had insisted on making them tea.

Craig had insisted on helping her in the kitchen. She was, after all, the devoted wife of a convicted serial killer. He didn't want to discover too late their tea had been drugged or poisoned. Not that he thought she shared any of her husband's inclinations. The killing of witches or anyone else probably wouldn't be in the category of what women were sanctioned to do in Raoul

Nicholson's heavily chauvinistic church.

Craig had watched the Lipton's tea bags come out of the box, and he laid out the home-baked little shortbread cookies on the tray himself, determined they'd watch her eat one before indulging themselves. Then they sat in the parlor and talked.

He didn't see a speck of dust in the handsome, well-kept room. The carpet showed signs of vacuuming, and the pillows on the sofa were plumped. The covers had been hand-knit — the yarn in colors that spelled out True Life.

"I came into the offices, you know. Your director, that nice Mr. Egan, asked me if I'd come in. I spoke with the psychiatrist —"

"Psychologist," Mike corrected.

"Psychologist?" Amy repeated, and smiled. "Well, whatever, that lovely Miss Finnegan. Raoul had told me she'd visited him and talked with him. I can't emphasize enough that my husband loved me. Loves me. He just wouldn't involve me. I'm a wife, a mother —"

"We've met your sons, Mrs. Nicholson. They're grown and gone," Craig said.

She shook her head, smiling serenely. "They'll come back, and they'll need me, and my husband knows this. He won't come near me. He won't put me in any kind of jeopardy."

Amy had consumed a cookie. Mike was living dangerously, trying one himself.

Craig leaned forward. "Amy, we need to know more about your church. I understand the men and women don't mix."

"We each have our roles in life," Amy said. She waved a dismissive hand in the air. "Oh, I hear all this talk about equality all the time. But there are just some facts that have to do with life. We're built differently. We're built to procreate, and the husband should be the breadwinner, and the wife the care-giver, the nurturer. That goes back to the dawn of humanity, when our higher power was arranging the great knowledge we would come into. Cavemen hunted. The women kept the home — or the cave, back then." She paused and smiled, as if showing them she did have a sense of humor. Then she sighed. "It's just so hard to make you people understand. You're just not among the chosen. I feel bad that I don't have Raoul's talent in helping you see the truth."

"Interesting," Mike said. "Jim Jones claimed his people were the chosen, and over nine hundred of them died. Not to mention they killed a congressman and oth-ers who wanted to leave. Imagine — giving cyanide to children and babies."

Craig nudged Mike's foot with his own. Yes, the thought made anyone rational ill.

But they needed information from this woman.

"What did your husband like to do for fun, Amy?" Craig asked.

"Fun?" she queried.

"Didn't the two of you ever have fun?" Mike prompted.

"Oh, I see what you mean. You had to have known him —"

"We did meet Raoul," Craig reminded her.

"Yes, of course, but you don't know him," Amy said. "Fun. He was a happy man when we went to the post office with supplies for the lost and the hungry. He was happy when we sat here together, sipping tea, knowing we were . . . we were walking a true path."

"Did you ever go anywhere on vacation?" Mike asked.

"Vacation?" She repeated the word as if she didn't really understand it.

"Some people go to the mountains, a way to get out of the city," Craig said. "Some like to head south to the beaches down in Florida. Some like to visit historic sites."

She smiled. "Our world was right here," she said.

"What can you tell us about the members of the church?"

"Nothing, and I know my legal rights," she said sharply. "My beliefs are protected. This is America. You just want to persecute us. I will not help you persecute my husband's flock."

"Is the church still going?" Mike asked.

"Isn't faith truly in the heart of the faithful?" Amy asked. She set her cup and saucer down abruptly and stood. "You may leave now. And you can have your judges throw me in jail, too, if you wish. I will not betray our church members. I'll — I'll sic Raoul's lawyer on you, I will!" she said angrily.

Craig lowered his head. "I'm so sorry, Amy," he said. "We're not leaving just yet. We have a search warrant for these premises. I have officers waiting just outside. They'll escort you to the street, or if you like, you may remain by the front door."

"Search warrant!" she cried. "You're searching for what?"

"Something that will give us your husband's whereabouts," Craig said. "Since you claim you love him but don't seem to want to get him safely back into custody."

She drew herself up to her full height, staring at them as if she were royalty about to go to the block. "You do your worst — just do your worst! You are nothing, do you understand? You are nothing, and my husband is a great man, and you will learn when the reckoning comes!"

"Let's hope you do, too," Mike told her.

Craig didn't bother to speak; he headed to the door where agents and officers from the local precinct were waiting with the search warrant to hand over to Amy — and then look everywhere they could, seeking anything that might be a clue, if not an answer.

An.

The beginning of the word *Annie's?*

Most probably. It was a place Nicholson loved. So she figured she'd stay downtown after dropping off her phone at the FBI offices. She could go over her notes for her afternoon appointment anywhere, since she had brought her laptop.

Annie's was downtown.

Finnegan's was downtown.

And her apartment wasn't far.

Kieran loved her city — New York. Some hated it; some loved it. Many came for the shopping, others for the theater. To some, it was a financial mecca, and to many an immigrant, the entry into a new world, a new life.

But there was so much more to love. The city offered spectacular museums and libraries, and history that was fascinating. And while the city had a past that included various prejudices and injustices, on the whole, people of any ethnicity, color, sex, and so on could find the American dream in New York City. New York remained, in her mind, one of the greatest multicultural cities in the world.

During their drives that day, she and Milo talked about New York. He was a native of Brooklyn, and enthusiastic about the city, as well. "I couldn't afford to see *Hamilton* when it came out. I finally got tickets through the lottery," Milo told her. "But my friends always reminded me I could go to Trinity Churchyard and visit the real thing — or the grave of the real thing anytime I wanted."

"My brother arranged for tickets for me," Kieran admitted. "Pays to have a theater guy for a twin."

"I look up so often people think I'm a tourist. Love the old buildings, the work you see on the exteriors."

He found legitimate parking in a lot about a block down from Annie's, and within easy access of Finnegan's and Kieran's apartment. As they walked to Annie's, he remarked that Wall Street had been a wall, and that Broad Street had been, of course, broad.

"The downtown area is to me so amazing. Traces of what went on hundreds of years ago, along with the fact the city is now millions and millions of people, and high-rises are here, there, and anywhere, right along with some really old buildings," he said.

He pointed to the modern frontage of the coffee shop as they approached it. "Wonder what happened around here? So many buildings went up flush against each other, and then you have weird alleys, sometimes barely wide enough for a human body. Well, I guess bodies fit."

When they entered, Annie was behind the cash register.

"That's Annie?" Milo whispered.

"It is."

"She looks a little like you. Well, with paler hair. A little shorter, but she is a blue-eyed redhead. Of course, she doesn't quite have your bone structure. Whoops, don't tell Special Agent Frasier I said that. Don't want him to think I'm horning in."

"I don't think you have any worries," Kieran assured him.

The lunch crowd was thinning out. By the time they had brought the phone up to Craig's office and turned it over to Egan, gotten back in the car and found parking, it was past two.

"Annie, is this one all right?" Kieran asked, pointing to a booth near the register.

"Of course — and welcome!" Annie smiled at Milo, who smiled back.

He'd apparently failed to note Annie was probably a few years younger than she was, too, maybe in her midtwenties, where Kieran had now reached — and just slightly passed — the grand old age of thirty.

"She's very cute," Milo said.

Kieran smiled, leading him to the table. "Yes, she is. I'm sorry to say I don't know her well enough to tell you if she's dating or not. We've only met once before. Anyway, take a look at the menu. It's extensive. The place is almost as good as Finnegan's," she said lightly.

He picked up his menu. She glanced idly out the window.

And that's when she saw him.

Raoul Nicholson.

He was in a trench coat, with a brimmed hat pulled low over his head. He had grown something of a scruffy mustache and short beard in the few days he'd been on the loose, altering his appearance.

He looked at her desperately through the glass, and then looked at Milo, shaking his head with dismay.

He turned away, heading toward the rear of the building.

She didn't think; she was just certain he had been telling her the truth, and she had to see him.

Alone, so that he didn't run off. Nicholson himself might be their best chance of catching a copycat killer.

She jumped up. "Ladies' room!" she announced, giving Milo no chance to react, and took off, hopefully slipping out the door without him seeing her.

She burst outside and looked up and down the street. She didn't see Nicholson. Then she realized there was a tiny opening — barely wide enough for two people to walk through — to the side of the building. It had not been built flush against its neighbor.

She moved along the street to that narrow alleyway.

And she turned, knowing he would be there.

He was, but he wasn't alone. He was far down the length of the building. For a minute she couldn't see what he was doing. He appeared to be with another man.

But the other man . . .

She began to scream, calling for help, calling for anyone . . .

Wishing desperately now she'd let Milo know what she was doing.

CHAPTER FOURTEEN

Craig and Mike joined the team searching through the Nicholson apartment.

The man had kept an office, obviously taken over by his wife in his absence. The tech team had already bagged the computer. Whatever files Nicholson had kept would be on it. He had no file cabinets and seemed to keep no files — not even bills — with a physical paper record.

Nicholson had, however, kept a notepad by his computer, but it was blank. Craig picked it up and walked to the window, playing with the light, trying to see if any written impressions were on it.

With gloved hands, Mike was going through the little wicker trash basket next to the desk. The NYPD had sent officers as part of the task team force — and it was a good thing, because it turned out they were needed to watch over Amy Nicholson, who had to be restrained from attacking the agents and tech team as they went through the apartment. For such a devout woman, Amy had a lot of venom to spew at them as they went through her apartment.

"I will have my husband's attorney sue the NYPD and the FBI, and you will be sorry! My husband broke your laws, but I did nothing! You have no right!" she had told them.

Craig wondered if she had spoken with Nicholson's long-suffering attorney. She had made a phone call, just one, after they'd informed her of the upcoming search, and since she didn't want to involve her husband's "flock," he could only assume she had called the attorney.

He didn't arrive right away, but that didn't surprise either Craig or Mike. They knew Cliff Watkins, Esquire, still wondered how he'd had the bad luck to draw this client when the firm had decided to take him on pro bono.

Amy continued shouting, calling the officers many things Craig hadn't heard in any kind of religious group — ever.

"I've got something!" Mike said, smoothing out a paper.

"Yeah?" Craig slipped the notepad he'd taken into an evidence bag and hunkered down by Mike. "What is it?"

"I don't know. What do you think this means?" Mike asked.

The piece of paper he'd drawn from the trash had been written on hard — so hard the paper had nearly torn. Mike held it carefully.

Whoever had written on it had been angry — very angry. They had written down one biblical line, with a bit of an addition.

Suffer not a witch . . . not evil asses!

"Interesting. Not so . . . perfectly holy, I'm thinking," Mike said.

Craig studied the handwriting.

"We have examples of Nicholson's writing at the offices," Mike said. "And if he wrote this . . . well, I'm wondering now just how pure his motives were. Witches — and asses. Maybe it's against Nicholson's higher power just to be a jerk."

"Maybe. And maybe his wife wrote it. She's hard to read. All her protesting may be too much. Maybe she wants out and a normal life like her sons," Craig mused. "Except . . ."

"Yeah?"

"Nicholson had a lieutenant — a right-hand man. If she wanted out so badly, wouldn't she just tell us who he is and get us questioning him?"

"Think she's afraid?"

"Could be. Though, if you listen to her now, she's the scary one." Craig grinned. "She's thrown out a few words I think I've only heard a handful of times in my life."

One of the special agents from tech paused at the doorway to the office. "We've been through the bedrooms — nothing but clothing. And it doesn't appear anyone male has been here anytime recently. No men's clothing, except for clean suits, etcetera, hung up in the closet. And neatly folded underwear, T-shirts, and so on in the drawers. It doesn't appear there are any pieces of men's clothing in a laundry basket anywhere. No papers of any kind in any of the rooms." He hesitated. "You know what's weird that we haven't found?"

"What?" Craig asked.

"A Bible, or any other kind of religious text."

"He paraphrases the Bible when he chooses, but maybe his higher power is different from anything we consider the norm," Craig said. "What about the kitchen, dining room and so on?"

"Everything clean, except for the tea service in the parlor area. Everything is put away."

"I guess cleanliness is next to godliness," Mike murmured. "Or higher power-ness, whatever."

"Are we done here?" the tech asked.

"Yeah," Craig said, handing him the bagged notepad and the little piece of paper. "We need to know if that is Nicholson's writing, or his wife's."

"We have Amy's writing?"

"She had to sign in when she came to the offices," Craig said. "Yes, we have samples from both. If Amy wrote them, well, we know she is one angry person. But if that anger is really against us, or the life she was forced to lead and the notoriety she'll now bear all her life, I'm not sure. If Nicholson wrote them, then there is a possibility he came here, and we can bring Amy back in with a subpoena."

They heard a commotion from the front hall and headed out.

Cliff Watkins had arrived at last, looking harried — and frustrated. He was speaking with Amy, trying to calm her down.

"Amy, yes, they have a right to do this. They have a search warrant, a legal document signed by a judge, allowing them to search," Watkins explained.

"They're getting their filthy hands all over my things! This isn't right — I didn't do anything."

"Amy, they're all wearing gloves," Watkins

said. "Their 'filthy' hands really aren't filthy, and a judge signed that warrant. It's legal. And, please, just calm down. It's natural. They're trying to find Raoul. You're his wife. This was his home."

Amy let out a breath and seemed to give up.

"May I sit?" she asked.

"Yes, of course," Cliff said. "Make yourself comfortable in the parlor, and the officer will just stand there. They won't touch you." He sighed deeply, looking over at Craig and Mike with weary eyes. "Are you almost done here? Was it necessary to upset her so?"

"We didn't do anything upsetting other than show her the warrant," Mike said.

"And we are almost done here," Craig assured her. He felt his cell phone buzzing in his pocket. Looking at it, he saw that Egan was on the line.

"Get over to Annie's Sunrise," Egan told him. "There's been — an attack."

Sirens filled the air. Police and medical personnel crammed against each other in the small alley.

Kieran was still there, next to Milo, who told the EMTs what measures he had taken while the man on the street was carefully lifted onto a gurney.

The victim was breathing.

Kieran's screams had alerted everyone on the busy street. She didn't know who had dialed 911, but she had to believe Milo De-Luca would one day be a very good agent. He had been there so quickly.

When Nicholson had seen her, he'd disappeared.

He'd been holding the man on the ground in his arms. At the sound of her scream, he had stood, looked down the length of the narrow alley right at her, then turned and run.

As the EMTs picked up the gurney and shouted for space to move, Kieran leaned against the wall, trying to make sense of what she had seen and what had happened.

First . . . Nicholson had looked into the window, shaking his head at Milo, then moving on. He'd worn a coat and a hat, but he hadn't been carrying anything — certainly not a container of gasoline.

Second . . . She had followed him, no time at all passing.

Third . . . She had seen him in the alley, down on the ground with the victim.

Fourth . . . She had screamed like a banshee, and a passerby on the street ran over in confusion. Someone surely had dialed for help at that point.

Fifth . . . Milo had run in behind her as she raced down the alley, praying the man on the ground might still be alive.

Sixth . . . She never made it down on the ground to help. Milo had pushed past her, immediately checking for breath and a pulse, then forcing air into the lungs of the injured man.

Seventh . . . Mayhem.

But she had seen Raoul Nicholson down with the victim. The man had been strangled to within an inch of his life, she thought, but had Nicholson done it? Had he had the time to find a victim, surprise him, strangle him, lay him down?

Or had Nicholson surprised someone else?

The gurney was being rolled away. Milo grabbed her hand to lead her out of the alley, warning her she was going to be answering a lot of questions.

"What were you doing there?" he demanded. "That was no ladies' room!"

"Okay, I was . . . well, I saw . . ."

"You started to the ladies' room, saw Nicholson and shouted for me?" Milo asked.

She looked at him. She'd get him into just as much trouble as she would be in for following an extremely dangerous convicted murderer — without her assigned body-guard. Her reasons for not telling Milo where she was going felt very flimsy now.

She nodded, hating the way she was lying, but knowing it was best, and only part of it was a lie, anyway.

She *had* seen Nicholson and screamed bloody murder.

They reached the street, and she saw there was already crime scene tape all around. Police were milling . . . and Richard Egan was there. Annie's Sunrise wasn't far from 26 Federal Plaza, and he could have walked to them easily in the time it had taken between her initial scream and now. The victim was secured on the gurney, being quickly trotted to a waiting ambulance by two EMTs.

"So, what happened?" Egan asked, eyeing her. "Imagine — you were so close."

"Well, we'd just dropped the phone off to you, and we were in this area, and I figured it couldn't hurt to stop by here for lunch. I mean, we're close to the pub, too, but I'll head in there tonight, so it just seemed like a good idea, and you never know what I might learn . . ."

Her voice trailed off.

"We had just gotten a booth," Milo contin-ued for her. "Kieran was on her way to the ladies' room when she suddenly headed for the exit. I realized she had to have seen something that caught her attention, and I leaped up to follow her to the street, and —"

He broke off then, too. Kieran turned to see what had caused his sudden silence.

Craig and Mike were standing by the ambulance as the gurney was placed inside, speaking with one of the EMTs.

They then came striding over. Their expressions were grim.

"Special Agents — leaving, all set to go!" an EMT called.

They heard a policeman in uniform shout to the crowd. "Back up, back up. Let these people through!"

"I'll go with the ambulance," Mike said. "Just meet me at the hospital when you can." Mike tossed a set of car keys to his partner. Dragging his hair back from his forehead, Craig stared at their little group — Egan, Milo, and Kieran.

"What the hell happened?" he said tensely.

"They saved a man's life," Egan said. "Stopped the killer in the act."

Craig's eyes were still on Kieran. She started explaining again — with Milo's help. With both of them explaining how they'd run into the alley and scared Nicholson off,

342

the situation sounded natural — and good.

"And you just happened to be at Annie's?" Craig asked.

"No. We came here on purpose. I talked Milo into it," Kieran said.

"And you saw him, and didn't call —"

"You asked me to drop my phone off at the FBI offices," Kieran reminded him.

Craig nodded. "Yeah, I guess I did, but Milo —"

"I called Egan instantly," Milo said.

"And there had to have been someone in this alley before Nicholson," Kieran said. "We — we followed right away. There would have been no time for Nicholson to have done that. Someone had to have come in from the other end of the alley and gone out that way, before Nicholson. I think, believe it or not, Nicholson was the one who interrupted the killer. I think he was trying to see if the man was alive. I mean . . . you'd have to be here to know how quickly this all happened."

Craig nodded slowly, looking at Egan. "Sir, what do you think? Is it possible?"

"I wasn't first on the scene . . ." He paused, looking back toward the street where the police were enforcing the yellow crime scene tape. Forensic crews had arrived and were spreading out in the alley.

Egan turned to look the other way, deeper into the alley. "Cops are searching the end of this alley, assessing anywhere someone could have run. But there's a subway line just the other side of the block, so if some-one came out over there . . ." He trailed off. "Kieran, you can describe Nicholson as he's looking now, right?"

"Yes. I know he has to be apprehended, but there's no way he had the time to do this. I believe . . . I believe the man who was attacked is going to live. Maybe he'll be able to tell you what happened to him."

Craig looked at her. "Do you know who that man was?"

She frowned, shaking her head. "No. Milo was working on him, trying to make sure he was breathing . . ."

She stopped speaking, frowning.

She didn't know who the man was, but evidently Craig did.

"Who was it?" she asked.

"Simon Wrigley, head of the security company that manages Charles Mayhew's building."

"Annie, did this man come in here — often or ever?" Craig asked.

Mike had reported from the hospital that Simon Wrigley was going to live. Mike wasn't allowed to talk to him as yet. Doctors were working. The near asphyxiation had caused distress in other organs; and while they had chosen not to put Wrigley into a medically induced coma, he was still unconscious.

Mike would be sitting right outside the hospital room until Wrigley could talk. In the meantime, Craig was determined to find out what a man who ran a company with an elite clientele on the Upper East Side had been doing in an alley downtown.

"I recognize him," Annie said gravely.

Despite the crime scene tape cordoning off a circle of sidewalk beside it, Annie's Sunrise was still open to customers. Now, people were piling in, and gossip was running rampant. There was a killer on the loose; a man had nearly died.

While the police had given out no specifics, including the name of the victim, the sidewalk and the street had been busy. The attack had been seen by dozens of people, and, perhaps, people believed that more news might be forthcoming if they lingered around the crime scene.

"So, you know Mr. Wrigley? He comes here often?"

"I wouldn't say *often.* A lot of my regulars work in this area, many of them on Wall

Street. It's just the way it is. You stop by for breakfast where it's conveniently on your way to work. But I believe I've seen him here . . . maybe four or five times."

"Did he come with anyone else?" Craig asked.

"I think so . . . yes, once he came with a young man in some kind of uniform. They sat at one of the booths. It was . . . early, I think. Breakfast. I didn't get to talk to him that day. We were busy," Annie told him.

"But was he in here today — before he was attacked?" Craig asked her.

She shook her head. "No." She kept looking to the register. Her staff was running about like a bevy of very busy bees, and he was about to let her go, saying, "Thank you, Annie. Just one more thing. Did you ever see him speaking with Raoul Nicholson when he was in?"

"I don't think so, but I don't notice everything that goes on here. I stop to talk to people in the booths and to those at the counter, but . . . I don't know. I'm sorry. I just don't know."

She appeared to be distressed. He smiled at her and thanked her for all her help.

"I'm sorry. I'm a little flustered right now . . . I . . . I'm happy to help you at any time you need."

He started to leave the shop, but paused when he heard someone at a table talking.

"Man, that could have been me. I come in through that alley from the subway all the time. But I know it's there and that it goes through. A lot of people don't, but . . . then again, I've seen people follow me — guess they figured I knew where I was going."

It was a young man in a suit doing the talking.

A Wall Street suit, he thought.

Craig paused by the table. The man was sitting with another slightly older man in a similar suit and a young woman in a skirt, tailored blouse, and jacket.

They looked up at him as he produced his billfold with his badge and ID.

"Hey, is the guy all the excitement was over going to live?" the woman asked.

"Hopefully," Craig said. He looked at the young man who had been talking about the alley. "You come through that alley all the time?" he asked.

"All the time."

"But not many people do?"

"If you walk around the block that way, you'll see — it looks like nothing. Like it ends at the building on the other side, but there's a little turn. You have to know it's there. Always surprised me. Most buildings are kind of wall-to-wall, especially down here. When you get to the ritzier areas, you may see more open spaces and fewer shared walls. But it makes it really easy to get over here, when the sidewalks, especially at certain times of the day, are as crowded as the streets."

"People gridlock," the other man said.

"I'd have never been in that alley," the woman said. "Once it starts getting dark, it's like no light penetrates at all. Creepy. But I guess those who hang around here do come to know it. Now that this has happened . . ." She looked across the table at the man who had spoken first "Don't you dare go down that alley anymore! If that man hadn't been seen . . ." Her voice trailed off.

Craig thanked them and went back outside. He walked down the alley, moving carefully lest he disturb the crime scene crew on-site, pausing at one time to show his badge to the head of the team.

He traveled down the narrow strip by the building that housed Annie's Sunrise, taking it all the way to the end and turning to where it led out to the sidewalk on the other side.

It remained narrow on both sides, little

more than enough space for two people to walk abreast.

When he reached the sidewalk, he saw the stairs down to the subway were just another twenty feet down the block.

Nicholson could have escaped that way.

So could have anyone else who might have been there.

He wondered if Kieran was right, and tried to put together the timing of the previous two hours. If she was correct in her assessment, someone had come through the alley from the end by the subway. That person had either followed Simon Wrigley or come upon him accidentally.

Wrigley had been strangled to the point of lost consciousness.

Had death been intended? Had the killer carried a knife to cut out the tongue and a grapefruit spoon for the eyes and a can of gasoline to torch the victim?

Raoul Nicholson?

Or had the Fireman actually stopped another from imitating his methods?

Two killers. They'd suspected it. And the other killer was someone who must have frequented Annie's Sunrise, someone who knew Raoul Nicholson.

His lieutenant, his right-hand man?

349

But what did it have to do with Simon Wrigley?

Craig headed back out to the street where the Bureau car remained, watched over by the officers still at the scene while the crime scene crew continued to pick up every bit of trash, every cigarette butt, anything they could find in the narrow alley.

Most of it would mean nothing.

But anything could mean something.

At the car he looked in the direction of Federal Plaza; he knew Kieran was there with Milo and Egan, and they were filing reports. They were safe; they were fine. He needed to get to the hospital. There was a solid chance Simon Wrigley might have seen his attacker.

And if so, all the answers might be waiting for them, locked in the mind of an unconscious man.

Kieran went over the events that had just occurred again, this time without Milo De-Luca at her side.

They were both supposed to report everything just as they had seen it occur.

The agent in charge took her testimony before she went to sit in Egan's office to wait for Craig to come back, which she thought might be a long time.

But then her phone rang, and it was Craig. "You just happened to be at that coffee shop," he said dryly, without preamble.

"No, I told you. I went there on purpose."

"Why? You already stalked Annie."

"I didn't stalk her!" Kieran protested. "Craig, I can't help it. I —"

"It's all right. You went to a coffee shop. You happened to see Nicholson, or maybe he followed you there. He was either in the act of attempted murder on Simon Wrigley, or saving Simon Wrigley from a killer. Either way, Simon Wrigley should be extremely grateful you were there. Because if Nicholson was saving Wrigley, he wouldn't have gone so far as to call the cops or EMTs."

"You haven't been able to talk to Simon Wrigley yet?"

"Not yet."

"Craig, I need you to know that I really don't believe Nicholson was trying to kill Simon Wrigley. I've said since the start that he only ever killed people the voice he heard told him to. And we know someone called him as the 'voice.' I think someone found people who did have problems, physical problems or mental problems. They might have been a danger to others, even inadvertently. The voice found these people and told Nicholson to kill them, but how did they choose the victims? Maybe they knew about them because of access to medical records, or maybe even just knew the victims. But Charles Mayhew was very rich, and probably had his fingers in a million schemes. If we just knew what kind of thing he was up to . . ."

"Egan has forensic accountants working on his books," he told her. "And on Olav Blom's accounting, as well, though honestly, I think Blom just happened to be a means to an end." He was quiet a moment. "I've started to think Nicholson's wife, beneath her tragic little housewife appearance, is more deranged than her husband, but she was at her apartment when all this happened today. There has been a man watching Thomas and John Nicholson, and they were at Thomas's apartment all day. They received a food delivery right about the time this all happened, as well. Right now, I'm hoping Wrigley wakes up soon, and he can tell us exactly what happened."

He paused for a second, then went on. "But I called you to tell you Milo has asked to stay on as your guard detail. He'll take you to the pub and hang around until I'm able to get there tonight. Don't go out the door chasing after people, huh?"

She chose to ignore his jab. "I think that

I'm going to head to the apartment first and pick up Ruff. That's all right with you, right?"

"Sure. Just keep Milo with you. He seems to be doing a good job of looking after you — whatever crazy thing you decide to do."

"Hey —"

"Since I can't always be there with you," he went on. She smiled, relieved he wasn't too angry at her. "Stay safe, Kieran, okay? I'll see you at the pub."

"I love you," she said softly.

"I love you, too. I just wish . . ."

"What?"

"That you'd stop being right in the middle of things when they're all going south!"

"Probably not going to happen," she said quietly, only half joking. "We'll talk."

"Yes, we will."

She hit the end button on her phone and sat behind Egan's desk, thoughtful. She knew the Bureau was a well-oiled machine, and there were a score of people dedicated to finding out everything that could be discovered. They could track money trails and activity; and in the age of the internet, they could even find out what kind of cologne a person might buy.

But there had to be something they should be looking for they didn't know they should be looking for — someone who needed to be investigated they hadn't investigated.

There was a knock at the door and she sat up. Milo poked his head in.

"Ready?"

The afternoon was nice, storm clouds and rain not on the horizon, and Kieran suggested they just leave the car in the lot and walk. Milo agreed; traffic was growing heavy. It would take about ten minutes to reach her apartment on foot. It might be a good twenty minutes if they sat in rush hour.

As they walked, she told him, "Thank you."

"For?"

"Saving my ass."

"Thank you for saving mine," he said with a grin. Then he grew somber. "Seriously, Kieran, if something happens again, please let me know."

She sighed. "Nicholson indicated he wouldn't talk to me unless I was alone."

"But tell me anyway. Because I can follow discreetly — and at least I'd know you might get into trouble."

"But I didn't get into trouble."

"No, we might have saved a life."

"We just might have!"

At her building, Kieran put a happy Ruff on his leash, and they started back out.

"He's not supposed to be in a restaurant, is he?"

"Not really. I'm planning on sneaking him back to the office."

"What if you have a nasty customer who wants to complain? Wait — I know. Finnegan's just doesn't get nasty customers."

"Well, we've had a few who weren't just nasty . . . they were criminal," she said. "But just because you're a criminal doesn't mean you're not a dog lover."

"I got you covered," Milo said. He reached beneath his jacket and produced a small folded cloth with a belt around it.

She looked at him with curiosity.

"It lets people know he is a service dog. It's cheating a little, but only a little. Ruff has been a service dog on this, providing a tremendous service, really."

Kieran smiled. "It will do for our present situation," she said. "Thank you."

She still intended to keep Ruff in Declan's office. She didn't know the little dog well enough yet to know how he'd behave in a noisy pub with all kinds of people. "I think," Milo said as they walked, "I might just start having breakfast before coming on duty. I saw on the sign that Annie's Sunrise opens at 6:00 a.m."

"You like Annie, hmm?"

355

"You think she's married or in a relationship?"

"I have no idea."

"You could ask her for me."

"Milo, we're looking for a killer."

"Yes, and her place seems a magnet for suspects, so . . . what's not to like about combining business and pleasure? You could ask a few questions for me. Nothing too serious — just, is she in a steady relationship? Is she open to a handsome G-man? I am kind of cute at least, right?"

Kieran laughed. "Adorable," she assured him.

"Hey, life goes on. I intend to rise in the Bureau, but it doesn't mean I want to spend my nights alone." He grimaced.

"Gotcha. We'll find out about Annie."

The pub was right ahead. She paused to dress Ruff in the little coat that proclaimed him a service dog, then swept him up. Milo opened the door for her and they went in.

When an alarm went off and a nurse rushed into the room, Craig shot a look at Mike and then, policy or no, he rushed in behind the nurse.

Thankfully, Simon Wrigley hadn't flatlined.

He'd awakened fighting, apparently en-

356

gaged in the battle in the alley that had almost killed him.

"Mr. Wrigley, Mr. Wrigley," the nurse said, trying to pin his arms and calm him. "You're all right, you're all right. You're in the hospital."

She caught one of the wild-eyed man's arms; she almost got a good wallop to the jaw with the other, but Craig got hold just in time and stopped the swing.

The nurse looked at him appreciatively.

"Mr. Wrigley, it's Special Agent Frasier. You're in the hospital. You're all right now. You're being guarded. You're all right."

The desperate look remained in Wrigley's powder-light eyes for several seconds, then his muscles eased, and he spoke in a hoarse whisper.

"Hospital."

"Yes, sir. You were attacked in the alley by Annie's Sunrise."

Craig heard Mike come in quietly and stand a few feet behind him. The nurse was still there, but she had backed away, too.

Waiting.

Wrigley frowned, confusion wresting across his features. He stared at Craig and demanded, "Why?"

"We don't know. Do you?"

Wrigley shook his head, at a loss.

"Sir, this is important. Who attacked you?" Craig said.

"Why?" Wrigley repeated. "I — I'm in the office most of the time. We never have problems. Mayhew . . . Blom . . . the ice chute. Those were the only . . . only failings we've ever had. Why?"

Craig could barely hear his words; he had to lean close.

"Sir, did you see anyone approach you?"

"I don't know," Wrigley whispered. "I got off the subway. I was taking the alley over . . ."

He paused, his eyes widening.

"I could see someone coming from the street, then I heard someone behind me. And then . . . then felt arms. Felt the lock around my back and my neck. And I saw . . . saw someone running, coming toward me . . . couldn't breathe. Knew I was dying —"

He broke off again and stared at Craig.

"I am alive. This is a hospital."

"You are alive. It is a hospital."

"He had me. I never saw his face, never had a chance to turn. I tried to shout . . . someone was coming from the other way . . . never saw his face either. Everything just all went dark. I thought I was done. I . . . never saw either man. I . . . . I am alive," he whispered, and he looked at Craig. His absolute confusion knit his face into hard wrinkles. "Why . . . who would do this . . . to me?"

Craig heard Mike sigh deeply and then speak. "Sir, that's what we were hoping you were going to tell us."

CHAPTER FIFTEEN

Walking into the pub was apparently a bit much for Ruff.

He didn't bark, but he whined and tried to press himself into Kieran's ribs, hiding his head beneath her arm.

She figured that was a good thing; she left Milo at one of the little booths between the bar and the front door and went straight to Declan's office. "Be good!" she told the little dog as she set him down.

He cocked his head at an angle, listening to her. What went on in his dog mind, she had no idea.

She backed out slowly, closing the door. When she turned, Declan was staring at her.

"You just put a dog in my office."

"That's Ruff. I thought I told you about him. Maybe I didn't. Declan . . ."

"Okay, whatever. It's all right. He's a service dog?"

"He's definitely in my service at the moment," she said cheerfully.

"Everything all right?" he asked her.

She stared at him, brows arching. She took a deep breath, then plunged into an explanation of what had happened, leaving him to shake his head.

"You just happened to be there?" Declan asked.

"Now, you're sounding like Craig! No, I went on purpose."

"Hmm. Okay, so you want to spend your time at Sunrise Annie's. Maybe we can get Annie to come here instead."

"Maybe. Milo has a crush on her."

"Oh, there is really an Annie, and she's young and cute? Well, then, invite her in. Oh, and quit trying to meet up with Nicholson. I know you believe you're safe, but the man is a serial killer."

"I'm not a witch."

"I don't know. I think that Kevin, Danny, and I could argue that!"

"Jerk!"

He grinned, and she shook her head. Growing up with three brothers, especially her three brothers, had not been an easy task.

"You need help anywhere?" she asked.

"We're in good shape right now. Where's Craig?"

"At the hospital. They're hoping that Simon Wrigley will know who attacked him."

"Wouldn't that be nice?" Declan said. "We're covered. Sit down with your bodyguard. Poor guy. What an assignment they gave him."

She made a face at Declan, pushed him out of the way as she came behind the bar, then poured herself and Milo glasses of soda, adding limes and orange twists just because they were there.

She decided to throw a cherry into each glass, too.

"Ah, there's the sorry man of the hour," Declan murmured, coming back beside her.

She looked up. Nicholson's attorney was coming in, making a beeline for the bar, just as he had the other day.

Cliff Watkins smiled weakly when he saw her. "Working a lot," he said. She poured him a shot of whiskey, and he drained it in a swallow. "A lot," he said gravely, setting his glass on the counter.

"I guess you're in a tough place," she prompted.

He shook his head, pursing his lips. "You know, this should have been easy. The man is certifiably insane. You must see that. He should have gone immediately to a facility, something really maximum security. He should have been put away, and this should have been over. And, you know I tried to help his wife. I thought she was a poor thing, a victim in her own way. Well, she's a raving bitch. They searched her apartment today. I tried to explain there was nothing that could be done about it, that the agents had a search warrant and that it wasn't unexpected, what with her husband on the loose and her claiming to love him despite his guilt. The kids . . . they're decent. You know, I got that business sold with his blessing and do you know what? She still didn't help her kids. Two boys who got scholarships — the first graduated with honors and the second is still working his way through." He shook his head. "Hit me again, and I'll pay my bill this time and go back to work."

She poured him another shot. "You know what happened this afternoon?" she asked.

"I do. Nicholson tried to kill Simon Wrigley, that man who manages the security at the building where those other men were killed."

She hadn't seen the news, and she didn't know how it was being reported, but apparently — and luckily — she and Milo had been deep enough in the alley that, as far as the media went, they hadn't been a part of it.

"You think it was Nicholson?" she asked.

He lifted his glass to her. "*Slainte* — may this end!" he said.

She nodded. "Yes, may it end."

He set his glass on the bar along with cash to pay for his drinks. "Well, back to work," he said glumly, and he turned and left the bar, a weary slump to his shoulders.

Craig didn't want to leave the hospital until he was certain that Simon Wrigley was well-guarded.

NYPD and the FBI were both going to provide officers to watch over Simon Wrigley.

His attempted killer might not know that the man hadn't recognized his attacker. He certainly didn't know that Raoul Nicholson had been there, either attempting to kill him or save him. Mike was worn out. He made it back to the offices to check in with Egan and get Kieran's phone back, then he dropped Craig at the pub, but didn't come in. He was going straight home to bed.

"My mind is exhausted," Mike said, letting Craig out on Broadway. "I'm hoping I can turn it off. And I know you. You'll be making lists in your mind all night, too.

Then again, maybe not. You've got Kieran. Other things to do at night. Sorry, too personal. I just meant . . ."

"I thought I needed more of a life — you need to get one!" Craig teased.

"Yeah, yeah. Then again, if I know Kieran, she'll be going over it all again and again . . . You know, maybe we should set it up so that Nicholson can get to her."

"You want to use Kieran as bait?" Craig said incredulously.

"He wants to see her, and we don't believe that he's the one who killed Mayhew and Blom. And Kieran doesn't believe that Nicholson intends her any harm."

"You want to use my fiancée as bait?" Craig repeated.

"We'd never let her be in any danger. We could just make it appear that she was reachable."

"Go get some sleep, Mike. We can't use a civilian as bait."

"She's not exactly a civilian."

"She's a civilian," Craig said flatly.

Mike shrugged. "Close the damned door then, huh? Let me get out of here."

Craig was tense as he went into the pub.

Milo DeLuca, true to his word, was seated at one of the enclave tables; Kieran was behind the bar when Craig entered, talking to one of the pub's longest-standing customers, a good old Irish fellow who drank nothing but soda water — but loved the camaraderie of sitting at the bar.

Kieran flashed Craig a grimace, excused herself from chatting with the customer, and glanced Declan's way so that he knew she was leaving the bar.

"I'm ready for home," Craig told her, taking her hand and pulling her close for a quick kiss. "So ready!"

"You ate?"

"We grabbed some sandwiches at the hospital. Good enough." He handed over the plain box that held her phone.

"What is this?"

"Your phone."

"Already?"

"They have everything off it," he said. "I'm sorry — everything. But don't worry, they'll destroy any records as soon as they're done."

She smiled. "I wasn't worried."

"No Big Brother complexes, huh?"

"Well, I live with Big Brother, so it would be a rather futile complex. I just have to get Ruff," she said. Craig gave a wave to Declan at the bar, then walked over to join Milo at his table.

"Nothing from Wrigley, right?" Milo said

by way of greeting. "Kieran told me."

"Nothing, and then again, maybe they found something in the alley. They'll be testing everything. Oh, and even though everyone was rushing to save Wrigley's life, we had a photographer take pictures of the bruises on the neck. It's a long shot, but sometimes photos can be enhanced, and fingerprints can be seen in the bruises. Another long shot — they might match a fingerprint. To be honest, I don't think we're getting him that way. He wears gloves. They didn't get a thing out of Charles Mayhew's apartment, and they tore it apart." He paused. Kieran had already come from the office, Ruff in her arms, and the dog was wearing a little jacket with the words *Service Dog* on it.

He arched a brow to Kieran.

"Courtesy of Milo," she told him.

"We had a few in the office." Milo shrugged.

"Shall we go?" Craig asked.

"I'll run over and get the car," Milo told them. "I left it parked at Federal Plaza. I'll come back for you guys. Then I can drop you off. Another agent should be at the building by now."

"We can walk Ruff," Kieran said. "By the time you get the car —"

"I'll be really quick."

"Sure," Craig said. "Milo can drop us. I'm tired. We can just take Ruff outside here while we're waiting."

They followed Milo out, and Kieran let Ruff down to the sidewalk, where he found a little cutout with a small tree.

"He is a good dog. He had a good master," Craig said.

"I think we're doing the best we can for Olav Blom, keeping Ruff," Kieran said.

Craig nodded. He looked at her. "You really believe that Nicholson was trying to help Simon Wrigley today?"

"I do."

Craig shook his head. "If he's not killing people again, why did he escape?"

"Maybe the voice told him to escape? We know that at times, at least, there was an actual voice."

Craig nodded thoughtfully. "Amazing when a higher power uses a cell phone, huh?"

She didn't reply, and he smiled. Yes, her mind was working. Mike did know Kieran.

As fast as he'd promised, Milo pulled around with the car.

Back in the apartment, Kieran played with the dog and checked his water bowl and his puppy pads.

Craig acknowledged that Mike was on to something — their minds were tired. Physically, he was tired, too, but he realized he was mentally creating one of the boards they used at the office. A list of all the involved persons. There were the people at Mayhew's building, all of whom had checked out. Then again, the tenants, except for the vacationing couple, had been there when Mayhew had been killed. There were the security guards/doormen, all of whom had passed background checks and been fingerprinted and bonded before being hired. There was Nicholson's family; there were the people at the coffee shop.

He headed up to their bedroom, stripping and heading straight into the shower.

A minute later Kieran joined him, soaping his flesh, rubbing her fingers over him, her touch, beneath the steaming spray, ever more erotic.

He whirled around and embraced her, whispering against her lips.

"You do turn my mind off."

"In a good way, or a bad way?" she teased.

He grabbed the soap and began to work his fingers over her smooth, naked flesh.

"In the best way," he whispered.

She rose on her toes, the length of her

body sliding over his.

"You turn my mind off, too . . . in the very best way."

He heard the strum of the water.

And he felt her.

It wasn't until hours had passed, when they had made love, curled together and dozed, that he realized Kieran was awake again. She was at the window, looking out.

"Kieran?"

"My mind woke up," she told him.

He rose and padded over to her, drawing her away from the window and back to the bed.

"Let me turn it off again," he teased softly.

"Oh, please do," she whispered.

He did his best to oblige.

"So, we are headed to Annie's first, right?" Milo asked hopefully as he slid behind the wheel of his Bureau car, ready to escort Kieran for the day.

She smiled. "Yes, we can go to Annie's for breakfast. I can see if I can get her to sit with us for a bit. Who knows? I had wanted to go there very specifically, just to see if she had anything to say that she might not have said before, something she didn't re-alize could relate to Raoul Nicholson or people that he knew. Now, of course, we can still hope for something and find out if there is a significant other in her life."

"I love the way you think!" Milo said, but then he glanced her way again. "No taking off without me again, huh?"

"No taking off without you again," she promised.

At the coffee shop, Annie wasn't behind the register, but Blake, the young man who had waited on Kieran and Danny when she had first come to the café, came around and greeted them enthusiastically.

"Hey, welcome back, take a seat. I'll have water and menus right away. Coffee?" he asked. They nodded.

"Blake Hunter, waiter and actor," Kieran told Milo.

"Great, thank you," Milo said. They sat and he said glumly, "Not that Blake probably isn't a bad waiter, but . . ."

"Ah, but he's not Annie!" Kieran said.

"No. He's not Annie," Milo said.

"That's all right. We'll just ask for her," Kieran told him.

Blake was soon back at their table, delivering water, coffee, and menus. Kieran thanked him and then asked about Annie.

"She hasn't come in yet," Blake said.

"Is she due anytime soon?" Milo asked.

"To be honest, she's never this late. But

371

she is the boss, a great boss. I mean, we all know what to do and our head cook is always the first one in. He's here by 5:00 a.m. like clockwork. Rita there runs the counter, so we're good. And Annie is the boss. Gets to be late, I guess."

"But," Milo said, "she should be in soon."

"I expect her to come walking through that door at any time."

"Thanks," Kieran said.

They ordered the special omelets of the day, a mix of cheeses and veggies.

When Blake had gone, Milo said, "Go figure. Wrigley gets attacked, but never saw his attacker. You saw Nicholson with Wrigley, but you don't believe that Nicholson attacked him."

"You didn't see Nicholson in the alley?" Kieran asked.

"I didn't see anyone but you. I guess both of them, Nicholson and the possible other guy, disappeared down the subway. Or blended in with a crowd. In the subway you move fast, you get low, and even if cops and agents were right there, it would have only taken a matter of minutes to get down to the trains."

Kieran hesitated. She had looked to see if Nicholson had been watching her building again last night.

She had not seen him.

Maybe he had given up on trying to reach her alone.

"Yeah, it would have been easy for them to run around the corner — and to the subway — in just a matter of minutes."

Milo was looking at the door.

He frowned suddenly and cleared his throat. "Kieran?"

"What?"

"I'm worried."

"Well, the whole thing is worrisome, but —"

"No. About Annie."

"Milo, I don't think that she's that late."

"Can we at least get someone to call her — check up on her?"

"Well, I can suggest it —"

"Do that."

Milo was truly worried. Kieran wondered if she should be, too. She stood and walked over to the counter and asked the woman called Rita if it was possible to call Annie and find out if she was coming in soon.

"Honey," the woman said. "You don't think that I haven't already called her? This isn't like her, not at all. She bought this place from her uncle and she is one hard worker, wanting to make it a real destination place — five stars and all that."

"So, you've tried to reach her?" Kieran said, frowning.

"She's not answering her cell phone. She doesn't keep a landline at her apartment."

"Where does she live?" Kieran asked.

The woman narrowed her eyes, looking at her suspiciously and said, "Honey, I know you've been here, I know that you've talked with her, but . . ."

Kieran motioned for Milo to come to the counter. "My friend here is Special Agent Milo DeLuca. FBI. If you're worried about Annie, we're worried about her, too."

Milo obligingly brought out the flat little wallet containing his ID and badge.

The woman studied it and grabbed the pen by the register and a napkin, scratching out an address.

Kieran handed her a card. "Call us if she shows up?"

"And you call me if you find Annie. Now you've got me really worrying!"

Milo looked at Kieran and took the napkin from her. Neither spoke; they just turned to leave, anxious to get to the address in Hell's Kitchen as quickly as possible.

The board of suspects Craig had been constructing in his mind was now a real one. He and Mike sat in the conference

room, staring at the large whiteboard available to every member of the Fireman task
force. On one side, pictures and information detailed the five murders of "witches"
Nicholson had confessed to committing.

There was a listing of Nicholson's family
members.

To the right on the board, one list that
detailed tenants of the building, and one
that listed Simon Wrigley, Joel Catalano,
and the rest of the security personnel who
worked there.

"Amy Nicholson," Mike said.

"She couldn't have attacked Simon Wrigley. We were with her when he was attacked," Craig said.

"Well, Simon Wrigley didn't attack Simon
Wrigley," Mike said. He shook his head. "So
where is the connection between Nicholson
killing witches, Nicholson escaping, and the
deaths of Charles Mayhew and Olav Blom."

"Blom — we figured that was a matter of
convenience," Craig said.

"Then why attack Simon Wrigley?"

"It all goes back to Annie's Sunrise somehow," Craig said. "We know that Nicholson
went there. And Wrigley went there."

"Charles Mayhew was really rich. What
we need to figure out is, did he do something that caused someone else problems?

Maybe lose a great deal of money? How are we doing with the forensic accountants?" Mike asked.

Flipping open his laptop, Craig pulled up the report that their people had been working on. "Charles Mayhew gave to every heart, kidney, diabetes, and cancer institution out there," Craig said, looking at the spreadsheet.

"Tax dodges?" Mike asked.

"Always a benefit, but okay, you want to kill Mayhew, and you happen to know a serial killer who hasn't been granted bail. But if you can make it look like the serial killer was on the loose and killed Mayhew, you get away with it," Craig said.

"So we're back to this — who wanted to kill Mayhew?"

"Killing Mayhew couldn't have benefited Raoul Nicholson. Since he was on the loose, it tightens the noose around his neck, so to say."

"But then again, where did the voices come from? Other than the cell phone."

Craig reached for a stack of manila folders containing profiles of each of the Fireman's victims. "The first woman," he muttered. "Gretchen Larson."

"The first victim whispered to Nicholson that she should kill him? Hey, maybe she was one of his flock, finding religion once she knew that she might not have long to live. She's the one we know to have tested positive for HIV. You think she had a death wish? That she wanted to die before she began a slow descent?"

"Maybe she did find religion. She had been arrested a few times for prostitution. Although how you find a 'church' like Nicholson's is beyond me. We're the FBI, and even we can't find out who the members are. We'd need subpoenas, but no one even goes by a last name and judges are very worried about trampling on the rights of citizens. We'd need more info on someone than what we have. But, say in jail she talked to someone, and then that someone who had been with her gave Nicholson the clue on her illness, and that if she had sex with anyone, she'd possibly be giving that person a death sentence. Do you have the reports from the ME's office? Was there anything wrong with or about the others that would suggest that they might be . . . witches, or, rather ordinary people, really, who could cause bad things to happen to others?"

Craig leafed through the sheets in front of him. "Well, hmm. Our second girl didn't have any other blood-related disease, but apparently she had been diagnosed with a brain tumor, and that tumor might have eventually caused 'erratic' behavior."

"Turn her into a killer?" Mike said skeptically.

"Hey, I'm grabbing at straws here," Craig said. "Is there anything in the third victim's medical history? Uh, she was a star student, right?"

"Nothing in the autopsy. She was a healthy girl, clean lungs, great heart . . . healthy, until she was dead," Craig said. "Ah! But she did spend time in jail!"

"A shoplifter?" Mike asked.

Craig shook his head. "Protester, animal rights group. They held her on mischief charges because she pelted a number of people wearing fur and leather with red paintballs. Oh, and she was known to shout out threats, as in 'Paintballs! Animals get knives and bullets — remember, people are animals, too. Maybe someone wants your skin!'"

"You made that up?" Mike asked.

"It's in her record."

"So, if you weren't an avid animal activist, you might think she meant those words and that she could turn into a killer," Mike said thoughtfully. "What about the fashion designer?"

"Victor Brava. I'm not seeing an arrest

record. Oh . . . but wait! His daughter, Viola, was arrested and held on some drug trafficking."

"Didn't mean she was held without bail, but she might have been. One more victim — the accountant. The guy we found in the street, still burning," Mike added quietly.

"Larry Armistice." Craig flipped through the massive pile of records before them and looked at Mike. "You're going to love this one. He spent time in jail, right here in New York. I don't know how our people got it, because he wasn't convicted, and the record had been expunged. He was brought in for child abuse."

"Okay, so Nicholson's victims might have all somehow come through our legal system. How did he come in contact with these people? And what about Mayhew. He wasn't ever arrested, was he?"

After a moment Craig shook his head. "I know who we can call. Cliff Watkins may know things that he's not sharing with us."

"Client-attorney privilege," Mike reminded him.

"He's an officer of the court. If he can stop further violence, death, or criminal activity, he is required to do so."

"I don't know. He may be unhappy with this case, but he's a good attorney. He's still

Nicholson's attorney of record. He can't tell us anything that was said to him in confidence."

Craig shook his head. "I don't think Nicholson said much in confidence. He talked to us before getting an attorney, and we almost had to push him to understand that he really needed to accept a public defender before Cliff Watkins came on, the pro bono sacrificial lamb from his firm. If there was a third party present — and there often was — things Nicholson said wouldn't be limited under the law. Especially since we are facing the fact that whether we think he killed Mayhew and Blom or not, he very well may kill again."

"Let's call him. We'll set up a meeting," Mike said.

"No, let's find him and talk to him *now,*" Craig said.

But as he spoke, his phone began to ring. Caller ID told him it was Kieran.

"Hey, what's up?" he asked her.

"Annie hasn't shown up to work," Kieran said.

"Maybe it's her day off?"

"Craig, obviously we asked. She hasn't shown, and she isn't answering her cell phone. I'm forwarding her address. Milo and I are almost there. She might be just fine, sleeping or something. But we're going to try to find out. To be safe. After yesterday. Hanging up and sending you the address — okay, see you here, unless I call right back, with everything all right."

"Kieran, wait. What is Milo thinking? Don't go —"

There was silence. She had hung up on him. He cursed softly, getting up.

"We're seeing Watkins?"

"No, we're going to find Kieran and Milo — who are searching for Annie Sullivan."

CHAPTER SIXTEEN

Annie's apartment was up a single flight of stairs; the building was only four floors, with one being the lower floor beneath her — a nice little space with something like a tiny courtyard.

The outdoor space was almost completely taken up with a recycling bin and a trash can, but Kieran could still imagine that it would have been a nice space for a little pup like Ruff.

But their attention was on the second floor, up a broad flight of stone steps from the sidewalk. Kieran rapped on the door; there was no answer. She saw that there was a buzzer, and she rang it.

There was no response. Milo stepped past Kieran and pounded on the door.

"Hello!" he shouted. "Annie, if you're home, please open the door!"

No one appeared at Annie's, but the door to the apartment below on the basement level opened. A sleepy looking young man with long tousled hair came out. "Hey!" he whined. "You're going to wake the damned dead. Annie is obviously not there!"

"Did you see her leave this morning?" Milo demanded, his tone sharp.

The man frowned, definitely feeling put-upon. "No. I saw her come home last night, and she goes to work real early. Go away. Come back tonight!"

Milo produced his credentials. "She didn't show up for work," he said.

"We're worried," Kieran said.

"Do you hear that?" Milo asked her.

She looked at him blankly. "Hear . . . ?"

He glared at her. "I think that someone is in distress in there. I hear screaming!"

"What you hear is kids playing in the park," the young man said, shaking his head.

Kieran didn't hear anything, but she did smell a funny, sweet odor. "Milo," she began worriedly. She didn't see smoke, and she didn't smell it. Just something a little bit sickly sweet.

She narrowed her eyes, frowning, but nodded at Milo. She was about to tell him that they needed to break in when the irritated young man spoke up again. "Did you leave this here? My brother visits with his kids and his dog. What the hell is this?"

He picked something up.

A gas can.

"Break the door!" Kieran told Milo.

He kicked the door to no avail; he tried again. Kieran was ready to help him when a car jerked to a halt on the street and Craig and Mike jumped out. The two hurried up the steps, and Kieran quickly said, "There's a gas can down there in the little courtyard —"

Craig and Mike each took a turn aiming a powerful kick against the door.

It held.

"What the hell is that smell?" Milo muttered, getting ready to slam the door again.

"Gas," Craig said.

"Ah, crap, it is," Mike grumbled.

"Gas?" Milo said. "There's a gasoline container down there, but I think it's still —"

"Not gasoline, kid," Mike said. "Knockout gas. Methyl propyl ether, maybe. Any number of other gasses or combination of gasses. Be careful breathing."

"Careful . . . breathing?" Milo repeated.

"We should have masks, but —"

"We can't wait," Craig said. "Together. On three, guys. One, two, three!"

They slammed the door again.

This time, Kieran heard a crack as the

wood around the bolt gave and the door flew inward.

The apartment was all on one level; Milo split off and went to the right, Mike on his tail. Craig was headed to the left, probably thinking that Kieran would follow him, for the sake of her own personal safety, even if it was a crime scene.

But it looked to her as if a dining area and small parlor were to the right, and the kitchen and pantry were to the left.

The bedroom was straight ahead.

She rushed in.

Annie Sullivan lay on the mattress. She was still in a lacy nightgown, and with her hair spread out around her, she looked like the sleeping princess in a fairy tale.

Kieran froze for a second; she covered her mouth with the edge of her blouse. She could see a small container that must have held the knockout gas on the floor at the foot of the bed.

She hurried forward, falling to her knees at Annie's side, seeking her wrist and a pulse.

She had a pulse. She was alive.

"Here!" she shouted. "Here — call 911. She's alive! We need an ambulance!"

Craig rushed in, and then the other agents. Milo cried out and pushed past Kieran, falling down on his knees, as well, shouldering her out of the way. "Oh, my God — oh, my God, oh, my God!" he cried.

"Ambulance is on the way," Mike said.

Craig, on the other side of the bed, felt for her pulse. Then, he gave Annie a tap on the side of her cheek, once, again, and then again.

"Craig!" Milo said indignantly.

He ignored him. Wasting no time, he swept her up, hurrying outside the apartment. Out into the fresh air of New York City.

May not have been the best ever, but it was better than the toxic air of the apartment.

"Annie, Annie, come on, listen to me, listen to my voice, open your eyes," Craig pleaded with the limp woman.

Her eyelids fluttered slightly. He thrust Annie into Milo's arms.

"There's a back door," he said. Craig dashed back into the apartment. The young man living in the basement apartment started exclaiming loudly and in alarm. "You said there was knockout gas? That could have come into my apartment! And this gas, here . . . oh, jeez! I shouldn't be living next to her . . . she knew that killer guy. That's it, right? That serial killer is on

386

the loose. He was going to burn Annie up, and I might have been knocked out and the whole place could have burned and oh, my God, gas —"

He started to reach for the gas can.

"Don't — don't! Don't even think about touching that!" Mike said. "You're fine. Gas is diluted out here. Go inside and wait. Emergency personnel are on the way."

"Oh man, I can't believe this is happening right now!"

"Shut up!" Milo roared, his voice loud, deep, and authoritative.

Annie was conscious, but just barely. She was looking up at Milo with wide eyes. As he shouted, she seemed to grow more alert. Her lips moved in a whisper.

"You saved me," she whispered.

In truth, he had. It had been his insistence that they find out why she wasn't at work, and why she hadn't answered her phone.

Kieran could hear that sirens were close; an ambulance was on the way.

"Stay with her. Get to the hospital with her," Kieran said, and she ran through the apartment, back to the kitchen, Mike close behind her.

There wasn't so much a back door as there was a fire escape. She looked up; escape stairs from the two floors above joined those on this floor. A little metal platform allowed one to get from the kitchen to the stairs. They didn't have to be dropped; they were permanent, fixed down the side of the building and landing on a narrow porch that circled the building.

Craig was already on the ground.

Mike followed him down and Kieran went after, but she paused, seeing that there was something glimmering in the morning sun, caught on the metal of the stairs.

She started to reach down, but paused when she realized she wasn't wearing gloves.

"Mike!" she called.

He looked up.

"There's something here."

"What?"

"I need gloves!"

He headed back up to her; his hands were already gloved by the time he reached her.

"What, where?" he asked.

She pointed. Mike withdrew the shiny piece.

Kieran gasped. It was small, but the bowl had jagged edges.

It was a grapefruit spoon.

"She should really just go through the Academy and maybe join a profiling team," Mike told Craig. He was referring to Kieran, of course. "She swears, though, that Milo was the one who wanted to check on Annie right away."

Craig nodded. "Good instincts on the part of Milo DeLuca," he said. "Except, of course, that his job is to watch over a civilian, one who has a true penchant for trouble, and he manages to drag her along on all his adventures."

Mike grinned; they were seated in the hallway at the hospital again. Annie Sullivan was going to be all right; in truth, they were only keeping her for observation. She had just been transferred from Emergency to a room, and the doctors were still with her.

Kieran was down the hall, trying to coerce the coffee machine into giving up a cup.

Milo was pacing.

Mike leaned back. "Well, face it. You've dragged her into things before — your cousin's situation. And then, of course, when you met her, her brother was involved, and then, a woman shoved a baby into her arms . . . trouble finds her. Can't blame Milo — or her — for that," Mike pointed out.

Craig shrugged.

"So what are we dealing with this time?" Mike asked. "Killer gassed Annie. Maybe he didn't want to have to see her face or feel her struggle when he strangled her. But he left his gas can outside, and he apparently escaped and lost his grapefruit spoon along the way. So, what are we looking at here? Nicholson or the copycat?"

"We're looking at us, a day late and a dollar short again," Craig said. He winced, leaning his head back to rest on the wall. "One of them was there. One of them came and knocked Annie out. He might have been waiting, hiding in that little courtyard-under-the-stairwell area. And that's why he left his gasoline can there. He was waiting, trying to make sure that his knockout gas had worked on Annie."

"We had to break the door down. How did he get in?" Mike asked.

"It was a small cannister. He might have knocked on the door. She might have let him in."

"Then she'd know who it was."

"She barely knows who she is right now. They're still cleaning the sedation out of her system."

"Was it laughing gas? The kind you get at a dentist?" Milo suggested. "I mean, too much of any sedation can be . . . too much. I'm sure the doctors will tell us. Thing is, why was she targeted? Was Annie a 'witch,' or do you think she knows too much?"

"Not laughing gas," Mike said. "It might have been methyl propyl ether."

"You think she's hiding information? That she might know more about Nicholson, or his lieutenant, than she's saying?" Craig asked.

"We do know now that all of Nicholson's victims had records," Mike said.

"Do you know who we haven't seen yet?" Craig asked.

"Who?"

"His old pastor. He went to a recognized Unitarian church before he went off on his own. The church wasn't strict enough for him. I never really knew if he left on his own, or if he was asked to leave," Craig said. He stood. "I'm going to go to find his old pastor . . . Axel Cunningham. Nicholson's son said that his father had a falling-out with him, or that he may know his movements now that he's out — a hideaway. The guy's rectory was right by his church. Then, I'm going to find Mr. Cliff Watkins, Esquire, and find out what he knows about Nicholson and the fact that his victims had all been jailed for various offenses." He started to walk away, but then spun and went back.

"Mike —"

"Aw, come on, Craig. I can talk to Annie just fine."

"I know you can. But —" He paused, indicating Kieran, who was finally getting coffee out of the machine, and Milo, who was still pacing.

"I'll watch the children, too," Mike said dryly. "Can't knock them, though. Looks like they might just have saved two lives now."

No, he couldn't knock them. He went to Kieran, who was smiling in triumph at having gotten the machine to work.

"I'll be back. Mike is staying. You . . . you guys did great. But this is getting pretty damned scary."

"I will stay right here!" she promised, then kissed him lightly. "Go. I'll be right here — or, wherever Milo and Mike may be."

He hesitated, not wanting to encourage her to include herself on dangerous outings; he'd come too close to losing her, a few times too many. But she was good — at people, and, it seemed, yes, for finding trouble — and at following the right twists and turns.

Saving lives. She deserved that recognition.

"You and Milo . . . great instincts today," he said.

"Thank you! I did call you right away. Great timing!" she said, returning the compliment.

He smiled. "I'll be back as soon as I can."

"I really could go home, or even to work!" Annie said, propped up on her hospital bed. She was no longer in her pretty nightdress, but rather a plain hospital gown in lifeless green.

She was still a pretty girl. And Milo was wide-eyed and happy by her side. He wasn't trying to talk to her; he was letting Mike do all the work.

Her eyes widened, and it seemed that her face grew pale. "But oh, if you hadn't come . . . I might be dead now. That's . . . terrifying. I love my apartment, but I don't know if I can ever go back there now."

"What were your movements yesterday?" Mike asked.

"My movements?" She shrugged. "I went to work. I came home. I was . . . kind of late. But still, I run a coffee shop. We don't stay open nights. We close at 6:00. But of course, if people are there, we don't throw them out. Then, there's cleanup and prep for the morning. So, late for me was . . . hmm, I think I got into my apartment at about 9:30."

"And then?" Mike asked.

"Well, since I work in a restaurant, I have

to admit, I sometimes feel a little bit like walking maple syrup, or barbecue sauce. I took a long shower, and I was in bed by 10:30. I know because I watched the news, and I think I fell asleep when they were doing a recap on the attack on Mr. Wrigley yesterday."

"Annie," Kieran said, speaking up, "this is really, really important. Do you think that there was something between Raoul Nicholson and Simon Wrigley that you maybe didn't really see, but might somehow remember?"

She shook her head firmly. "I never saw Raoul and Mr. Wrigley speak. I'm not even sure they were ever in at the same time." She trembled suddenly. "Someone meant to kill me. To knock me out and come in and . . . strangle me and burn me!"

"But they didn't," Kieran said. She smiled at Annie.

Mike, seated by her, just seemed frustrated.

Kieran's phone rang, and she excused herself, expecting it to be one of her brothers. Again, no details were out, but with crime scene investigators coming to search for clues at Annie's and a gas can left at the neighbor's, they had certainly seen something on the media by now.

She should have called one of them already to tell them that she was fine.

But it wasn't one of her brothers. It was the attorney, Cliff Watkins.

"I just tried to reach Richard Egan or Craig Frasier," he told her. "I couldn't get through. Is it true? Has there been a Nicholson attack on a young woman?"

"There has been an attack," she said.

"But the young woman is all right?"

"Yes, she's going to be all right."

"Well, thank God for that." On the other end, Cliff Watkins hesitated. "Was it Nicholson who tried to kill her or a copycat? He hasn't reached out to me, his wife, or his kids . . . Has he tried to reach you?"

Kieran paused a minute. She didn't know just what she was allowed to say to whom. Cliff Watkins was an officer of the court, bound by professional rules and regulations.

That didn't mean that there wasn't something that he knew that he wasn't saying. He was, after all, human.

"I'm not sure. I think I see people in crowds who might not be there . . . Maybe he is out there, trying to figure out how to get to me, talk to me. You know, of course, that both Craig and Mike go by the book. Every move they make is legal, so you will be advised right away if they do find him or have any news of him."

Her words weren't strictly the truth.

Close enough for now.

"Well, thank you," Watkins said, and hung up.

Kieran stared at the phone, reflecting on it for the moment.

He was an attorney — a defense attorney. His firm had handled some of the most high-level cases in the city.

He'd spent plenty of time out at the island with those he was defending. He was privy to all kinds of information. He knew details of the killings that had never been out in the media. Could he be involved in this new wave of murders?

Why would Cliff Watkins want to kill Charles Mayhew, and try to see that it was blamed on Raoul Nicholson?

She paused in the hallway and called Craig. She got through no problem, unlike Watkins, apparently. Craig had just reached Pastor Axel Cunningham's rectory.

She quickly told him which way her thoughts had turned.

"Watkins," Craig said. "The one man close to this all that we hadn't considered. Hard to imagine that an attorney of such note could possibly be involved."

"He could have known about the people

Nicholson killed as witches, known about their past records. He'd have access to so much that others might not have. He saw Raoul Nicholson the day that he escaped. He might well know enough about the workings of jails and infirmaries to have laid out the plan for Raoul Nicholson to have escaped. And he just called me and asked if Nicholson had tried to reach me. Look, from what I've seen of the man, he's a straight shooter, but . . . who knows? The only thing I can't figure is why he'd want to kill Charles Mayhew."

"We've had the task force going through records. Mayhew had to have done something that angered somebody enough to make them want to kill. I'm going to call Marty Kim. If anyone can find dirt on someone, it's Marty. Stay in touch. Call me if anything changes."

"You are number one on my speed dial," she reminded him.

"Thanks," he said softly, and ended the call.

Kieran paused in the hallway for a minute, at an angle where she could look through the doorway to Annie Sullivan's room.

Mike was still seated by her legs, right on the bed.

Milo was next to her. They seemed to be

talking about something that had nothing to do with the attack; she was smiling.

Milo was looking at her, the stars in his eyes evident.

She frowned.

Timing.

So much came down to timing.

It was *possible* for Raoul Nicholson to have escaped and killed Mayhew, but not very probable. He would have needed to get a key, get Olav Blom outside . . . gotten back in through the ice delivery chute . . .

He had to know more than just how to escape from the island — he had to have known something about the building ahead of time.

But due to his past, a prosecutor might well have made a case that Nicholson had been the killer.

She knew in her gut that he wasn't.

She was about to head back into Annie's room when her phone rang.

Craig couldn't possibly be getting back to her again this quickly.

She looked at the number; it was an unknown.

"Hello?"

"Miss Finnegan?"

The voice was hushed and low. *Raoul Nicholson.*

"Mr. Nicholson, yes, it's me."

"Can you talk?"

"I'm standing alone in a hospital hallway. Annie Sullivan was attacked."

"I thought that might happen. I . . ." He stopped speaking.

"Please, if you were to come in, or tell me something, we could help you. You will get help. Even if you go to prison, you'll be alive —"

"There's construction at my old shop. Seven p.m. Please, I'm begging you. Say nothing, and come alone."

"Wait, please, you have to understand —"

She broke off; she was talking to air. He had already hung up.

Tonight — at 7:00. Come alone.

She couldn't do it, of course; she couldn't do it. But . . .

Something had to be arranged. It might be her only chance to reach him.

Their only chance to stop a killer before more people died.

"Pastor Cunningham," Craig said. The man had answered the door to his rectory, a little room off the main body of his church. A Unitarian church, somewhat strict in its teachings, but nowhere near as fanatical as

399

the True Life church Raoul Nicholson had created.

Cunningham was somewhere in his early fifties, tall, distinguished looking, with platinum hair going white and cool blue eyes that were probably a blue fire when he was passionate in the midst of a sermon.

"Special Agent Frasier," Cunningham said wearily. "I've been expecting you. Come in, please. Can I get you anything?"

"No, no. I've come for help."

"I wish I had help to give."

Cunningham led him from the entry to a sparse parlor. There were chairs by a fireplace, glowing with an electric set of logs, and a bookcase holding religious texts. Cunningham asked him to take a chair.

Once seated, Craig launched right in. "You were once Raoul Nicholson's spiritual adviser. Someone he might come back to now."

"You do realize that while I'm not a Roman Catholic priest, what members of my congregation say to me in confidence must be confidential. I'm protected by the law on that."

"So, he has come to you."

"If I had something that would help you, I'd give it to you."

"But Pastor, you're behaving as if you do

know something. You don't have to betray a confidence. If you know where Nicholson is, I'm hoping you'll help us, so that an overzealous officer doesn't kill him in the line of duty. We need Raoul."

Cunningham frowned. "You don't think he's guilty of killing again?"

Craig shook his head. "No. We don't."

Cunningham hesitated. "Well, honestly, I didn't hear from him at first. He must have gotten hold of a cell phone today. I didn't know the number when my phone rang. But of course, being who I am, I answer my phone. And before you think it, I don't hear voices of any kind."

"I didn't think it," Craig said.

Cunningham stared toward his fireplace. "He sounded frantic. He told me that he hadn't killed Charles Mayhew, that he didn't even know Charles Mayhew, and he hadn't even been in the Upper East Side in years. He says no one will believe the truth — his word against another's word. And he's afraid to show himself to anyone anywhere. Oh — and he's questioning himself now. I think he hates himself. He now believes the voice was from an earthly source, and not that of a higher power. To be frank, I'm afraid he's going to commit suicide."

"You have no idea where he was?"

"I haven't. I did tell him that he could find sanctuary with me. But he said that he just called to tell me that he had been wrong, that I was a good man, and that he was going to burn in hell for what he had done. But also, he'd been used. I, naturally, told him that he was confessing, and that all sins could be forgiven when they were truly repented in the heart. I did encourage him to come in. He sounded . . . wild. I'm sure he's been painted as a lunatic, but he was different than I remember."

"You didn't think to call any of us with this information?" Craig said lowly.

"He said that he didn't know who to trust. Like I said, I begged him to come to me and get help, but he said again that no one could be trusted."

Craig nodded. "Do you know anywhere he might be? Would he have gone home?" He didn't mention that they had searched the man's apartment that day.

Cunningham shook his head. "I don't know — I really don't know. Amy Nicholson . . . well, I'm not sure she wanted him coming home. The attorney arranged for the sale of Raoul's business and set up a trust for her. I think she intended to get rid of her apartment and relocate somewhere she wasn't known. Then again, Amy was his . . . well, she was his chief supporter. In fact . . ."

"In fact, what?"

"I think that Raoul felt his children might not have left if it weren't for her. Do you know much about the Amish, Special Agent?"

"A bit, why?"

"Well, they allow their children to go off into the world and then come back to the church if they choose. I think Raoul saw it that way. Amy was the strict one. They were bound in their marriage . . . and, the way he saw it, women had their place. Amy was happy with that place. I don't know more than that. Honestly." He grimaced. "I am a man of God, sir, and I would not lie to you."

But you did withhold information, Craig thought. "Sir, may I have your phone?"

They could try to pin Nicholson if they could coordinate his location by the cell towers his call had been routed through, though Craig was sure he'd be constantly changing phones and moving about the city, too.

Cunningham smiled. "He called on my landline. You're welcome to my records."

"Thank you," Craig said, rising.

"I hope you're able to bring him in. He

caused tremendous pain, but . . . in a way, he's an oddly good man. The world isn't all just good and evil. There are areas in between."

"Yes, I know. And I told you — I am trying desperately to bring him in alive, and have him help us find the killer who is using him."

Craig headed out, thinking that it was time to find Cliff Watkins.

Watkins, who knew prison and jail systems. Who knew Raoul Nicholson.

And, still, why had Charles Mayhew been targeted? There was no motive.

His phone rang; Marty Kim was returning his call.

He answered it, listening intently.

"The building, Craig, that Mayhew lived in — he owned it. Well, he didn't own it on his own. The first two holding companies on the contract were owned by him, but there were others in on the purchase. I started to dig into a holding company that holds a good share of the building. Someone had something to gain if he died — someone wanting to get control of the building. I'm not sure who it is yet, I'm still digging, but I wanted to let you know."

"Thank you! Keep going!"

Craig thought he just might know who the

other owner could be.

He moved quickly.

Marty had just given him a very big puzzle piece.

One that might very well make all the others fall into place.

CHAPTER SEVENTEEN

Annie was doing well. The sedation seemed to be entirely out of her system. She was happy to shake off what had happened, and happy to talk to Milo about movies, plays, sports — anything that kept her mind off what had happened, and being afraid.

Kieran managed to get Mike out in the hallway alone and tell him about the call.

"We have to let Craig know, and Egan. And see what we know about the furniture shop."

"We know that his shop was sold, that Watkins helped Amy get rid of it fairly quickly, and that he made some money for her. I believe, however, that there was a bunch of construction going on. He had a two-story warehouse just north of Canal and the buyers were ripping it all out. Nicholson was a furniture maker — he did a lot of special designs and one-of-a-kind pieces. The new owners are going for a much larger employee roster and mass-market work. I think, because of some of their machinery, they were ripping it down to the foundations."

Mike had his phone out as he spoke.

"I'm calling Craig. And then —"

"Egan. I guess we need some kind of plan if we're going to figure out a way for me to safely connect with Nicholson. I know he doesn't want to hurt me, though, Mike. I'm convinced of it."

"Craig first," Mike said.

He must have answered right away; Mike immediately gave the details about the call Kieran received. He frowned, and he listened, and he seemed to listen a very long time, just throwing in a word here and there.

Mike hung up, smiling at her. "We're set," he said.

"We're set — to do what?" she asked.

"Go to the furniture shop at 7:00."

She stared at him, stunned. "What about —"

He smiled. "Craig is going to head straight there, survey the situation. He's going in alone to make sure that he isn't seen or followed, or that anything gives away the fact that you're not going alone. He is, however, informing Egan, but even then, this whole thing will be on the down low. We can't spook Nicholson. We have to get him in. This might be our only chance."

"Okay," Kieran said slowly. "What do we do about . . . well, Simon Wrigley is still in the hospital, and —"

"Simon Wrigley was discharged. But don't worry. Agents are watching over him," Mike said.

"And now Annie —"

"And Annie has Milo, and . . ."

"And what?"

"They're going to add on a man from the NYPD. Just to be safe."

"Mike, what's going on? Are we suspicious of the FBI?"

He shook his head. "No, but Craig did just get some very interesting information."

"Which is?"

"I guess it took some digging, but Marty Kim was able to discover that a holding company owned another holding company."

Kieran shook her head. "Mike, I'm lost. What are you talking about?"

"Charles Mayhew didn't just live in that building, he owned it."

"Well, we knew he was a billionaire. How does that help us find his killer?"

"Marty and Craig are working on it. Craig believes that he was doing something with the building that might have infuriated someone. Apparently he bought it a while back, and was just starting to make changes. The changes he was making might have caused someone to want him dead before those changes could be made."

"What kind of changes?" Kieran asked.

"Well, we don't know about that yet," Mike said. "Craig is trying to make a connection between the attorney, Cliff Watkins, and the building. But if we can bring Nicholson in, or even if he talks to you, we may get the answers." He paused for a minute. "Craig is showing some real faith in you, you know. A little while ago, I suggested that we use you to draw Nicholson out. Well, you know, normally, we do everything we can not to involve civilians, and, of course, Craig is rabidly protective when it comes to you. But he's showing tremendous faith in your intuition and training . . ."

"And he intends to be there himself," she said.

"Exactly," Mike admitted.

"So, when do we go?"

Mike looked at his watch. "We just go. We head to the area. Oh — by the way, we'll be giving the entire place a major sweep. That's where he was calling you from, and Craig believes he called his old pastor from there, too. So Egan is placing a few special agents nearby, and I need to get you dropped off by the closest subway station and appear to disappear. I imagine that Nicholson will know that you're not really intending to come alone, so he'll have an escape route planned. Craig is getting all the blueprints, so he'll know what that escape route might be."

Kieran nodded.

"Now we go in and I tell Milo that we're leaving him on to watch Annie through the night, and that I'll be taking you home and staying with you there."

"You don't trust Milo?" she said.

"We're not trusting anyone right now."

"Okay," Kieran agreed. She turned and walked into Annie's hospital room.

Milo was on duty; he turned immediately, and she knew that he was ready to pull his weapon if danger threatened.

Annie looked at Kieran, smiling hesitantly. "I guess I'm not in that big a hurry to go home. I'm safe here, with Milo and you and Special Agent Dalton."

"You're safe as can be," Mike assured her. "The hospital is on the alert. There are cops everywhere."

"I am good at what I do," Milo said.

"You are," Annie said, giving him a brilliant smile.

"I'm going to take Kieran home. She's had some busy days, and after today, well, her bosses are going to be expecting her bright and early tomorrow. You're going to be safe, I promise," Mike said.

"Of course, you have to go home," Annie said. "I have complete faith in Milo. Please, go get some rest. You've been so wonderful to me. I'm so grateful!"

"Annie, we're just happy that you're going to be okay," Kieran said. She smiled at Milo. "But this is the guy who was worried first, so . . ."

"Absolutely — my hero!" Annie said.

"All right, then. We'll see you tomorrow," Mike told her. He and Kieran left the hospital room. "We've got an hour," he said. "Have to get you in view of the agents on the street, and out of view of me . . . by the subway. Don't see how he can be in the old shop and see you on the street, but since he's afraid . . . Well, we'll be on you the whole time."

"I don't need to be wired or anything?"

"Craig will be in the building with you," Mike assured her. But she could tell Mike was anxious.

As they drove, Craig called her. "You sure? You sure you want to go in there?" he asked.

"Craig, I know that Nicholson won't hurt

411

me. I'd stake —"

"You'd stake your life on it. That's just about what you're doing."

"But you'll be there."

"You bet I'll be there."

"I love you," she said, glancing at Mike, a little embarrassed to be personal at the moment, but then again, when if not at this moment?

Mike, driving, kept his gaze ahead but smiled.

"I love you, too. Oh, Kieran, you had better be right," he said.

"Hey, Ruff can't lose two owners, you know," she said lightly.

"And I can't lose one fiancée," Craig said. "I'm in. I'm here. I came in by the construction entry, covered over. Nicholson didn't come this way. I'll be making my way to the front, so make sure you come that way. I don't intend to lose sight of you from the minute you come in."

She smiled; they ended the call.

In another five minutes, Mike dropped her off. She headed straight to a newsstand and bought a pack of gum, then turned and headed down Canal, ready to enter the old warehouse.

Something was wrong. Craig wasn't sure

what it was, but something was going on here that didn't feel right.

He had the plans on his phone, including intended changes and those that had already been made.

It would have been easy enough for Nicholson to hang out here. Construction had been put on hold for a few days while the builder was getting a permit.

The place was large, but Craig had no trouble easing around from the hard-hat entrance to the center. He was hidden by pillars, but he had a solid visual on the front door.

But Nicholson should have been here by now. Kieran would be arriving any minute.

He leaned against the pillar, wondering what it was that wasn't right. It was the place. Dark, but there were construction work lights here and there. The new owners were being careful of any lawsuits should the unwary or the homeless stumble in.

The place smelled to high heaven, though. Rats? Dust? The concrete that had been dredged up in the pursuit of a new design?

He wasn't sure. There was something else about the smell, but he couldn't place it yet.

For a moment he tensed, remembering a knockout gas had been used at Annie Sullivan's place. But he knew that kind of scent, and this wasn't it.

He should be able to place the smell. And then he did.

Death.

Something had come into the old warehouse and died. Maybe the construction crew had set out poison and traps for rats and other vermin.

No. This was really the scent of death.

He pulled out his cell phone, not wanting to give away his position, but anxious that Kieran not come in.

Too late.

He saw her as she tried the doors to the street — doors that should have been securely locked, but were not.

Nicholson had unlocked them.

But Nicholson wasn't going to be there to greet her now.

Craig saw the doors open, and Kieran stepped inside. He watched the killer come out to greet her. Craig drew his Glock, and then he knew his weapon wouldn't save her. And if he gave himself away . . .

They would all die.

Kieran thought that the door gave surprisingly easily, but of course, Raoul Nicholson had been making use of the place. He must have known that the construction was on hold, but then again, that would have been public record.

He had known to be careful, but he had known, too, that New York was massive, with millions of residents, millions more commuting in during the workday. It was easy to get lost in a crowd, especially when a man knew the city, and Raoul Nicholson was a lifelong New Yorker.

He'd escaped from jail and an island — easy enough for him to leave open a door that should have been locked and secured.

She walked in, letting the door close behind her. There was dim lighting from temporary work lights around the vast space, despite the fact that the building was closed up for construction with boards on many windows. Odd bits of equipment left about lurked in the gloom.

When Kieran entered, she saw the figure coming toward her. She frowned. When she'd seen Nicholson before, he'd been wearing his trench coat and a hat.

Now he was wearing a black sweatsuit with an oversize hoodie, the shadow of the hood covering his face.

He carried something in his hands that looked like a gun but wasn't — it was a flamethrower.

And he smelled of gasoline.

Then she realized that she might have been right about Raoul Nicholson and that he never meant to hurt her in any way.

The problem was that this wasn't Raoul Nicholson.

"Welcome, dear Miss Finnegan. You know, you could have just minded your own business, let those illustrious doctors you work for manage the state of his sanity. Let this manhunt play out. But you wanted to see Raoul? Come, I'll bring you right to him. Far be it from me to break up a meeting. I'll let you be with him. Right with him! Come — come with me now, or . . . well, I'll have to start singeing that beautiful auburn hair of yours right here."

Kieran refused to be afraid.

Except, of course, that she was. She felt the trembling that began, and the thunder that took over the beat of her heart.

Craig was here, she reminded herself. Craig was here, somewhere.

Unless the killer had already gotten to him.

Craig watched as the dark-clad figure indicated that Kieran should walk in front of him, displaying the direction by waving the flamethrower about.

Craig's phone trembled in his jacket; he cursed himself, but he had turned off the ringer. He kept his eye on Kieran and managed to slip his hand into his pocket and look at the phone.

Marty Kim was calling, but he didn't dare answer.

The vibrating stopped. A second later he received a text. He grimaced. Too late, just a few hours too late.

They had been able to take a thumbprint off the bruises on Simon Wrigley's neck.

And they'd matched it.

Craig glanced from his phone screen to the figure leading Kieran.

As he did, all the strange pieces began to fall together before him.

The killer had nothing to do with the court system. Or the prison system. Though it was true he would have connections there.

"You're foolish, you know." Kieran's voice echoed in the big space. She sounded bizarrely calm for a woman being forced to what was surely intended to be her death by a man with a flamethrower, a man who seemed to be carrying gasoline on him.

He could rush him, Craig thought. Rush him hard and fast, bring him down . . .

But not before he could pull the trigger and send Kieran bursting into flame.

Shoot him, just shoot him, shoot him in the back here and now . . .

And still risk Kieran's life by causing the man's finger to trigger the flamethrower.

Craig realized that the killer was forcing Kieran toward stairs between two of the back walls that were heavy with plaster dust. Craig waited until they reached the head of the stairs, then moved closer, aware that he had to stay on them — right on them. But he couldn't be noticed.

"I'm assuming you know that I'm going to say this, but you will be caught. I could tell you that you will go to a federal court and get the death sentence, but then again, I think you'd rather be dead than in prison, and they would put you in prison," Kieran went on. She was speaking a little louder than strictly necessary, and Craig was proud of her — she was both distracting her captor and making sure Craig knew where she was. "Maybe you think you'd get out, but I don't think so. You see, they'd know that you know just about everything when it comes to security, but by the way, I am a little surprised. You just got out of the hospital. How did you get here? They had agents guarding you, Mr. Wrigley. How did you strangle yourself? Wait, why am I asking you that? I believe I know the answer. You've been into that kind of sex play during your life, I imagine. Autoerotic-asphyxiation. Naturally, a man like yourself would have been interested in how far a person might go. But what surprises me is that you did such a good job!"

Simon Wrigley laughed softly. "You're so young, Miss Finnegan. Yes, I have a lifetime of experience. When I was a child, it was all locks and keys. As I grew older, computers and more came into it — ways to get anywhere, do anything. Oh, of course, you're thinking that I had a master key, that there was no reason to kill Olav Blom. That's not my fault. The nosy bastard started to get into my business with the building. I was trying to get the majority share, of course. Blom, well, he had no problem with Charles Mayhew intending not only to fire me — the idiot thought that if he fired me, no more worries! As if I wouldn't still be involved in decisions about the apartments. Then to say that my company was worthless! I showed them both just how worthless my abilities were."

"But," Kieran said, "you couldn't have been working alone. I mean, the plan might have been yours, but what connection did you have with Raoul Nicholson?"

"Ah, my dear, connections come with

other connections. You just have to make sure that all of your accomplices are on the same boat." He paused. Craig couldn't see his face, but he imagined that the man was smiling. "You can always add in someone who is . . . not all there. Like Amy Nicholson."

"She's helping you?" Kieran asked.

He laughed, enjoying the questioning, Kieran's confusion. It seemed Wrigley liked feeling smarter than everyone. "Well, in her convoluted way. You see, I convinced her that I was the voice of her higher power, and that women are now supposed to rise up to their rightful places. I managed to get into her apartment often enough, and whisper what she should be doing — you know, telling him to kill. My voice even let her know why. They were all expendable — people about to kill other people, people who were wretched and horrible." He paused for a minute, smiling. "Okay, okay, yeah, I like to be in control. I mean, seriously, how idiotic is it? A great voice calling for sacrifices to save the earth! And, yes, I love to sit back and know that I caused some real carnage!"

"So, she was helping you, but not on purpose?" Kieran stopped on the stairs.

Good, Craig thought, she's slowing him down.

"She's truly going mad," Wrigley said. "On the one hand, defending her husband. On the other, she's thinking of herself as a new kind of prophet, but that, in her power, she should have much more freedom, curse, drink — do whatever the hell she wants. Hey, I liberated that woman! She's absolutely convinced that a higher power told her how to give her husband instructions on escaping. But the lady — lady is a kind term — was not my knowing, willing accomplice. I have to admit, I am enjoying thinking of myself as a criminal mastermind, so, who am I to judge? And then again, you must be ready to make any sacrifice — make sure that your accomplice is in it all so deep that they could never turn on you," Wrigley said. He started to laugh. "Raoul Nicholson! What an imbecile. I think he had half of it figured out, as a man will do, but . . . only half. I mean, seriously, why would I be involved with him?"

"You got to his wife," Kieran asked. "Interesting. She's delusional, too, and a liar, but she didn't kill anyone, right?"

"She did not kill anyone." They were halfway down the stairs.

Craig followed. He moved quickly.

Simon Wrigley was coming dangerously close to his final act.

Kieran should have seen it; she should have sensed it coming.

The terrible smell of fire — of burned flesh.

They reached the basement, and there he was. Raoul Nicholson, dead on the floor — at least she presumed that it was Raoul.

A blinding and terrible fear swept over her.

Fire.

She couldn't think of a more painful way to die. But if Wrigley wanted law enforcement to believe that Raoul Nicholson had killed her before the final act of suicide himself, he was going to have to strangle her first.

Then the attacks and the killing were going to have to stop. But Simon Wrigley would have accomplished what he needed for his agenda — Charles Mayhew wasn't a roadblock anymore, and he'd be able to get his hands on the building, for whatever purpose.

"You are a psychopath, you know," she told him.

"A brilliant psychopath. Well, I don't know if that's right. I love the power of knowing that someone's life — their very life — has been snuffed out because I, and not God, had the power to make someone do it."

"Not so brilliant. You will be caught."

"How? You might have noted, Nicholson is lying there dead. He killed you — and then, hey, go figure, the voices said that he should kill himself!"

"You're not brilliant at all — just very sick. And they will catch you."

Yes, they would get him somehow. But right now Kieran was worried about herself.

"Well, here we are, my dear," Wrigley said, pointing the flamethrower at her. "I would like to be merciful, even though you're just not smart enough to stay out of things, but —"

"Damn it, Simon, just do it!"

Kieran was stunned to hear the female voice that suddenly shouted.

She was so startled that she, like Simon Wrigley, spun around.

Annie Sullivan!

"You — you're in the hospital," Kieran heard herself say. Stupid — the woman wasn't in the hospital. She was standing right there.

"Poor Milo! Such an easy mark. He's out cold. When they find him, they'll believe that I was spirited away before the police could come, but not even that would matter. Do you realize that no one pays attention to you when you wear one of those silly apron things that the employees in the lab wear? They'll think that I was kidnapped by Simon — oh, but of course, I'll be found having turned the tables on Simon. He'll be dead. I'll be a beautiful and charming victim on the floor, just coming to — amazed and grateful to be alive!"

"What the hell are you doing?" Simon Wrigley demanded. "Waving a gun at me — at me!"

"Men. You can't trust them." She looked at Kieran and shrugged and smiled. "You and that FBI agent of yours. You need him now. Where is he? And Simon . . . he knew that Nicholson saw me every day. I could be a little voice in his ear. Nicholson — poor bastard. He never knew what was going on. He really thought he was on a mission. Now, here we have a greedy, greedy man who is one sick son of a bitch! And that's just it. Men. They can't be trusted. See, Simon here is going to die tonight, and do you want to know why?"

"Love to," Kieran said dryly.

"He promised me everything. He promised me a whole new life. Luxury. A huge wedding. He said that if he could just get rid of Charles Mayhew — the ass who didn't appreciate talent and was keeping him from making a fortune — everything would be perfect. But then he laughed at me. Told me that I'd go to prison all my life just like him if I ever said anything. He laughed — laughed, I tell you. He was too good to marry someone like me. So now, I'm going to shoot him. See, Simon, you know all about security. But you forgot that a gun can beat a heck of a lot. I could have already killed you, of course, but I wanted you to know why. Exactly why. And now I think I want to make you suffer, too." She walked closer. "Let's see — who first? Maybe I should let you see Simon die, Kieran. I mean, after all, like I said, men are dirt. Simon may be more dirt than most." She took aim, her gun directed at Simon Wrigley. "He said that Amy was truly stupid, dumber even than her husband." Annie's gun swung toward Kieran. "And you — you're so in love! That big, hot agent. Where the hell is he now?"

"Here, he's right damned here!"

Craig jumped out of the shadows near the wall at the foot of the stairs; he took careful aim, and he fired.

The bullet hit Annie's hand, and her gun went flying.

Kieran shoved the man away from her — far away. He was still carrying a flamethrower.

She seized her chance and dived to the floor, rolling as far as she possibly could from Simon Wrigley and his accomplice, Annie Sullivan.

Simon had jumped at the sound of the bullet.

Jerking, his hand spasmed.

The flamethrower spewed fire.

But it was Simon Wrigley who burst into flames, screaming in agony and rage. Somewhere on him, he had carried a small cannister of gasoline, and he had lit himself afire.

He staggered forward; Annie saw his intention. She screamed and screamed again — in pain from the wound to her hand, and fear of the flaming figure stumbling toward her.

Too late.

Simon Wrigley plowed into her and encompassed her in his arms.

And, together, they burst into flames.

CHAPTER EIGHTEEN

"Horrible, just horrible," Cliff Watkins said, shaking his head. "But you and I were both right. As crazy as he really was, as tragic his crimes, Raoul Nicholson was nowhere near the monster that Simon Wrigley proved to be. And Annie Sullivan! So sweet — there's a lesson. Watch out for charming women."

"Yeah," Milo said glumly, turning a dark shade of red. He winced and admitted, "She had me. I had no idea of what went on . . . I don't know how she managed to stick me, or how she managed to get whatever it was she stuck me with. She really was out of it when we reached her. And Simon! He strangled himself? Man . . . but wow. I'd better stay away from women for a long, long time."

"Hey, we're not all evil," Kieran protested.

They were, naturally, at Finnegan's.

Monday night had turned into Tuesday with no one sleeping; there had been paperwork that seemed endless — after police and agents had swarmed the old warehouse; after the ambulances had come for the corpses of Nicholson, Wrigley, and Annie Sullivan. After meeting with Egan, finding out if Milo was all right, discovering how Annie had slipped out, drugging Milo before the police officer had come on duty, leaving in a stolen labcoat, just walking out with a smile as if she belonged there, unnoticed by those who didn't expect a frightened patient to be attempting an escape.

Now, Tuesday night had come, and while everyone was exhausted, Finnegan's had seemed the place to come to try to shake it all off. To come to terms with the fact that one man had caused the deaths of so many people — because of something so simple as greed. Well, greed, wanting a building, hating a man who didn't appreciate him — and being so deranged it boggles the mind.

Milo shook his head. "I was just taken so easily."

"Hey, we were all fooled by Annie," Kieran assured him.

"And Simon Wrigley. Sometimes, the obvious is the obvious. We were so focused on the fact that it couldn't have been Nicholson who had killed Mayhew and Blom that we accepted the fact that he was head of a security firm, and so a very unlikely suspect," Craig said. "But we did research him. His record was clean as a whistle."

"Yeah, well, that kind of record doesn't show that the guy was into some wicked sex practices. We talked to Nicholson's wife, but too bad we didn't talk to one of Simon Wrigley's ex-wives. If we'd known why they were ex-wives, we might have had a clue that he could knock himself out — strangling himself!" Mike said.

"I kept thinking that Nicholson's wife had to have been the one who helped him," Milo said. "Well, I guess she did, but because of what bull was fed to her."

"She's disturbed herself, and dangerous, too, I think. I'm out of it — completely," Cliff said. "The prosecutor is trying to decide if there are charges he can bring against her, but she'd have to be really involved somehow, and he's not sure." He grimaced.

Richard Egan spoke up. "It's not against the law to be crazy. But we're still delving into whatever part she might have had in what her husband did. She was pliable and usable, but Nicholson would have gone away for the rest of his life — if Wrigley hadn't murdered him."

"I do just thank God that I'm out of it!" Cliff said. He lifted his glass and took a long swallow of his draft; he'd opted for beer that night. Maybe he didn't need the straight shots, now that he saw an end to the Nicholson affair.

Kieran smiled weakly, glancing over at Craig — and feeling bad that she had suspected the attorney and suggested that he might have been in on it.

Craig grimaced back at her, reminding her that they had both suspected the attorney.

"I'm still feeling like an idiot," Milo said.

"Hey, in a way, I read people for a living, and she had me convinced, too," Kieran said.

Milo nodded glumly. "So, you're going to marry Craig, right? Did you all set a date yet?"

Kieran looked at Craig. "Ah . . ."

"Yes," he said.

"We have?"

"Well, almost," he said. "I was thinking Christmas."

"And the reception will be here!" Kieran turned. She hadn't heard her brother Declan come up behind her, joining the conversation at the table.

She looked at him and saw that both Danny and Kevin were there, as well, and

430

that Mary Kathleen was rounding out the group.

"The pressure is on!" Mike said, grinning.

Kieran grinned. "Christmas — a few weeks before. And, yes, we'll have the reception right here."

"*Slainte!* Finally!" Declan declared.

The toast went around.

It had grown late. Assistant Director Egan and Cliff Watkins left at the same time. Then Milo said that he was going to go to bed and get a start on the days off he'd been given for the extra hours he had put into the case.

Mike looked at Craig. "No one gave us a day off."

"Yeah, aren't you the one who taught me that the lead agents would be needed to sort out the last details on a high-profile case — for days?"

Mike shrugged. "Yeah, that would be me. All right, then, I'm out of here. Oh, let's make it a late morning though, huh?"

"I'm sure that will work," Craig said.

He looked at Kieran and smiled. "Tired?" he asked softly.

"Exhausted. I'll grab Ruff." She hesitated. "I feel so bad . . . but I hope that we really are doing the best thing for a stranger who lost his life the way he did. Ruff is . . ."

"He's a good dog, and I sincerely think that Olav Blom would be grateful to know that he was going to be taken care of the rest of his days. Grab our adoptee. Let's get going."

Kieran headed to Declan's office for the pup. Apparently her brothers had taken turns spending some time with the little guy and let him out for breaks while Kieran had been off being bait for a serial killer.

They said good-night to her brothers, and walked the distance to their apartment.

As they headed up in the elevator, Craig turned to Kieran and said softly, "You know, you handled yourself like the best of our agents. Mike joked that you should go to the Academy. I'm afraid every time you become involved in something, and yet you have as much right as I do to go after what you see as right. If you wanted . . ."

"I like my job," Kieran said. "I like working with those who could be in trouble, but who just need to learn to understand themselves and work past the bad parts . . . I don't think I really want to do what you do."

He smiled. "Good. I'd like to think you're safe sometimes."

"I'd like that, too," she assured him.

He opened their apartment door, closed

and locked it, and keyed in the alarm. Then he looked at her, an arch in his brow.

"It has been a long, long couple of days," he said.

"Sure has."

"But here's the thing . . . We're tired. We have to wind down. We now need a certain kind of rest. You know — we need to turn our minds off."

She laughed softly.

"Well?"

"My mind needs to be turned off, too."

He pulled her into his arms. "A Christmas wedding . . . and for tonight, a vacation for my mind and pure luxury for body, heart, and soul." He grew sober suddenly, smoothing back her hair. "That's life, you know. Living while other stuff goes on — taking moments in the midst of everything else and remembering just how special some moments are."

She stood on her toes and very gently kissed his lips. "I cherish those moments," she assured him, and added, "Just let me put junior to bed, and I'll race you up the stairs. I very much want to seize a special moment with . . . with my mind magnificently turned off!"

She hurried to put the dog in his room for the night.

"Hey!" Craig called. "The dog can be in the wedding party, too, you know!"

She smiled, set Ruff on his pillow on the floor, and turned.

Then they raced up the stairs, ready to forget the case, and remember all that was so special and precious in life.

EPILOGUE

The day came.

New York was beautiful at Christmastime. The church was decorated with lights and garlands of greenery.

Neither Craig nor Kieran were much for details; they'd even contemplated getting married on the courthouse steps.

But Declan was so honored by the concept of walking his sister down the aisle as the oldest Finnegan sibling, and Danny and Kevin had been eager to be groomsmen.

Craig had his own cousin, Finn Douglas, anxious to be his best man, and Mary Kathleen wanted to be Kieran's maid of honor.

And so, it all came about, the church decorated for Christmas and their wedding. He and his groomsmen were dressed in kilts — he was wearing his family clan's Frasier colors, and the others the Irish Finnegan plaid. The bridesmaids all wore beautiful green dresses and were adorned with plaid shawls to honor the bride.

Kieran looked so beautiful. All brides were beautiful, but Craig thought there couldn't possibly be one as stunning as his bride. All the empathy and honor and integrity and humor of the woman seemed to shine through. And the mischief, of course. Because Kieran was going to be very traditional to honor her family, but she was also going to stop and kiss a few kids and friends on the heads or cheeks as she came down the aisle. He supposed they were a playful family. After all, Ruff was the ring bearer.

From the rehearsal to the real deal, Ruff moved with his ears up and his head high, regal as he walked straight down the aisle to take his place at the altar.

Father Anthony had been fine with it — he, too, had fallen in love with the little creature.

Ruff was just that kind of dog.

Then there were the vows. Craig had written his own, as had Kieran. In those vows, he told her that it wasn't so much that she had changed his life — rather, she had become his life. And he was so grateful, and so in love. Grateful that he'd found someone like her: passionate, caring, amazing. They never seemed to detract from one another;

they just gave, and he prayed that he could make her life as complete as she made his.

She thanked him, too, for coming into her life — even if it had been in the middle of a diamond heist. That admission got a few chuckles from the gathered guests.

She went on that she was amazed that she could love so deeply and with such appreciation for the respect he gave her in return.

Ruff barked in the middle of her vows. Kieran laughed it off and went on, "And I just love you. I love your face in the morning, and at night, and the world is always good just because you're beside me."

Craig could hear Mary Kathleen quietly sobbing. She later claimed she always cried at a good wedding.

Then there were pictures, dozens of them, Kieran and Mary Kathleen and the bridesmaids. Craig and his cousins and the groomsmen.

Him and Kieran — and Ruff. So much smiling and celebrating.

Then, at last they headed for Finnegan's.

Their wedding dinner would be the shepherd's pie that was considered the best in the city.

And the cake. Craig would always have the memory of sharing the first delicious slice with Kieran in front of the crowd.

And toasts! Toasts and more toasts!

Because there were Kieran's brothers who each had something to say. Her bosses, the Drs. Fuller and Miro. Richard Egan, Mike and Milo and so many other friends and coworkers. Regulars from Finnegan's filled the space to standing room only.

The musical entertainment was arranged by Kevin — he'd managed to get a host of his Broadway performing friends to perform at the church, and for the reception — continued throughout.

Finally, it came time for the beautiful white limo — generously provided by the Drs. Fuller and Miro — to take Kieran and Craig to the airport.

Their destination was Central Florida.

It had been funny when it had first come up, but then the idea had taken hold — what better way to spend time away from lives that contained murder and mayhem and incredible tension than with nothing but fun and fantasy?

Then Richard Egan had done some research — or maybe had Marty do it for him — and discovered an amazing suite at one of the parks with a gorgeous whirlpool tub right in the bedroom, high up and with a view of spectacular fireworks each night.

So, the time to leave came. Mary Kathleen — and even Declan — had misty eyes. There were more toasts, and the party called out, *"Slainte!"*

"Slainte!"

They returned the toast together, laughing, and then Ruff barked, and even his bark sounded a bit like the word.

They were covered with rice as they climbed into the limo, and apologized to the driver, who laughed and informed them that he had a car vacuum.

Then they were at the airport, bags checked in, and almost to security.

Craig stopped. Kieran halted, questioning him with arched brows.

"Wow. Mrs. Frasier."

"Ah, yes, you're a married man, Special Agent."

"Does it feel any different?"

She smiled. "I've known I've loved you for a very, very long time."

He nodded. "But still . . . It's amazing."

She slung her arms around his neck, looking at him. "We're about to start on an adventure."

"You know, I never did get to meet Mickey Mouse when I was a kid."

"You poor, deprived child! We'll make it the first thing we do."

He grinned, shaking his head. "First thing is trying out that whirlpool tub — and watching the fireworks."

"I was rather thinking we'd create our own," she said.

He smiled. "So was it all you dreamed of — today?"

"Honestly, the wedding was beautiful, but if I dreamed of anything, it was finding someone like you. Who understands that I have passions in life, who cares about my wacky family, who would . . . respect me and love me, the way that you do."

"Wow!" Craig murmured, and he pulled her into his arms, kissing her deeply. Forgetting they were in one of the country's busiest airports.

When he pulled back, people were staring.

And then they started clapping.

Craig looked around and realized that someone had stuck a big *Just Married* sign on his carry-on bag.

He could feel that he blushed. Yep, tough agent. That was him.

Kieran thought to call out, "Thank you!" Then she caught his hand, and drew them to the security line ahead.

Richard Egan had managed to get them lovely first-class tickets.

Once the plane was in the air, Craig turned to Kieran.

"Really, the adventure is just beginning. You were so . . . eloquent. And all I said was *wow*. Let me add to that. I am so grateful that you're my wife. I am so grateful that I can wake up and see your face every morning, and when I'm down or frustrated, I can come to you, and that you will do the same with me, and that . . ."

"Yes?"

"Well, it's not quite as eloquent."

"What?" She was smiling.

He grinned and kissed her.

"And there's a lot to be said for fireworks, too!"

ABOUT THE AUTHOR

New York Times and *USA Today* bestselling author **Heather Graham** has written more than a hundred novels. She's a winner of the RWA's Lifetime Achievement Award, and the Thriller Writers' Silver Bullet. She is an active member of International Thriller Writers and Mystery Writers of America. For more information, check out her websites: TheOriginalHeatherGraham .com, eHeatherGraham.com, and Heather Graham.tv. You can also find Heather on Facebook.

The employees of Thorndike Press hope you have enjoyed this Large Print book. All our Thorndike, Wheeler, and Kennebec Large Print titles are designed for easy reading, and all our books are made to last. Other Thorndike Press Large Print books are available at your library, through selected bookstores, or directly from us.

For information about titles, please call:
  (800) 223-1244

or visit our website at:
  gale.com/thorndike

To share your comments, please write:
  Publisher
  Thorndike Press
  10 Water St., Suite 310
  Waterville, ME 04901